The Nameless

K.M.Bishop

—Shellville Press—

Printed by Shellville Press in the United States of America

Cover illustration, map, and chapter illustrations by Dirk Macorol

ISBN: 978-1-7334487-0-3

Shellville Press
a division of Shellville Design LLC
www.shellvillepress.com

10 9 8 7 6 5 4 3 2 1

The Eternal Realm

Part 1

UNBREAKABLE VOWS,
UNSPEAKABLE TRUTHS

CHAPTER 1

THE ELDEST PRINCESS OF SKAHRR'S CARAVAN PULLED ITS WAY ALONG the Desert of Vremir in the late afternoon, a few days after the summer solstice. The sun was unforgiving and the only thing the wind brought with it were bits of sand that stung the faces of those outside and pelted the polished wood of the royal carrier.

The caravan was hoping to make the week-long journey through the harsh desert and beautiful coast of the Dormant Sea to the lush city of Harpren in the country of Thren where the princess' betrothed awaited her. Princess Rain had never met the prince of Thren, but like most women of her position her marriage was nothing but a political move. A hope for continued peace and trade between the two countries; a physical treaty between the two that was seen as a slight by their shared neighbor Bornnen, a bloodthirsty country full of ruffians and degenerates. Bornnen was home to the barbaric King Ahlenwei who lost the bid for the princess' hand and bore a grudge toward Skahrr.

So it was no real surprise when Bornnenian soldiers blocked the path of the caravan, their blood red banners whipping and flailing in the desert wind. The royal guards of Skahrr rushed into position in front of the royal carrier, all of them trained and ready to give their lives for their princess. But Bornnen's soldiers, who were known for their ruthlessness, outnumbered them.

It was over in a few gut-wrenching minutes. The sounds of death rang out across the vast desert as the men were cut down; and then it was over. The wind ceased as the women inside the caravan waited for news from the guards. But when the door opened they were met with the crazed eyes of a Bornnenian soldier.

The women screamed as bloodied hands pulled the hand maidens out one by one until only the princess remained. She trembled in the corner as she listened to the women screaming, the men of Bornnen enjoying their spoils.

After what seemed like an eternity, the screams and cries stopped, and another face peered inside the princess' keep.

He held out a sullied hand, baring a disgusting smile.

"I have me orders. I ain't gonna hurt ya," he said in his unpolished accent.

The princess merely stared at him, her eyes wide with fear, her entire body shaking.

"If ya don't come out nicely, I'll have tuh pull ya out not so nicely," he said when she didn't move.

The princess, knowing she had no choice, moved toward the opening of the carrier ignoring his hand and stepping out on her own. She gaped behind her sheer veil at the dead bodies sprawled out all around her. The guards, the hand maidens, all of them dead.

The men laughed at her disgust and without a word she was pulled onto a horse and raced toward Bornnen.

THE CAPITOL OF BORNNEN, PORTCHREN, WAS GROTESQUE. THE streets were covered with the sick, the poor, and the dying. Filthy children ran around in the streets and the smell of sewage burned inside the princess' nose.

The decrepit stone road was littered with discarded items as well as drunken men and women. The princess pressed her back against the chest of the man that rode with her and felt him laugh.

"Scared, are we, royal highness?" he said. "Don't worry, we're almost thar. Won't be long 'til ya meet King Ahlenwei."

The princess continued to look around at the city that seemed to be falling apart at the seams. Most of the mud and stone houses had cracks in them. They were built one on top of the other with barely enough room to allow a breeze between them, creating a stagnant, dark atmosphere as they moved along.

The princess' heart sank and her stomach churned when she thought about how little the people of the city were taken care of.

The castle was by no means as dilapidated as the city leading up to it. It was as grand as any castle of any selfish king would have been. She huffed as she looked at it. Disgusted by the grand display of wealth amongst its poverty-stricken subjects.

The soldiers were let into the gates and the princess was handed down to two different soldiers that led her through great wooden doors. With each of her arms held tightly by a guard, she was all but dragged into a large hall where banners of the country hung from high windows.

She cringed as the sound of harsh laughter hit her ears and she turned to see a bulky, dark-haired man with a long beard sitting on a gold and red throne. He sat there slouching, a leg of some animal in his hand and some flecks of its meat in his beard. Her stomach lurched when she caught sight of him.

The guards brought the princess to the foot of the throne and forced her to kneel.

"Muh king," one of them said, both of them raising their right hands and placing them palms open over their hearts. "We bring ya tha princess of Skahrr."

The king smiled, bits of flesh stuck between his teeth. "And so ya have!" he said in a bellowing voice. He laughed a low, guttural laugh. "We shall certainly feast tonight, boys," he said rising from his seat. He placed the meat on a plate being held by a servant standing by the throne and wiped his hand on his cloak. "For now, let me feast my eyes on tha beauty of Skahrr," he said all but strutting down the couple of steps to her.

He put his hand under her chin and lifted her face up toward him, yanking off her veil. "Your hair is curlier than I imagined, a little different from those of your country but ya have the greenest eyes as anyone of Skahrr." His voice was just as harsh as his soldiers'. He caressed her cheek with his rough, greasy hand. "And ya have tha smooth, perfect skin of a princess." He licked his lips.

She turned her head away from him, disgusted by the stale scent of meat and ale lingering on his breath.

"Ya should've been mine," he said looking down at her. "But your father decided that a man of Bornnen would never be good enough for his daughter." He spit to the side. "A king not good enough for a princess!" he bellowed. "Sending you across the Dormant Sea tuh the ignorant people of Meht would have set better, but I'll be damned if I lose ya tuh a prince of Thren!"

The princess remained silent while those in the hall shouted in agreement.

The king laughed. "Won't matter soon enough," he started. "The prince of Thren won't want anythin' tuh do with ya when I'm through." He made a gesture with his head to the soldiers. "Take her tuh muh chambers."

The men pulled her back onto her feet and dragged her out of the throne room, down a hallway, and up a winding staircase until they came to a door. They threw her in without a second thought and closed the door standing guard in front of it.

The princess slowly stood from the floor scoping the bed chamber of the king. She shuddered. She knew what was about to happen. She took deep, calming breaths preparing herself as she walked over to the far window and peered down the wall that came to a cliff overlooking Gher River. The other window looked down into a garden where a group of high-class women, or the king's chosen women, walked and talked amongst themselves.

She didn't have too much time to walk about the room before King Ahlenwei burst through the door. She whirled around to see him not even pausing before he began taking off his long black cloak, leaving it in his wake.

He gave a growl-like laugh as he continued to undress, eyeing her with an animal-like intensity. "I don't take tuh losin,'" he said dropping his belt. "And when I have been denied somethin' I want, I take it."

The Princess walked about the room, watching him, trying to keep her distance, but knew that she could only stay away from him for so long. He had finally backed her up to the wall and grabbed her by the arm, pulling her close to him.

"Please, put up a fight," he said ripping away at her clothes with his free hand, his breath stale and hot against her. "I love muh women a little feisty." He threw her to the ground, her clothes hanging loosely off her, revealing her skin. He laughed as she lay there facedown. "Come now, princess," he said walking over to her. "Don't spoil muh fun." He leaned over her laughing again.

Suddenly and quickly, she turned, jumping off of the floor and grabbing a fist full of his hair she plunged a dagger into his throat. She smiled at his surprised expression and watched as he stumbled backwards grabbing at his throat, sputtering wildly as the blood flowed from him.

"I would never dream of spoiling your fun, your highness," she replied. She removed her tattered, outer layering of clothing and threw it on the floor revealing the 'X' tattoo on her left wrist. She sneered at him. "Well, I wouldn't spoil my fun at least." She walked toward the wide-eyed king who was struggling to breathe. "I'm sure by now you have realized that I am not the princess and that you are very soon going to die."

He reached out for her, stumbling.

"Tsk. Tsk," she said clicking her tongue. "You're not as clever as you might think." She walked up to him and plucked the necklace with the Bornnen seal on it from his neck and placed it in the small satchel she had on her hip.

She then made screaming noises and began knocking things over putting on a ruse for the guards outside the door as she ripped the king's sheets into long pieces and tied them together. She tied the makeshift rope to the bed and gave it a good pull to make sure it was secure before she walked over to the window leading down to the cliff.

"Oh," she said walking back over to the king. "I almost forgot." She yanked her knife from the king's throat and wiped it on his shirt. "It would have been a shame to lose." She looked down at his silent body, the look of surprise still on his face and scowled at him before she returned to the window and gently crawled out.

By then, the moon was high in the sky giving just enough light to see where she was going. Once she was far enough down the wall, she clung to it and cut off a good portion of her rope letting it fall down the cliff. She then scaled the wall toward the garden using her knives to help her climb. Once she made it to the garden wall she jumped down onto an awning and rolled back to the ground.

The sounds of the women were not far off. She crept around in the dark finding a heavy shawl that she used to wrap herself in when the shouts of the guards were heard from the King's window. The ladies rushed out to the garden and looked up in a panic wondering what the fuss was about while the assassin slipped out of her dark corner and disappeared into the night.

CHAPTER 2

THE ASSASSIN PULLED THE NECKLACE WITH THE SEAL OF BORNNEN out of her bag and held it up for the king of Skahrr to see.

King Breht clapped his monstrous hands. "The Tigress has done it," he exclaimed. "You are worth every penny." He walked forward from his throne and took the necklace from her. He laughed as he clutched the necklace in his hand. He snapped his fingers at one of his men. "Pay the lady," he said taking his seat once again.

A robed man walked out from the shadow of the pillars and handed her a tied leather bag.

The Tigress took it and stared at it. "Forgive me," she said, "but this amount is nowhere near what we agreed. Unless I am mistaken, it is about half the amount that was promised to me."

The silence of the king's hall amplified as everyone held their collective breath.

The king slowly turned around to face her. "You will take what I give you," he said in a poisonous voice.

She stood her ground. "I saved your daughter's reputation so that she could still marry the prince of Thren and you can still have your precious treaty. I traveled four days with your caravan, another three with the tasteless soldiers of Bornnen and then another four just to get back here and deliver that to you," she said pointing at the necklace dangling in the king's hand. "I have done my duty. I have even come back two days before I was expected." She gave a slight shake of her head. "And just in case you have forgotten, I killed a king for you. Kings carry a high price."

The king's face was beginning to redden. "You will address me as 'your grace' or 'your highness' when you talk to me, girl."

She blinked. "I have done my duty, your grace," she said almost spitting out the last bit. "I all but started a war for you and I think that I deserve more than this handful of," she opened the bag and frowned, "silver," she said. "A handful of silver?" she said angrily. "You insult my intelligence, *your grace*."

The king laughed. "The Tigress seems angry," he said. "I will pay you a handful of silver and a handful of silver is all you shall receive."

"Is that really all your daughter is worth to you?" The Tigress said not budging. "I have done less for men of lesser status for more than this."

He glared at her.

"Is this how you want to be known?" she said holding up the small bag. "As the Cheap King?"

"How dare you speak to your king that way!" he yelled at her.

She didn't flinch. "You forget, your grace, I hold no allegiance to any king."

"Yes," he said nastily. "You and all of The Nameless scum all live out your bastardly lives together in that gods forsaken land. The whole lot of you unwanted and discarded! As far as I'm concerned, you're no better than a common whore! For sale to the highest bidder! A whore with a different game to play!"

"This whore just made you a lot of money by saving the alliance between your daughter and the prince of Thren," she said, still calm. "It was my careful planning and skills that made all of that happen and such things do not come at the cost of one lousy bag of silver." She dropped the bag on the floor and listened as the entire room gasped.

The king took a step forward. "How dare you!?" he growled.

"There is a code among The Nameless," she said. "We are bound by a sense of loyalty, an honor among assassins, if you will. We do not kill those who have employed us before," she said looking up at him. "But if I don't *receive* payment, it wasn't a job." She kicked the bag further away from her and stared back into the King's flickering eyes.

The king gave a nervous laugh. "You couldn't get past my guards."

She gave a small smile. "You will only think that until my dagger has pierced your throat. And then you will know better."

The sounds of swords being pulled from their sheaths echoed throughout the hall. Four guards emerged from the shadows.

"My men have been training since childhood, each one hand-picked to be part of my royal guard. Do you honestly believe you can take them on all by yourself?"

The smile never faded from her face. "You seem to forget who I am and how I was trained, *your grace*," she replied. "I was trained to fight such men as yours all at once since I was able to drag a sword."

The guards advanced.

"I have no qualms killing to save my life, though I would prefer not killing senselessly, but if your men continue to come toward me I will kill them all and then you," she said not moving.

The king stood smiling at her. "Good luck."

Without warning one of the guards rushed her, sword at the ready. She stood until the last second before spinning around out of his path and driving a hidden blade into the back of his neck. Another guard ran for her but barely took five steps when she hurled another blade in his direction, hitting him through his eye. He fell to the floor screaming. A third tried to take her while her back was turned but she ducked and swept her leg under his feet causing him to tumble and clatter to the floor. She then took the sword from the first guard and stuck it in the third's leg. She turned to the fourth guard who was standing there watching her, gauging her moves. They both stared at each other circling around the hall.

Her eyes scanned the area looking for anymore possible threats, her ears in high alert as well.

"If you are not afraid," she said to him, "you should attack me now for I am all out of weapons." She took a step forward and watched as the guard took a step back. "You're not afraid of me, are you?" she asked watching him narrow his eyes and raise his sword. "Good," she replied.

She ran full speed ahead, taking in everything as she closed the distance between them. She took each breath slowly, watching the guard raise his sword as she came closer and just as he was about to strike she ducked, pulling out a pair of brass knuckles from her boots, and jumped up, giving him an upper cut right under the jaw.

She could hear his teeth cracking and his sword falling to the floor as he fell backwards. She hovered over him, blood coming from his mouth. She then looked up at the king who stood frozen on the steps of the throne and made several strong strides toward him before he scrambled backwards.

"I will pay you!" he yelled frantically just as she reached out for him. "I will pay you what I promised. Just leave!"

She stopped and took a few steps backwards. "I will wait here for my payment," she said in a voice just as calm as before.

The king looked at the man who had handed her the silver. "Two bags of gold, now!" he said sending the man off in a hurry.

The man bowed deeply and rushed back out of the hall following the king's demands.

She stood there staring calmly at the king who was breathing heavily and wringing his hands.

When the man finally returned with her bags of gold she bowed. "It was a pleasure doing business with you, King Breht," she said taking them. She then took a few steps forward picking up the bag of silver and slipping it into her satchel.

"You are to rob me of my silver as well?" he asked, a little tremor in his voice.

She winked. "This is payment for me teaching you a lesson," she replied. "Sorry about your men, by the way, but I did warn you."

"I will find a way to have your head for all of this," the king said as she began to depart.

"I suppose you can try," was all she said as she walked out the doors of the hall and disappeared into the crowds of the capitol Cragg.

CHAPTER 3

"People are beginning to talk, T," the monk walking next to the assassin said.

"Beginning?" she replied. "Haven't they more or less always talked, Marten?" She secured the pale colored shawl over her dark curls.

He huffed. "I was talking about them talking about *you*," he emphasized.

She shot him a side glance. "How can they talk about me when most people don't know who I am?" she picked up a pear from the market and handed the man a coin. "I am a nameless face in a sea of names. I hide what little I know about myself and live in the shadows surviving off blood money."

"They're talking about something that you have done."

"How do you know I have done it if they don't?"

He shook his head. "Have you heard about the king of Bornnen?" he asked.

"Should I have?" she replied looking solemnly at a poor young boy and girl huddling together, their faces and hands dirty.

"You mean to tell me you have no idea that the king of Bornnen was assassinated last week, supposedly by the princess of Skahrr or someone who posed as the princess?"

She shook her head. "Sounds curious," she replied. "I am not sure how something like that could have escaped my notice."

"She then scaled down the side of the castle and escaped into the night?"

She shook her head. "Amazing," she responded indifferently. She pulled out the small bag of silver she had and dropped it nonchalantly in front of the children. "Did not the princess of Skahrr just get married or will be married soon?"

"I believe her caravan will leave for Thren in the next couple of days," he told her. "Her real caravan."

The Tigress didn't reply.

"Did you also not hear about the attack on the King of Skahrr?"

"Attack?" she repeated, sounding astonished. "One king murdered and another one attacked? What is the realm coming to?"

"Something tells me that you had something to do with this," he concluded as they continued to walk along. "I should like to think that you know better than to go around starting wars, but then again I'm not confident in that presumption."

They walked inside the tavern and took a couple of seats.

"You once told me that a job is a job as long as you get paid," she replied.

"I said that?" he asked.

She nodded.

"And you listen to that trash?" he laughed. "And did you get paid?"

She flashed a small smile. "After some convincing, yes, I did."

He laughed again. "They named you well," he said. "The Tigress, you are as aggressive as your name leads one to believe."

She looked away. "My aggression is not the only reason they presented me with that. It was because I saved that girl and sought revenge for myself." She took a deep breath and shook her head trying to release the memory from her mind. "And it is not a name," she retorted a little bitterly. "Not a real name anyways. It is a title. I was titled, not named."

"Are you still on that?" he asked.

She met his gaze. "You wouldn't really understand, Marten," she replied. "You were old enough to remember your name when they took you in. I don't really remember anything before the coven. I was as lost as our name truly implies. The Nameless."

He motioned for the barmaid to bring them two ales. "Does it still truly bother you after all of these years?"

She looked up at the low rising ceiling of the tavern and shrugged. "I suppose it does. Sometimes I just feel like something is missing and that my past is the key to fill in that gap."

He laughed and shook his head.

"You always laugh, Marten," she said. "And because you remember your mother's and father's names and that you had brothers and sisters, that you had a place in the world before the coven, you don't understand what it is like not to know any of that."

He frowned.

"You had an identity."

"Is that what this entire thing is about?" he asked incredulously. "You finding yourself?"

She lifted an eyebrow. "Well, when you put it that way it sounds ridiculous."

There was a strange silence between them while they waited for their ale.

"Do you remember anything at all before the coven?" he asked when the barmaid put the mugs down before them.

She shook her head. "No."

"What about that necklace you always wear?"

She pressed her hand over the silver wing dangling around her neck. "No. And no one can seem to tell me anything about it either. Or they just refuse to."

"Maybe it means nothing," he said gauging her.

She shrugged looking down into the mug frowning as she pushed it away. "I have dreams about a woman."

"Really?" he said with heightened interest.

"A woman I believe is my mother," she said shooting him a look. "She has the same eyes and hair as me, a soft, loving voice. She says something to me and I can hear the tone but not the words." She paused glancing among the crowds of people. "Perhaps they are memories."

"Is that why you came here seeking me out?" Marten asked.

"I want to remember my name," she persisted. "I was hoping that you might be able to help."

"How?"

She shrugged. "You were already there for a few years before I came. I was wondering if you remember anything about the day I arrived."

He took a gulp of his ale. "That is like taking a shot in the dark," he said. "I remember very little about that day. You were brought along with a few other kids, another girl and two or three boys. All of you seemed scared and shaken, confused. I remember one of the boys didn't live long after being brought there and that the others struggled with the coven's way of life. I remember the other girl crying every day and one of the other boys being scolded all the time for misbehaving. And I remember that you adapted to the coven's rules and training quicker than any other person that came through." He swirled his mug not meeting her eyes. "But I cannot remember where you came from or whether or not you told me your name."

She gave a small nods. "I didn't think that you would."

"Why now?" he asked a little sharply. "You never asked me these questions before."

She pursed her lips. "I never had a need to know like I do now, I guess. My dreams have been more frequent and have become longer, raising more questions."

Marten finished off his ale and slammed down his mug. "Are you not going to drink that?" he asked motioning toward her mug.

She slid it indifferently to him. "Do you think The Master will know?"

He creased his brows as he drank. "Though The Master has always regarded you as his own I doubt he would ever tell you anything even if he did know," he replied putting the mug back down. "The coven has secrets, T. It's best if you don't go looking for them."

"I don't want to know secrets about the coven," she retorted. "I want to know facts about my past."

"And what do you hope to find?" he said. "What is so great about what your past might hold? Suppose you are nothing more than a fish monger's daughter or a whore's daughter?" he asked getting a little heated. "Would it make you feel any better about your life right now? Would it make you feel better knowing where you come from if you knew you were the daughter of a murderer or rapist?" he asked. "Why not just know that you are great as you are. A feared and powerful assassin, trained by The Nameless, the underworld coven, brotherhood. Let that be your family and forget what life you came from before." He drained the rest of her ale slamming the mug down once again.

She breathed heavily out of her nose. "Forget it," she said. "You're right."

"Damn straight, I am right," he agreed ordering more ale. "Be proud of your training, your accomplishments. That is what makes you, not where you have come from. We had the rare opportunity to jump above our roots and get out." He shook his head. "You want to know where I came from?" he asked her.

She looked at him.

"I came from a copper mining town in Bornnen, born the thirteenth son of a blacksmith," he said. "Thirteenth," he repeated. "My father was a cheating bastard who screwed everyone and everything." He looked down into his empty mug. "He sold me to a man when I was six to help him pay off his gambling debts." He cleared his throat. "You know all too well how an unwanted hand feels against your skin," he said looking at her. "I spent four years as a boy whore to sick men. Four years of pain and self-loathing. The coven saved me from that."

She shifted her eyes.

"The coven gives those unfortunate souls the ability to be more than what society would have allowed them to become."

She silently nodded.

The barmaid came with another mug of ale.

"If you were nothing but a whore's daughter, you would have grown up to be nothing more than just that. A common whore." He began to wolf down the third mug when she stood up to leave.

She huffed, half annoyed as she stood. "Maybe knowing just that would have been enough." She turned to leave.

"Don't go poking around, T," Marten called after her. "As someone whom you trust, heed my words. Don't go asking questions you don't want to know the answers to."

She flashed him a grin. "You know, something else you told me was not to trust anyone," she said before giving him a small nod and bidding him a good day.

"Truer words have never been spoken," he yelled after her.

She walked out of the tavern and into the crowded streets of Cragg, the setting sun casting an orange hue over the rooftops. She had been hiding as a nun the past few days after the squabble with the king's guards. The Tigress never regarded herself as an overtly religious person. She only wore the garbs because of the cover they provided. She was taught the realm's religion growing up in the coven of The Nameless, but she wasn't sure how much she truly believed. There were times she bowed her head in thought or, perhaps, prayer, but it was never directed to any of the gods or goddesses. It was just something she did; she never wondered if anyone was listening.

She sulked as she walked. Marten was never one to deny her information if ever she needed it. He was the closest thing to a friend or brother that she had ever known. He had always tried to look out for her when he could. He encouraged her never to give up or to give in. She had never felt like he was hiding something from her until that moment.

He almost seemed angry she even asked him about it.

She squeezed through the crowds of people in the market and made her way to the small house she had been renting with Marten for the past few days.

She turned a corner just past the market when she noticed that she was being followed. She slowed for a minute to gauge the stranger's reaction, watching him from the corner of her eye. When she slowed, so did this man. When she stopped to inspect something at a merchant's cart, he tried to appear interested at an adjacent one. She almost laughed. This man was making it too obvious.

She picked up her pace slightly, pushing her way past carts of nuts and fruit, and ducked around the next corner. She scaled the walls between two houses and crouched in a window, cursing the long garbs the nuns wear for hindering her movements. She waited, silently, for the man to turn the corner. When he was right below her, she jumped from her hiding place and pushed the tip of a knife into his back and grabbed a fistful of dark hair.

"Might I ask why you are following me?" she asked, a harsh whisper in the man's ear.

He grimaced. "Ah," he said. "Following you? Why would I be following you? Are you always this paranoid?" he asked, swallowing hard.

"I call it being cautious and it keeps me alive. So, yes, I am always this cautious." She pressed the knife harder into his back, the blade almost piercing flesh. "Answer my question."

"Remove the knife and I might think about it," he replied.

"Avoid my question again and I will be removing the knife from your dead body."

He paused. "Understandable," he replied after a moment. "Could you at least release the grip you have on my hair?"

She pulled back harder on his hair, pressing her knife on his exposed throat.

"Alright! I get it," he said, his hands up in defense. "The king sent me."

She narrowed her eyes. "The king of Skahrr sent *you* to kill me?" She laughed. "I knew he wanted me dead but I thought he would have at least tried harder."

The man grunted. "He didn't send me to kill you," he said. "He sent me to find you."

She paused. "What for?"

"He has a job for you."

She laughed again. "Now I know you're lying. The king would never hire me again after our little misunderstanding."

"The king is not one to trust someone too easily. And even if he doesn't trust you as a person, he does trust you as someone to get a job done."

She regarded what he said for a minute before she let go of his hair, but she kept her knife out.

The man rubbed his head, his dark grey eyes shining in the dying light of the sun. "You sure do have a death grip on you," he said almost smiling. "You certainly live up to your reputation."

"How did you find me?" she asked not amused.

"I'm a," he paused, "tracker. I get paid to find people or things," he replied.

She lifted a brow and looked him up and down. "A tracker?" she repeated annoyed. "You mean you're a bounty hunter?"

He licked his teeth and nodded his head. "Technically," he said once again pausing, "no. I don't usually get sent to find people. Most of the time I find things people have lost or misplaced. You're the first person I have tracked." He looked a little proud of himself.

She scowled, obviously irritated. "What's the job?" she asked impatiently.

He shrugged. "I wasn't hired to find you and tell you what the job was. I was hired to find you and tell you there is one."

"Were you expected to take me there in chains? Or on my own accord?"

"Depends on how compliant you are."

She let out a small, dismissing laugh and began to walk off. "You can tell the king that I said he can go hang himself for all I care."

"He had a feeling you might say that," he said.

Before she could respond a lasso was tightened around her and she was pulled back.

"I am not as incompetent as you might think," he said pulling the rope in.

She laughed as she sliced the rope with her knife. "Obviously you are just as incompetent as I think you are," she replied jumping back to her feet.

The man looked dumbfounded at his cut rope. "Was that really necessary?" he said sounding dejected.

"Did you think it was going to be that easy?" she said. She rushed him, swinging at his face with her fists.

He yelled in surprise sloppily blocking her punches and stumbling backwards. "We could just talk about this," he yelled trying to dodge each blow.

"I wasn't trained to 'talk,'" she said taking a step back.

"I just want to know how you manage to be so swift in all of those long flowing garbs," he said. "I mean, I am pretty amazed that you aren't tripping over yourself and falling on your face with all of that fabric in your—"

She sighed and took a hopping step forward crushing his foot under hers and hitting him across the face with the back of her arm.

He grimaced as he fell to the ground. "Ah!" he exclaimed as he fell. He pressed his hand to his nose and looked down at the blood. "Again! Was that necessary?" he said trying to wiggle his nose.

"I am not sure what you expected. But I do not bend to the king's every whim," she told him. "And I am not so sure how much I really trust this 'new job' that you have for me." She turned to walk away again. "This is me declining again. Don't follow me because the next time I won't hesitate slitting your throat."

"He said he will raise the price from the last job."

"Not interested!"

"I owe him this favor!" he said shouting after her. "Please! He spared my life last time and I am not so sure he will spare it again after my last screw up."

"Not my problem." She continued to walk down the alley not looking back.

"I can help you find what you want!"

She yawned and waved without looking back.

"Your family, that necklace, I can help you find who you are."

She froze and turned her head to the side.

"I heard you talking to your friend in the tavern about your past," he said. "I can help you find what you're looking for."

She stood there thinking.

"I'm good at finding people," he said. "I found you, didn't I?"

"You found one person and now you think you're some kind of expert?"

He shrugged. "I would be more help than your friend who didn't even care to try."

She turned and faced him walking back toward him. "So, you think you can find out about something that happened almost twenty years ago?"

He thought for a moment. "I could at least help you find out more than you already know."

She narrowed her eyes at him considering his offer. "But you can't guarantee you'll find anything."

He opened his mouth to speak, but closed it again without having said anything.

She sighed. "It would be a start in the right direction at least."

"But you have to help me out by accepting the king's offer," he reiterated.

She thought for another minute before she pulled the veil from her face revealing her long, dark curls. "I accept," she finally said watching him staring at her.

"Good," he said swallowing hard, his eyes wide. "I am really glad that I am going to be able to keep my head for another day."

She lifted an eyebrow at him. "Shall we get this over with?" she asked walking back toward the way they both came.

"Eager, aren't we?" he said limping slightly on one foot. "You know, since we are going to be working together soon for quite a bit I feel like it might be necessary for me to introduce myself."

"Working together?" she repeated. "I do not 'work together' with people," she said. "I work alone and I prefer it that way."

"Yes, but I have a feeling that the king is going to want me to tag along with this job. You might need my help tracking down someone. And how am I supposed to find what you're looking for if you are not there helping me?" he asked. "Anyways, back to me introducing myself."

She shook her head. "You talk too much," she said.

He cleared his throat ignoring her. "My name is Tristan Stahrs, third son of Drakus Stahrs."

She gave him a sideways glance. "Your father is Lord Drakus Stahrs of The Hills?" she asked almost laughing. "What is the son of a lord doing as a bounty hunter?"

He twitched his mouth. "Not the reaction I was hoping for, but like I said, third son. I can't inherit unless by some tragedy both of my brothers die and I didn't have the discipline to become a soldier. And I am not a bounty hunter. I'm a tracker or a finder of things."

She didn't respond.

"I didn't catch your name though," he said after a brief moment.

"I didn't give you one."

He nodded as he pushed through the crowd, the sky becoming darker every minute. "Well, are you going to give me one?"

She pushed her lips together in an annoyed manner. "I don't really have one," she replied, bitter that the subject had come up twice in the same day.

He looked at her incredulously. "How do you not have a name? Your parents just forget to give you one?" He laughed. "Seems a little strange."

She flashed him an angry glance that made him pause.

He gulped. "So what am I supposed to call you then?"

"Listen," she said, "we are not friends, you and I. So there is really no point in you calling me anything."

"Well, if we are going to be traveling together then I have to be able to call you something. How am I supposed to get your attention in a crowd if I don't know what name to shout across it?"

"You're not."

"Does anyone call you anything?" he asked. "Nickname? Made up name? Haven't you ever thought of giving yourself a name?"

Her breath caught in surprise at the thought of what he said. It was such a simple idea, and, yet, she hadn't. She had never before thought to name herself. Why would she? Her title had, until now, seemed enough. She then furrowed her brows and pursed her lips. "If I tell you something that I am called will you shut up?" she said.

"For the time being, I guess," he replied.

"The Tigress."

He didn't say anything for a moment. "Your name is Tigress?" he asked.

She huffed through her nose, annoyed that she had to explain. "*The* Tigress. It's more of a title than an actual name," she replied.

"A title for what?"

She shot him another glance. "You told me if I gave you something that I am called you would cease talking."

"Well, now I'm just curious."

"Fine," she said. "But I swear if you do not give me at least five minutes of peace after this, I will cut your head off myself."

He held his hands up. "I give you my word."

She sighed. "I am part of The Nameless coven. If you need me to explain what that is, I won't. After a member reaches the end of their training, decided only by The Leaders, they receive a title. A title that The Leaders believe describes their spirit, or essence. Mine was The Tigress." She looked at him. "That is all I'm going to say—so if you want to live, please continue being silent."

He nodded and pursed his lips but after a few moments he opened his mouth again unable to contain himself. "How about I give you a name?"

She held in a groan.

"What about Mahtrren?" he said. "Fun, ancient name that means mother."

She glared at him.

"You're right," he said. "You don't look like a Mahtrren." He tapped his chin as he thought. "Esther?" he said and then shook his head. "I have a sister named Esther, that would be weird."

The Tigress shrugged her shoulders in a bothered manner.

"Glorna, another ancient name that means—"

She turned around and waved the knife in his face.

"You're right, Glorna is an old sounding name. You are much too young for a name like that," he said shaking his head.

"You are supposed to be silent," she hissed at him.

He looked down into her eyes and smiled. "Dahker, meaning dangerous," he said. "That could be your new name. Or maybe Sohlen, meaning sunset." He motioned to the setting sun. Then his eyes widened for a second. "Or Dahlen, a mixture of the two meaning dangerous sunset."

She closed her eyes and breathed out of her nose. "If I didn't want something from you, you would already be dead," she said turning back around.

"Everyone wants something from someone, Dahlen," he replied.

"Do not call me that," she said.

"But it suits you so well," he replied. "You are beautiful like the sunset," he said pointing to the sky, "and yet you are also dangerous. Very befitting name for you."

The Tigress shrugged her shoulders again and rolled her neck as she pushed through the dwindling crowds of the streets to the castle.

CHAPTER 4

THEY BOTH ARRIVED AT THE PALACE JUST AFTER DARK, ONE WAS IN good spirits the other annoyed. Guards surrounded the entrance and were checking people's cargo as they walked in through the gates.

"The king's feast is tonight so they're being extra careful, but don't worry," Tristan said. "I have papers to get in so we won't be-," he turned to look at her but she was gone. He spun around looking for her among the people going through the gates, but couldn't find her.

His heart raced in a panic. He was supposed to bring her back to the castle. If he returned to the castle without her, the king might definitely kill him this time. He has tested the King's patience more than once over the years. He moved to get away from the gate when one of the guards noticed him.

"Have ya lost somethin', Lord Bounty Hunter!" one of them shouted sending the others into a fit of laughter. "Come over here!"

Tristan froze and slowly turned to face them. He waved two fingers at them and nodded. "How are you, fellas?" he said walking slowly, begrudgingly toward them.

"We've been waitin' for ya," one of them said.

"That is very sweet of you to do so, but I don't really have feelings for you that way."

The guard frowned. "I might have orders to bring you in alive, but that don't mean I can't rough you up before hand."

"Noted," he said. "Well, I am not ready to meet with the king yet. I am just scoping the area. You, sirs, have yourselves a pleasant evening." He turned to walk away when the one that called him over placed a strong, large hand on his shoulder.

"Our orders are to take you to the king and that's what we're gonna do."

Tristan nodded. "Well, I am never one to miss a party," he said solemnly.

The guards took him to the king's hall where the king was greeting several of his guests. His rotund belly shook with laughter as he accepted the gracious gifts of his noble subjects and exchanged a jovial word or two.

When the king caught glimpse of the guards with Tristan, the laughter stopped and he immediately sent the guests to the courtyard where the festivities were going to be held. After everyone dispersed he waved the men forward.

"Tristan, my boy," he said in his normal loud voice. "I see you have returned."

Tristan bowed. "Your grace," he started. "I have found the assassin you have been looking for and she has agreed to come and meet with you."

The king drummed his fingers on the arm of his throne. "Then why is it I only see you and not her?"

Tristan swallowed and cleared his throat. "Trust issues, I am afraid. She seems to think that you are still out to kill her. I told her you had a job for her, not a price out for her head, but it didn't seem to matter."

The king continued to drum his fingers, a frown on his face. "You told me that you could bring her here and yet I see you have failed to do that. Just like you failed to bring that bird back alive for my daughter's birthday."

"I don't actually remember you saying the word 'alive' when we talked about bringing the bird back," Tristan replied tilting his head to the side.

"Enough!" the king bellowed. "I grow tired of your antics! Your father is a friend, but I can only take so much of your idiocy!"

"Technically, your majesty, we are rel—"

"How dare you try to correct me!"

Tristan flinched at the sight of the red-faced king.

"Take him down to the cells and throw him in there. I will not have him ruining my celebration."

The guards laughed. "Yes, your grace!"

Before the guards pulled Tristan very far, The Tigress slid down from the rafters on a banner. "There is no need, your grace," she said walking up to the king. "I am here."

The king balked.

Tristan breathed a sigh of relief, but then scoffed. "What the hell do you mean hiding away like that and trying to get me killed?" he said.

She and the king flashed him small glances before ignoring him completely.

"How did you get in?" the king asked slightly shaken.

"There is a small gap in your security on the western tower facing the sea," she replied. "I very easily climbed up and into a window. You might want to place a guard there. There is easy access to the roof from that point."

The king nodded. "Yes, I shall certainly see to it. I thank you."

The Tigress bowed slightly. "What is this job that you have for me?" she asked.

"You don't waste any time, assassin. I admire that."

"I have no time to waste, your grace," she replied.

King Breht nodded and took a deep breath before letting it out in a huff. "This information goes no further than this room," the king said.

"Discretion is a virtue I hold near and dear, your grace," The Tigress replied bowing once again. "What you tell me shall not be told to anyone else through my lips."

"That goes for you as well, Tristan," he said.

Tristan nodded. "I am a vault of secrets, your grace," he started. "Whatever it is you wish me to keep secret will not escape even if I were on my last thread of life. I will never—"

"Good," the king said holding up a hand for Tristan to stop talking. He cleared his throat. "My spies have brought some disturbing news to my attention," the king said. "They tell me that before the death of their king, Bornnen was planning and preparing for another war. Ahlenwei had raised an army larger than Bornnen has ever had before," he continued clearing his throat again. "My spies also tell me about a new weapon Bornnen has. They were unable to smuggle some back but they have told me they have seen a demonstration of its awesome power." He took a deep breath. "They described a weapon that sounded like thunder and burned like fire. A weapon that blew dirt and stone into the air creating holes where the earth once was."

The Tigress frowned. "I have heard of many strange weapons, your grace, but this does not sound familiar to me," she said. "It sounds like a dream or magic."

The king nodded. "But I am forced to believe my spies," he said. "They told me that they have laid witness to its power. They watched as they used the weapon on a cow sending it in pieces all over the place." He shook his head. "That kind of weapon could mean trouble for the rest of the realm if Bornnen were to go to war again. Fortunately, enough, the death of King Ahlenwei has bought us some time as the Bornnenians will wait to retaliate after they make the funeral procession around the country. They will not start a war without burying their king and they will not bury him until they honor him."

"I am not sure why," The Tigress thought. "He did nothing right by his people."

"What I need for you to do," the king continued, "is to go back to Bornnen and steal me one of those weapons so that my weapon makers can harbor that same power. You must also kill his weapon makers so that they are unable to reproduce the weapon again."

She waited for him to continue. "Is that all, your grace?" she asked when he remained silent.

"Is there something else that you want to know?" he retorted.

She thought for a moment. "What, might I ask, are your true plans for the country of Bornnen, your grace, after all of this?" she asked.

He rolled his shoulders. "My brother has long wanted a throne of his own and the rich mining country of Bornnen will serve him well."

"You mean the people of Bornnen will serve him well?" she asked.

The king stared down at her from the thrown rubbing his thumb over his fist in an obviously annoyed fashion. "Have you become soft since the last I saw you?" he asked her.

"No, your grace, I am just my usual curious self."

"And you will remain curious. Anything else concerning what we have discussed has nothing to do with the business I need handled."

"And my fee?"

"Double what I paid you last," the king replied.

"Two bags of gold and one bag of silver?" she asked raising an eyebrow.

The king all but snarled. "Yes," he said. "So you shall receive four bags of gold and two bags of silver."

She thought for a moment considering how much she didn't want to work for this man again, but the proposal that Tristan told her earlier was very enticing. The gold that the king offered was more of a need, but what Tristan had was something she desperately wanted.

"Do we have an accord?" the king finally asked after her long hesitation.

She took a deep breath and nodded. "Yes, your grace," she answered. "We have an accord."

The king snapped his fingers and the guards let go of Tristan, pushing him to the ground.

He frowned picking himself back up and brushing himself off.

"But," The Tigress hesitated, "I will not start until a contract is written up and is signed by the both of us."

The king's lip twitched.

"You know the drill," she continued. "This time, the price will be paid *before* I leave."

Tristan glanced from the king and the assassin in amazement.

The king, who had remained silent finally nodded. "Agreed," he said. "You shall have your written contract and fee before. Just bring me back what I ask."

The Tigress's lips curled into a satisfied sneer.

"Now," the king said clapping his hands together. "I cannot be late to my own celebration." He spread his arms out wide as if he was going to embrace them. "Let business resume tomorrow for tonight we feast!"

The Tigress lifted her brow. "Forgive me, your grace, but I have no clothes fit for a feast. I am severely underdressed. I must decline."

"I can find something for you," a soft, gentle voice said coming from behind them.

All of them turned to see a small, lovely framed girl gliding up the hall to them, two ladies in waiting trailing behind her. The guards immediately bowed. Tristan bowed as well.

"Ah, my dear daughter, Rain," the king said. "Why are you not with the guests?"

"I was on my way when I heard voices in here. River is there entertaining." She turned to The Tigress. "If you will follow me, miss, I can certainly find a dress that will fit you."

The Tigress gave a slight bow. "I thank you, your highness, but it is not necessary."

She smiled. "I insist. It is the least I can do for the woman who saved my life."

The Tigress paused but then slowly nodded.

"Follow me, if you please," the princess said.

She silently followed the princess and her ladies in waiting to the princess's chambers.

"I have wanted to formally thank you for saving me," the princess said when they were inside her room. "My father, I know, does not seem as grateful, but I want you to know that I am."

"There is no need to thank me," she replied. "I was only doing was I was being paid to do."

"Still, you risked your life for mine and I thank you." The princess nodded to her maids who walked over to a large wooden armoire and began to pull out dresses. "You might be a little taller than I am, but it shouldn't be a problem." She held up a dark teal, silk dress against the assassin's skin and smiled. "Perfect," she said. She turned to the ladies in waiting again. "Help her dress please."

The ladies led The Tigress back behind a screen where they began to remove her borrowed nun clothing. When they got down to her underclothes, they gasped. Several scars littered her body and her undergarments consisted of brass and leather, a belt holding multiple knives hung from her hips. She twitched standing there half naked and uncomfortable.

"Shall we provide for you proper undergarments, my lady?" one of the maids asked sheepishly.

The Tigress looked down at what she was wearing. "What is wrong with the ones that I have on?"

The maid that spoke before blushed and bowed her head as if she had done something wrong. "The dress will not fit properly with the ones you have," she replied.

The Tigress frowned and sighed.

Since she made no objection, one maid went to fetch them while the other stayed behind. The maid reached out to unbuckle the belt that held the knives when The Tigress grabbed her by the wrist.

"What are you doing?" she almost yelled.

"Is there a problem?" the princess asked in her soft, smooth voice. She poked her head around the screen and covered her mouth in surprise.

The Tigress shifted uncomfortably again. "I cannot walk around without my knives," she said.

The princess nodded. "Quickly bathe her and do her hair, then dress her."

"What about her weapons, your highness?" the maid asked.

She met The Tigress's gaze. "As long as they are not visible, I can't see why she cannot have them."

The maids did as the princess asked and within the hour the assassin was primped and polished. The dress was a little tight in the bosom but fit just about right everywhere else. Her long tresses of curls tumbled onto her bare shoulders, creating a soft glow on her skin.

The princess smiled when she stood from the vanity chair. "You are a vision," she said. She reached out and fingered her necklace. "What a beautiful piece of jewelry."

"It is a family heirloom," The Tigress explained, "I think."

"You think?" The Princess have her an inquiring look.

The Tigress gave a bow of her head. "I have never had such personal treatment," she replied, changing the subject. "Thank you for your kindness."

The Princess gave a solemn smile before her bottom lip quivered and tears fell from her eyes. The Tigress took a confused step back.

The maids rushed to the princess's side but she waved them away.

"Leave us!" she said through the tears, her voice slightly raised.

The two handmaidens shot each other glances before they obediently and silently walked out the door.

The Tigress stood looking everywhere in the room except at the young princess crying on one of the cushioned benches.

"Forgive me," she finally said dabbing away her tears with a handkerchief. "I am sure you are baffled by my sudden outburst. I can only imagine how awkward it must be for you to listen to a stranger cry."

"It is not my most comfortable moment, your highness, but I have been in worse if it makes you feel better."

"Yes," the princess sniffed. "What adventures you must have seen in your lifetime already and you cannot be much older than I."

She pulled the vanity chair out from the table and sat down. She had the feeling that the princess was about to ask her a favor.

"No, I believe I am only a few years older."

The princess nodded. "What is it like living on the road?"

She met the princess's gaze knowing what was about to happen. "It is interesting," she replied slowly. "I get to sleep under the stars and meet intriguing people, but," she paused, "my line of work also puts me in a lot of dangerous situations."

"But you are a free woman, are you not?" she asked, a flicker of hope in her eyes.

She regarded the princess for a moment. "I make my own decisions, yes, if that is what you mean. But my life is not as glamorous as your romantic view of it might be."

The princess let out a sigh. "No, I suppose it's not. Nothing is as you ever wish it to be."

They fell into silence for a few moments, one of them ready to leave while the other trying to word what she was about to say carefully.

"I know you are probably thinking 'poor, pitiful princess, what could she possibly know about the real world,'" she finally said.

"Not at all, your highness," The Tigress responded trying not to sound as bland as she felt.

The princess smiled weakly. "You don't have to lie. I know you are thinking it because I am thinking it as well." She paused in her thoughts. "I just want to know what it's like to live free like that, to not have to bend to the pressures of society and duty."

The Tigress stood not wanting to hear where this conversation was going. "I think you are very kind to have lent me your dress and maids, your highness, but you are right to say that I think you know nothing of the world. You are comfortable having more than you could ever need or want. You will always be provided for. There will always be a place for you. I, on the other hand, have to provide for myself. I have to make my own money sometimes barely scraping by. Be grateful for what you have. I see others in your kingdom and in all the others who do not have a single coin to their name. Who cannot afford to feed themselves or their children." She paused. "You have been blessed to be born in your position." She gave a bow and made her way to the door.

"I cannot marry that man. I have never met him," she said after her. "Please, let me hire you to kill him so that I might be free of this marriage contract."

The Tigress turned and looked at the sad girl pleading with her eyes. "You want me to kill your betrothed? Have you heard anything ill of him? Are you scared that he will not treat you well?"

The princess bowed her head. "I have not heard anything ill of him. I have heard he is quite generous."

The Tigress shook her head. "Do you understand what you're asking me to do? I cannot kill a man just because you don't want to marry him. I am not even going to mention the conflict of interest it would cause. I have already done so much to save this marriage. You are a princess; it is your duty to marry for political gain."

"And you are an assassin! It is your job to kill!" the princess yelled standing up from the bench.

She gave a small nod. "You are right, but as we had discussed before, I have the freedom to choose." She gave another bow and left the chambers.

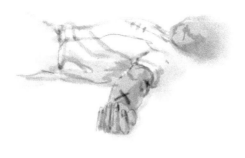

CHAPTER 5

THE TIGRESS MADE HER WAY TO THE COURTYARD FOLLOWING THE noise of the guests that floated down the stone walls of the halls. She only found the right corridor when a servant saw her and led her through the doors to the grand garden of the castle.

Thousands of different colored lanterns were hung around the perimeter casting a wonderful glow of colors all around. She had always heard about these magnificent parties that the Skahrrians throw but she had never before been present to see the splendor for herself. Even the guests displayed their own arrays of colors and lights as the flicker of the lanterns reflected off of their jewels and silken robes.

She lifted a hand to brush back a curl and took a single step toward the crowd wondering how long she had to stay before she could leave.

"You clean up quite well," a gruff voice said next to her.

She turned to see the king coming up to her and bowed slightly, stiffly, more from the constraints of her dress than from distaste for the king. "Thank you, your grace," she said out of duty.

"Had I not seen that defining 'X' on your wrist, I would not have known you from a lady." He held out his arm for her to take.

"I am a lady, your grace," she said emotionlessly hooking her arm in his.

"In the physical aspect, I believe you are, but it certainly does not go beyond that," he replied leading her down the few stairs toward the table.

"Yes, by all social standards you are correct," she said trying to hide her annoyance. "I wonder why, then, you would invite me to your feast. If word were to get out that you let a commoner to your fete you might be laughed at."

The king produced a thick bracelet and handed it to her motioning for her to cover up her tattoo. "I was hoping that we might be friends."

The Tigress hesitated as she took the bracelet, placing it over her tattoo. "Friends, your grace? If I am not mistaken you wanted to have me killed just a few hours ago. That is hardly the beginning of a friendship."

The king laughed. "It took a lot of faith to trust a woman to do a man's job," the king replied.

She tried to hide a scowl. The sexism she encountered in the rest of the realm had been a culture shock. She had never encountered gender restrictions while at the coven. Women are held to the same standards as men where she was raised.

"But you more than proved yourself the other day with my guards."

She turned to look at him. "Proved myself?" she repeated. "You mean that whole thing was a test?" She scoffed. "Forgive me, your grace," she said, "but you are far more clever than I originally gave you credit for. You are quite the actor."

The king laughed. "Perhaps, I am not as harsh as I first appear." They came to the large table where the king led her to a chair only a few down from his own. "This friendship would of course be out of a need," he whispered as she stood next to her seat. "A king is always in need of a good assassin."

She gave a slight nod. "I guess that means us being friends has nothing to do with it. This is more like a business-ship?"

He laughed. "I see we have come to an understanding," he said. "Please, enjoy yourself tonight. For tomorrow you will begin your journey."

The king walked to his chair at the head of the table and in his booming voice invited all of the guests to take their seats so they could begin the feast. Within moments of everyone sitting, servants appeared carrying large platters of roasted meats, fish and fruit, placing them on the table for the guests to partake.

The Tigress ate silently listening to the chatter of all of the lords and ladies of Skahrr as they stuffed their faces and drank glass of wine after glass of wine, laughing and snorting amongst themselves. When they had eaten their fill, the guests stood and walked over to where a band of men were set up to play music.

She got up from her seat and walked the perimeter keeping her eyes on the high-class men and women making drunken fools of themselves. She gave a small huff, laughing at their ridiculousness.

"My gods!" a familiar voice grated on her ears. "What a spectacle you are!"

She sighed and turned to see Tristan walking up to her, a glass of wine in one hand and a girl on each arm.

"Excuse me, ladies," he said caressing both of their cheeks. "I am going to have a little talk with my friend here."

The girls pouted but obediently walked away.

He turned back to her, looking her up and down, a pleased smile on his face. "It is quite difficult to be angry at you when you're look-ing like that, Dahlen," he said slightly slurring his words.

"Please don't call me that," she said annoyed. She looked away from him and out into the crowd again. "Is there even a reason you should be angry with me?' she asked indifferently.

"Yes!" he said taking a sip of wine and nodding his head. "You left me to the dogs back there! We were supposed to go to meet the king together and you left me."

She slowly turned to look at him, a confused look on her face. "I told you that I would go to see the king. I did not say we would walk in together."

"It was implied that we should," he said pointing his finger at her.

"I kept my word and showed up. You are not rotting away in the dungeons and are instead enjoying yourself at a feast, indulging in the rented whores that the king has provided for the party. I don't see why there is any reason for you to be upset."

He smiled at her. "I am willing to forgive you for your mishap," he said. He then reached out and gently took one of her curls in his hand, softly rubbing it between his thumb and forefinger. "If you and I could," he paused and winked at her.

She glanced down at his hand and pushed it away. "Forget it."

"You're not shy are you?" he asked playfully.

She lifted an eyebrow at him. "Let me share a few simple words that will dissuade you from ever touching me again," she replied.

He laughed. "There is nothing a beautiful woman could say that could ever dissuade me from wanting to lay with her."

She smiled, reaching out to grab a piece of his garbs and slowly pulling him toward her so she could whisper in his ear. "I kill men for a living."

He swallowed hard and nodded his head as he took a step back. "That would about do it," he said taking another sip of his wine. "You have yourself a wonderful night, Dahlen."

"Stop calling me that," she said through clenched teeth.

He winked at her. "I shall see you in the morning." He gave her a light bow and then walked back toward the two girls that held his attention before he had walked over.

She resumed her walk around refusing several servants that approached her with trays of wine and more food. She finally made her way to the other end of the courtyard where a balcony looked out into the Dormant Sea. She could just hear the pounding of the waves on the cliffs down below. She closed her eyes and listened to the sound of them, breathing slowing in and out of her nose, putting herself in a light trance. She let the breeze blow freely through her hair and caress her skin as she concentrated on pushing out the sounds of the lords and ladies.

She was finally feeling comfortable when she heard the scuffling of shoes behind her. She bent down and pulled out one of her knives that she had strapped to her ankle and turned to see a young man coming up toward her.

He held his hands up. "Whoa!" he said. "Forgive me. I didn't mean to startle you, but I mean no harm. I promise."

She noticed the emerald seal of Skahrr on the man's cloak and put her knife away. "You are the crown prince, I assume."

He bowed to her. "I am," he replied. "Prince Mohrr." He made a fist and held it in the air flexing his arm.

She blinked at him.

He smiled and let his arm fall to his side. "It is ancient Skahrrian for strength," he said. "Royal tradition dating back to many generations. The men get names with ancient meaning and the women get names of what the king wishes for his country."

"Rain and River," she replied.

He nodded. "Yes, we have plenty of farms to wish for a healthy water supply. Though my father's name is my favorite. Breht means life or breath. So if someone tells you to take a breht," he said, "what do they mean?" he took a couple of steps forward his hands opened.

She smiled. "Take a life or take a breath?"

"Ah!" he said coming to stand beside her. "I figured that would be something you could appreciate."

She didn't reply.

"You saved my sister's life," he said after a moment. "I appreciate that. You will never meet a more gentile soul than my sister Rain. River is young and like her name implies, wild. But Rain will make a good queen someday."

The Tigress smiled thinking of the conversation she had with the princess earlier in the evening. "I am sure once she accepts her position she will be."

He nodded again. "I see you have spoken with her. Her notions of marriage are still immature. She reads too much into those romantic plays and stories. Something I assume all women do."

She shot him a glance. "You would assume incorrectly, your highness. Not all women dream of love and marriage."

"Forgive me. I am still trying to figure out the mystery that is woman." He flashed her another smile. "I did not offend you, I hope, by my assumption?"

The Tigress shook her head. "No, your grace," she replied.

"Good," he said. "I would very much hate being on your bad side."

"Because I am an assassin?" she asked lifting a brow at him.

He shook his head. "No," he replied. "Because you are a beautiful woman and I would hate for you to shun me."

The Tigress felt her cheeks flush and she looked back toward the sea hoping that her companion had not noticed.

"You do my sister's dress justice," he said filling the silence.

She nodded and slowly turned back to meet his eyes. "Thank you, your grace."

"Do you dance—" he paused shaking his head, "I'm sorry. I am not sure what to call you. 'Assassin' just seems rude. Yet, I know you do not have a traditional name."

She was about to answer when she looked up and noticed a dark figure running along the roof of the castle, jumping from stone to stone. She watched as the figure stealthily came up behind a guard and broke his neck.

She gave a worried look to the prince before she hitched up her dress and ran toward the fete, pausing only to take out a couple of her knives. She pushed through the dancing couples causing an uproar from the guests who yelled after her. One of the males grabbed her by the arm but she turned and pushed her elbow in his face causing him to let go.

She watched as the dark figure scaled the wall and jumped down, landing on the table right in front of the king, dagger raised in his hand. Before he could strike, she threw one of her blades hitting the man in the back. She continued to run, jumping on the table and thrusting her other knife into the back of his neck just as he slashed at the king giving him a small cut on his face. The king fell backwards in his chair letting out a yell of surprise as his would-be killer fell on top of him, dead.

The king looked up, scared and confused from the ground at the cloaked face of the man that tried to kill him. "Gods be praised!" he said breathlessly.

Suddenly guards swarmed the area circling The Tigress as she removed her blades from the dead man and stood. All of them raised their swords and spears pointing them at her as she wiped the blood from her knives on the dead man's cloak. She slowly panned around looking at all of them. She took a step forward and the perimeter tightened around her.

"Put your weapons down!" a deep voice yelled across the courtyard. "This woman just saved my father and you are treating her like a hostile!" Mohrr stepped through the now silent and stunned crowd toward the table. "If you want to do something useful, help my father up!"

The guards turned and bowed at their prince, doing as he said. Mohrr walked over to her through a gap the guards made and held out his hand to help escort her out of the confusion. She put her knives away and allowed him to lead her away.

"I apologize for their idiocy," he replied. "And once again I thank you for saving a member of my family." He then let go of her hand and went over to his father.

"I'm fine! Leave me!" the king yelled swatting away the helping hands around him. He pulled a handkerchief from his chest pocket and pressed it against his cheek. He stood and breathed heavily as he glared at the dead body of the assassin on the ground. "Take him to the council room!" he barked. "You!" he said pointing to The Tigress. "Come with us. You might be needed."

She nodded and followed the guards who carried the body through the castle to where the council room was. The king and Prince Mohrr stormed in behind them.

The Tigress walked up to the body and picked up his limp left arm pushing back the long sleeve to reveal an identical 'X' tattoo to her own. She dropped the arm and fell to one knee.

"I have killed one of my own," she said.

"Sir Tohrn," the king said.

"Your grace," a guard responded stepping forward and kneeling.

"Take some of your men and scan the rooftops. Be on high alert. And get a small group of men to escort my daughters to one of their rooms and guard them there until the whole castle is searched and cleared."

"Yes, your grace," he stood and walked out of the room taking the other guards with him.

"You shouldn't find anyone else," The Tigress said when the guards left. "We do not normally work in groups and if you were the only target then only one would have done the job." She pushed herself off of the ground and stepped forwards toward the body. She put one of her hands over the dead man's heart and another over hers bowing her head. After a moment of silence, she removed the cloak from his face and gasped.

"Do you know this man?" Mohrr asked.

She nodded. "He was called The Shadow," she replied. "He used his dark skin and speed as an advantage, using the darkness as his own weapon." She closed his eye lids over his dark, vacant eyes. "I did not know him too well, but we used to train together. He received his title the year before me."

"You seem extremely upset about the death of the man who tried to kill the king," Mohrr said casually.

She turned and gave the prince a light glare. "As I told your father a few days ago, I hold no allegiance to any nation. The coven was my home, my family, and I just killed one of my brothers."

"Can you tell who sent him?" the king asked dismissing what she had said.

She searched the body of the corpse removing several hidden knives a little larger than her own and a thin rope with a grapple on the end. She finally found a money sack and pulled out a gold coin with a wild boar on it, the symbol of Bornnen. She held it up for the king and prince to see.

The king furrowed his brows and growled. "A revenge killing."

"It seems that Bornnen is asking for a war sooner than what was expected," the prince said.

The Tigress remained silent. She knew the people of Bornnen enough to know that they were less likely to send an outsider to do their own work. She had fulfilled more contracts to kill people of Bornnen than she had been hired by them.

Just then Tristan burst into the room and gasped when he saw the dead body. "Incredible," he said slightly stumbling.

The king turned to glare at him. "There is no reason you should have come in here," he slightly growled at him.

"She is a very handy person to have, your grace," he said ignoring his comment. "She saved your life." He shook his head. "I saw the way she threw that knife. Amazing," he said shaking his head again and sipping from the glass of wine still in his hand.

Mohrr nodded. "You're right," he agreed looking at her with a smile in his eyes. "She is amazing."

The Tigress and Mohrr made eye contact for a moment but she turned away, slightly blushing. She frowned, confused by her reaction.

"Perhaps she might be a nice edition to the royal guard, father," Mohrr continued. "She acted very quickly and efficiently."

The king nodded and looked up from his thoughts. "I will pay you twice the amount I offered if you were to escort my daughter to Thren tomorrow," he said.

The Tigress was taken aback. "But, your grace, if I delay my task it would give the Bornnenians more time to complete the funeral tour and build up their reserves. If I were you, I would not give them any more time to retaliate," she said.

"Certainly, they have already done that," Mohrr said motioning toward the dead assassin on the table. "I will also be in the company of the caravan. But I think that it would be in our favor to have someone with training such as yours to help us."

His soft way of speaking toward her brought the hint of a smile to her face and she pursed her lips to try and hide it.

"Agreed," the king said.

The Tigress nodded. "If I may be so bold as to suggest that we hide the royal caravan among tradesmen and merchants," she said. "If we camouflage the princess's carrier to make it look like a common lord, perhaps there will be less of a chance she will be targeted by an ambush."

The king gave what she said some thought before nodding. "It makes sense," he said. "There is always a large group of such men and women traveling in and out of the cities. We will get some men on that right away." The king's face became pale and he took hold of his son's arm for support. He pressed his hand to the back of his head and winced.

"Are you alright, father?" Mohrr asked.

The king pulled his hand away from his head and was taken aback to see some blood. "I must have fallen to the ground harder than I thought," he said.

"You should see the healer," Mohrr said holding his father at the elbow. "Tristan, could you escort my father to the healer's room?"

Tristan scowled at him.

"I do not need that idiot to help me," the king said. "I am capable of walking myself."

"None-the-less, your grace, I will walk with you to make sure you make it there," Tristan said.

The king grumbled as the two of them walked out of the room.

Prince Mohrr then turned to the last two guards in the room and ordered them to remove the body elsewhere before he turned his attention back to The Tigress. "You certainly are worth every gold coin my father is paying you," he said.

She frowned.

"Forgive me," he said realizing his mistake. "That truly did not come out the way I intended it to."

"How," she said slowly, "did you intend it to sound?"

"I meant for it to sound like you are intelligent," he started getting closer to her, "and insightful." He stood in front of her and brushed back a lock of her hair.

She could feel the heat rise in her face.

"Not to mention beautiful."

She gave a soft smile. "If I didn't know better, your highness, I would think that you are trying to sweet talk me."

He laughed. "Perhaps I am. Before this unexpected event happened, I was about to ask you to dance."

She gave a small smile. "I believe you were," she replied. "And I was about to refuse."

The Prince gave a small laugh. "As is your right, though I can't remember ever being refused before."

"There is a first time for everything," The Tigress replied.

He smiled and gave a small nod. "I still do not know what to call you," he said taking another step closer. "Perhaps you could enlighten me."

"The only name that I am called other than my title is 'T' which is just a shortened version that an acquaintance of mine calls me."

"'T' it is then," Prince Mohrr said taking one of her hands and pressing it to his lips.

She was taken aback, her body going a little rigid, but she did not pull away.

She lifted an eyebrow. "Are you always this charming, your highness, or am I just this lucky?" she asked him.

He smiled. "Maybe a bit of both," he replied. "But I must say that you somewhat inspire me."

"Forgive me," she said, "if I do not automatically buy what you are trying to sell. My experiences with men never usually end well."

He laughed a good hearty laugh that filled the room they were in. "For those men, I can imagine it does not. Do not fret," he said. "I do not expect you to follow me to bed."

A laugh escaped her. "Ha!" she said. "Men always expect a woman to follow them to bed, your highness. I cannot imagine you are that different."

"Are you calling me a liar?" he asked playfully stepping closer.

"Everyone lies," she replied.

"But I am a prince," he said his eyes as green as the emerald on his chest.

"You are still included in everyone, your highness, no matter what your status may be," The Tigress replied, her eyes searching his.

"But how can I lie when so much beauty is before me? I am having trouble speaking normally."

"I imagine it is easier than you are leading me to believe," she replied.

He shook his head, a smile still on his face. "You are not going to trust me so easily, are you?" he asked leaning closer.

Her cheeks flushed. "I don't trust anyone so easily," she replied almost breathless.

"Maybe you could make an exception this one time," he whispered, his breath warm against her ear.

The Tigress froze as a strange chill climbed up her spine. She opened her mouth to respond, but the sound of someone clearing their throat interrupted her.

"Forgive me," Tristan's indifferent voice said breaking the silence, "but your father sent me to get you."

The Prince stood staring down into The Tigress's eyes for a few more seconds before he took a step back and kissed her hand again.

"Duty calls," he said turning and giving Tristan a glare as he walked out of the room.

"Is it because he is rich or is it because he is a prince?" he asked her as she went to move out of the room. "Perhaps it is a bit of both?" he continued turning out of the room with her.

"What are you talking about?"

"I'm talking about your flushed cheeks and gleaming eyes. The prince obviously had some affect on you."

"I do not have time for your childish babble," she replied, scowling. "I think I will call it a night before our long journey. I advise you to do same. Especially since we are now traveling with the royal caravan to Thren."

Tristan laughed. "The night is still young!" he replied picking up the wine glass he left when he escorted the king out of the room and holding it in the air. "I have plenty of time to rest when I am dead!"

cHapteR 6

THE TIGRESS PATTED THE NECK OF HER HORSE AS IT TROTTED ALONG the road. It was perfect weather to embark on their journey to Thren. The coastal breeze followed them as they moved along, gently urging them along the path. She scanned the caravan making sure that everything was in its place. The king ordered extra guards to escort the princess, most of them in normal merchant clothes so as not to raise an alarm.

Half an hour into the journey, she heard a long groaning sound coming up behind her and she turned her head to see Tristan looking grey in the face.

"Why is everything so bright?" he asked to no one in particular. "I feel like my head is slowly being spilt open by a dull axe."

She faced forward again, ignoring him.

He pulled right up next to her. "I finally caught up with you," he said. "Do me a favor, Dahlen, and keep a hold of my horse's reigns so that I might nap while we travel." He tried handing the reigns to her.

"Are you mad?" she asked shaking her head. "I am not your stable boy. My job is not taking care of your horse. If you want someone to take care of you and hold your hand go back home to The Hills. And stop calling me 'Dahlen.'"

"You seem very bitter about my upraising," he said after a moment.

"I am bitter about your arrogant attitude and your incessant talking."

He gagged and placed his hand over his mouth. "Why am I the only one hurting this much?" He slouched on his horse.

"Because you're the only one idiotic enough to drink as much as you did the night before a long journey," she replied.

He rubbed his forehead with the heel of his hand. "Like you have never drunk too much before." He put his hand on his stomach making an uncomfortable face.

"I don't drink," she replied simply. "It dulls the senses."

He looked at her incredulously. "You have no joy in your life, do you know that?" he asked. "I am sorry if I like to enjoy my time while I am alive. Not like all of you stiffs who can't seem to let loose."

She lifted an eyebrow at him. "No joy?" she repeated. "You're the one complaining like a spoiled mama's boy."

He scoffed. "I am not complaining!" he retorted. "I am merely stating that it is much too early to leave the day after a grand feast. It just doesn't make sense." He paused and groaned again squinting. "Me stating a fact is not a complaint but I am wondering when we are going to break for a nap."

"Serious question for you," she said once again patting her horse.

"Yes?"

"How do you survive on your own acting like this?"

"What do you mean?"

"I am just confused as to how no one has killed you out of pure annoyance," she mused.

He scowled.

"Or how you even make it traveling from town to town without dying from something stupid you have done, like talking up the wrong man's wife or riding your horse off of a cliff. The way you talk I'm sure you would never have noticed a cliff until it was too late."

He frowned deeper. "I'm sorry. Have I done something to offend you?" he asked.

She shook her head. "You don't actually listen when people talk to you, do you?" she replied.

"My mother used to tell me that I only hear what I want to hear," he replied.

"Must be why you're so happy considering everyone around you finds you utterly obnoxious."

"It's called optimism," he retorted. "Maybe you should give those frown lines a break and try it." He made another face. "Ugh! What is that smell?" His face turned a shade of green and he put his hand over his mouth as his stomach heaved.

"It is probably that dead boar, baking in the sun over there," she replied pointing to the rotting carcass on the side of the road.

He turned to see the half-eaten carcass of a boar with several vultures feasting on its flesh. "Oh, gods," he said as he leaned over the side of his horse and threw up.

The Tigress smiled as she made a clicking sound for her horse to speed up, leaving Tristan retching by himself. She caught up to the royal carrier and slowed back down to a walk.

She made a glance around the area looking for any signs that an ambush might take place but noticed nothing unusual. This caravan, as opposed to the fake one she was in, was enormous. The king sent his best men along the road with them and, per her request, they traveled along with the tradesmen bringing their silks, and wheat to the luxurious city of Harpren to sell. The royal carrier itself had been bought from a merchant that morning, making it look the same as all the others. The only giveaway were the few scattered guards that rode along with them that were not incognito.

Before she had been riding alongside the princess' carrier for too long, one of the windows was opened and a face appeared behind it.

"I am guessing you are still not going to take me up on my offer," the princess said to her.

The Tigress shot her a short glance. "Your highness," she started, "me taking you up on your offer would almost be a conflict of interest.

Your father has already employed me on missions in favor of this union. I cannot simply go against it. I have a sense of honor."

The princess scoffed. "How strange," she said. "A common murderer like you knowing the meaning of honor. It's like a dog knowing the meaning of love."

She frowned a bit. "I understand that your speech was meant to insult me, your highness, but it goes to say that you have never owned a dog. For they know how to love better than anyone."

The princess pouted and slammed the window shut again.

"She really is a sweet girl," the smooth, deep voice of Mohrr said off to her side. "She is just a little naïve with the ways of the world." He smiled at her, a dashing tooth-filled smile.

She looked forward again. "I do not doubt either of those statements," she said back to him.

"Tell me about your travels," he gently urged pulling his horse closer to hers. "Where have your adventures taken you?"

She gave a half smile. "I have nothing worth telling that isn't something I shouldn't say," she answered.

His smile was relentless. "Are all of you assassins shrouded in mystery?"

"How unalluring is an unmysterious assassin?" she asked grinning back.

His smile deepened. "Is this you flirting with me, T?" he asked her.

"Of course not," she replied her heart making a slight jump at his calling her 'T'. "Women of my position are much too serious for things like flirting. No, we are all about business."

He laughed and they shared a glance, his emerald eyes sparkling back into hers. She quickly looked away not allowing herself time to process the strange feeling she got when he smiled at her.

"That breeze is nice," Mohrr said after a moment. "It takes away the harshness of the sun."

She nodded. "It is definitely a relief."

"Harpren is a beautiful place," the prince continued. "Have you ever been?"

The Tigress nodded. "Yes," she answered. "It is a wonderful city with beautiful gardens and buildings. The market place smells like roasted almonds."

The prince agreed. "Yes, it is quite lovely. The castle is perfectly situated on a rising cliff looking out into the sea.

"I have never been to the castle," she said. "I have seen much of the capitol, but I have yet to see the castle up close."

"Then you are in for a surprise," the prince continued. "Though I am partial to my own home I cannot deny the beauty that Harpren has to offer." He nodded. "My sister will be happy there, I am sure."

The Tigress pondered if she should comment on what the prince said when she decided against it. She simply tilted her head slightly. "Perhaps," she replied not really agreeing.

A few minutes later Tristan came riding up still moaning. He leaned over on his horse but immediately sat up again. "I can't escape the terrible smells around me," he said making a face.

The prince huffed and shook his head in disdain.

"Forgive me," Tristan said coming up between them. "Am I interrupting something again?" he asked.

"Would it make a difference if you had?" the prince responded.

The Tigress sensed a strange animosity between the two men. She could all but feel the tension emanating off of them since she first saw them together the night before. She regarded them both as they shot each other glares and threw half hidden insults at each other.

Finally, Tristan looked over at her to engage her in conversation. "How about you, Dahlen?" he said.

She raised an eyebrow and looked over at him. "How about what?" she asked back.

"Oh, you're not even paying attention," he said waving his hand. "Not important anyways, Dahlen."

"Dahlen?" the prince said leaning over his horse to see her, a confused look on his face. "Is that your name?"

The Tigress opened her mouth to respond when Tristan cut her off. "I came up with it," he said. "She told me that she did not have a proper name, so I came up with one for her. A mix of Dahker and Sohlen. It is very fitting don't you think?" he asked.

"Dangerous sunset," the prince whispered staring off in front of him. He looked pensive for a moment before looking back at her. "Yes, I believe it is very fitting for her."

WHEN THE CARAVAN STOPPED TO CAMP THE SECOND DAY, THE TIGRESS once again found herself in the presence of Tristan. He, like the night before, invited himself to her campfire.

Tristan took a large gulp of water that he got from a tradesmen that joined them from the Small Mountain area where fresh water springs gurgle out from the Desert of Vremir.

"Aaahh!" he said a little louder than necessary. "Worth every penny," he said.

"I cannot believe you paid for water," The Tigress said looking at him.

"Doctors say that the water from Small Mountain has healing powers. And I have to say that I feel extremely refreshed."

"It's a shame it can't cure idiocy," she added. "That would be a miracle."

"You cannot bring me down today, Dahlen" he said putting his hands up. "The stars are beautiful and this haunch of meat smells absolutely delicious. And they both tell me that I am about to be a very satisfied man."

She watched him for a moment. "Do you not know some of the silk traders that are riding with us?"

He froze in his seat. "Why?" he asked.

"The silk trade is your family's business, is it not? If I am not mistaken, that trade gave your family the money to buy The Hills and Stahrs Lake."

He chewed the piece of meat in his mouth and slowly swallowed. "You are correct," he said nodding. "Yes," he added after a pause, "I do know some of the traders that you are referring to."

"Then why is it you do not dine with them in the tavern?" she asked pointing to the small building along the side of the road with light dancing in the windows.

"Are you so opposed to me sharing in your company?" he asked her. "Yes."

He scowled at her. "You really know how to kill the mood, don't you?" he asked a little perturbed.

She was taken aback by the rise in his voice. "I think it a fair question," she retorted simply.

"Why are you not dining with the prince?" he asked. "You two seem to be getting along quite well."

"He is eating with his sister and after a long day in the company of many others, I decided to eat out here. Alone. By myself." She lifted an eyebrow at him.

"Well, I wouldn't trust the prince just because he has a pretty face and dashing smile."

"I don't trust him," she replied. "And stop changing the subject. I asked you a question."

He took another sip from his canteen. "It's none of your business," he finally said. "I don't want to talk about it."

She gave a small laugh. "Of all the other times I tried to get you to stop talking you wouldn't. Then I actually ask you a question, an invitation to talk, and you don't want to talk?" She laughed again.

"Well, it is none of your business," he shot back.

"That never seemed to stop you from trying to pry into *my* life."

He remained silent for a few moments as he continued to eat, staring into the fire. "I'm a bastard," he finally said picking up a stick and poking the fire.

"I could have told you that," she replied.

He looked up at her, a hurt look on his face. "No, a real bastard." She blinked at him.

"You know, my mother was never married to my father but bore him a child?"

She raised an eyebrow. "I know what a bastard is," she said back to him. "I'm just not sure what difference telling me was supposed to have made."

He shook his head. "What's it like?" he asked her.

"What is what like?"

"Being cold and unpleasant all of the time."

She narrowed her eyes. "Liberating."

"Then you are by far the freest woman I have ever met," he said angrily snapping the twig in his hand and throwing it into the fire.

She pursed her lips and creased her brows slightly. "What I meant about my earlier comment about what difference it would have made, was that I have known plenty of bastards and parentless children that have grown up to be something more than a mistake or a burden. They become something great." The Tigress paused for a moment, thinking how much like Marten she sounded.

He looked at her, a thoughtful look on his face. "Did you just say something nice to me?" he asked.

"I do have feelings, you know?" she answered shooting him a glance.

"It is difficult to tell sometimes between the hard glances and stonewall exterior you have going on."

She stared at him blankly.

"Like that, right there!" he exclaimed pointing at her. "How do you get to be devoid of all emotion like that?"

"I have learned to not let my emotions affect me or to let them show," she replied.

They fell into a silence for a few minutes, both of them eating quietly.

"Why does it matter to those silk traders whether you're the bastard of a lord or not?" The Tigress asked. "You are still the son of a Lord."

"If this is you pretending to care, you are terrible at it."

She didn't respond.

"Alright," he said shrugging. "I was never treated as a bastard by my father, not for a while anyways. He paid for my schooling and saw that I had what I needed. I lived in a nice bedroom in the house. His first wife was even kind to me, raised me as her own because she was unable to have children after her first stillborn." He cleared his throat. "But after she passed away and my father remarried I was treated as a second-class citizen. My stepmother chopped me down whenever my father's back was turned and it only got worse when her sons were born. She convinced my father to write me out of the will. She turned almost the entire house against me, threatening everyone with their jobs if they showed me pity. So, what I meant the other day by me being the third son of a lord was I am illegitimate. First in birth, but last in line." He sighed. "Those silk traders would just laugh at me if I asked to sit down with them."

"I am sorry," she said.

"Somehow I feel like it is difficult for you to feel pity for anyone," he replied looking at her.

She blinked at him. "You are very quick to judge what you do not understand."

"What was the coven like, then?" he asked. "Is it really a brotherhood where you look out for each other and learn the secrets of the realm?"

The Tigress opened her mouth to respond when a man walked up to them from the darkness, his face covered by a hood. "That is a question only those that have suffered through the coven know the answer to," the man said stepping into the light of the fire and removing his hood.

The Tigress stood up from her seat. "Marten!" she said in surprise. "What are you doing here?"

"You know this monk?" Tristan asked sizing up Marten.

"He is a friend," The Tigress replied.

Tristen looked at her, surprised. "You have friends?"

Marten turned to him. "I was wondering if you would allow me the pleasure of a private audience with my *friend* here."

Tristen looked at The Tigress who nodded. He stood after a moment and walked off toward the horses.

"You are not sharing secrets, I hope?" Marten asked after Tristan left and sat on the log that he had just vacated.

"I would never have answered that question in depth, Marten. You know that." She looked up at him. "What are you doing here?" she repeated. "I thought I left you in Cragg. I had a message sent to you and everything about my departure, but I did not tell you by what means I was travelling."

"I have been summoned back to The Rest," he replied. "I am needed for something. I always make a point to travel with caravans and when I heard that you were in this one as well I had to find you." He picked off a piece of the meat that was warming over the fire.

"Heard?" she repeated skeptically. "You heard I was here?"

"People are always whispering, T," he replied. "You just have to know how to listen."

"Well, however you came to find me, I am glad," she said. "You can do me the favor of bringing my yearly contribution with you." She dug through one of her bags pulling out a small satchel.

"If I am not mistaken," he started, "I did that for you last year as well."

"Yes," she replied. "So, I figured since you have done it for me before and are on your way anyways then you wouldn't mind doing it again," she said in a flat tone, her eyebrow raised.

He lifted his own eyebrow at her, but nodded. "I have a feeling you are avoiding the coven," he said catching the bag of money she threw his way.

She shook her head. "No, just not quite ready to go back yet," she replied. "There is not much for me there."

He nodded and took another piece of meat off of the roast. "I heard some disturbing news about the demise of one of our brethren in Skahrr," he said placing the meat in his mouth.

She closed her eyes and didn't respond.

"T," he started, "what happened?"

She didn't answer right away, thinking about what she wanted to say. "I was protecting an investment, Marten. He was going to take a great opportunity right out of my hand."

"So, you killed him?"

"I couldn't let him kill King Breht," she whispered harshly.

"Why didn't you come to me when you realized?" he asked. "I had to hear it from someone else."

She avoided his gaze. "One of these days you are going to tell me how you find out everything."

"Who was it?" he asked after a moment ignoring her comment.

She closed her eyes and took a deep breath. "The Shadow," she finally replied looking at him again. "I have already sent word for the body to be collected."

"The Shadow?" he repeated. "Are you sure?"

She nodded slowly.

Marten sat there staring at her, a baffled look on his face. "The Shadow disappeared off the map over two years ago almost since he left the coven. We all feared that he might have gone rogue."

"It was very strange, Marten," she continued. "He had gold coins from Bornnen in his bag. But why would anyone from Bornnen pay to have the king of Skahrr killed? They would never hire someone to do something they are capable of themselves. And if there is one thing that the people of Bornnen are capable of it is killing."

He rubbed his stubble, thinking. "I see your point, but that doesn't go to say that they wouldn't. Maybe they realized that it would be easier to hire an assassin; that an assassin could slip in and out unnoticed better than some clumsy, barbaric Bornnenian could."

She thought about it for a moment and nodded. "Yes, I guess if you put it that way, it does make more sense."

"I hope you were not cooking up some conspiracy theory, T."

"I was just thinking that it was curious, Marten." She paused. "How much trouble am I going to be in with The Master when he finds out?" she asked.

He laughed. "The Master would give you a slap on the wrist, I am sure," he confirmed. "But, the coven has been looking for The Shadow for years now. The last time I was at Dead Man's Rest, The Master asked me to find out what I could about The Shadow's whereabouts."

"You always have a magical way of finding out information," The Tigress said. "They should have given you the title The Ear."

Marten avoided her eyes but laughed. "It certainly would have been a little more fitting. But unlike before I was unable to find anything out about him. If you had not told me he had passed I would have continued my search."

"You never told me why they gave you the title The Monk," she said.

He nodded. "Perhaps one day I will but it is not a story I want to tell tonight," he replied.

They fell into a short silence, nothing but the sound of the crackling fire between them.

"So who is this boy I see you talking to?" Marten finally asked.

"Boy?" she repeated. "He is older than I am."

"I hope you are keeping your distance," he continued.

She scowled. "Are you here to give me information or are you here to spy on me?" she asked. "Neither of which I am fond of, but I can tell you that I will absolutely not tolerate you spying on me."

"I am just looking out for you, making sure you keep to your vows."

She glared at him. "I have always been true to my vows to the coven, Marten," she said defensively. "And you are certainly one to talk. I know of your personal parties at the local brothels. The Monk but only in disguise."

"I am only looking out for you, T," he repeated standing.

"Well, like you keep reminding me, I do not have a father, so stop trying to be one to me. I have been out on my own for over two years now and I have been doing just fine without you."

"You are still young and vulnerable, T," Marten said gathering his things. "You might be smart and ruthless, but you are somehow forgiving and naïve." He walked up to her giving her shoulder a light squeeze.

She glared up at him but was taken aback by the odd look on his face. His mouth was slightly open and his eyes, though fixed on her, seemed to look through her, a strange, dull haze over them. The Tigress started and was about to ask if he was alright but before she could react, Marten took a deep breath and shook his head blinking.

Marten took a step back, his breathing picking up like he had just been running. He looked over at The Tigress and swallowed hard.

"T," he began, trying to regain his breath, "promise me that you will be careful."

"Marten," she said furrowing her brows, confused, "I am always careful."

He shook his head. "Sometimes a handsome smile is a ruse for danger. Keep your mind open but do not be quick to trust."

"Marten, what are you talking about?" she asked.

He shook his head. "You are smarter than that," he said ignoring her question. "Let go of what you think you want and learn to respect and appreciate what you already have. Do not let your desire for answers cloud your judgement."

Before The Tigress could find words to speak again Marten turned and walked back into the darkness from whence he came.

CHAPTER 7

"Ah! Now I remember," Tristan said randomly, breaking his unusual silence. "That monk was with you at the tavern the day I found you."

The Tigress turned her head slightly to look at him.

"Who is he?" Tristan asked.

"He is an ally of mine," The Tigress responded knowing she was not going to get away with ignoring him.

"He seemed very concerned with your affairs," he added. "I never thought an assassin would be friends with a monk. Seems like a very unlikely friendship."

She gave a soft smile. "He is no monk," she said.

"He certainly dresses like one."

"That makes no difference. When you found me I was wearing a nun's habit, was I not?"

He nodded. "Yes."

"So, shouldn't that teach you to not assume someone is who they portray themselves as?"

He lifted an eyebrow. "I suppose so."

In spite of the warning that Marten had given her, The Tigress tried to warm up to Tristan. She still thought that he talked too much but she forced herself to actually open up and share with him. Though The Tigress agreed she should not trust him, he was, perhaps, her key to finding out about her past and he was also part of her cover to get into Bornnen.

"So, when you say 'ally' do you mean he is another assassin?"

She pursed her lips. "That I cannot say."

"I'll take that as a 'yes.'"

"There are more than just assassins at the coven," she replied. "Everyone knows we train mercenaries and spies as well."

They fell into silence as they rode along, the noise of the caravan rising in the cool sea breeze.

"Have you ever been to Harpren?" Tristan finally asked.

She nodded. "Several times," she replied. "It is a beautiful city and the people are usually less pushy and rude. They tend to be a little more welcoming than other cities I have been to."

"How many people have you killed?" Tristan said, the question bursting from his lips.

The Tigress was taken aback. "That is not really a question I should answer either," she replied.

"Why not? You are an assassin, are you not? Are assassins not proud of how many people they have killed?"

The Tigress sat silently, moving along with the motions of her horse letting his words run through her mind. "Yes," she said after a long moment, surprise apparent in her voice. "We are."

He tilted his head looking at her. "You seem upset."

She shook her head. "I just never thought about what you said before. Assassins being proud of their kills."

"What was the coven really like?" he asked. "You never answered my question from last night."

"And I will not answer it now," she responded. "Marten was right. Only those who have suffered through the training know the answer to that question."

"Why ask for answers you cannot know?" Prince Mohrr said

trotting up next to them. "Sometimes it is more fun to make speculations about such things, Tristan."

Tristan scowled at him. The Tigress turned her head to hide a smile.

"Dead Man's Rest, in my mind, is full of dragons," the prince continued giving The Tigress a playful wink. "Not the gigantic fire-breathing dragons of folklore, but tiny little dragons you can hold in the palm of your hand."

Tristan shook his head, irritated.

"They are a delicacy where you are from," Mohrr said.

The Tigress gave a short laugh. "You believe that we eat dragons?" she asked.

"Speculate," the prince said. "It's a little different."

"It is a stupid speculation," Tristan mumbled to himself. "Dragons are not even real."

"That is part of the fun," the prince replied, smiling back at The Tigress. "It is called imagination, Tristan. Do you not have one?"

The Tigress was about to add a comment when she saw movement in the sky and looked up. She squinted in the bright sun but was able to notice the red tipped wings of the eagle flying above them. She pulled back on her reigns turning her horse around. She pointed to the sky and the prince gasped.

"My sister," he said fearfully and rode back toward the royal carrier as fast as his horse could carry him.

"What's wrong?" Tristan asked watching the prince speed off. "What are you doing?"

"Do you know how to use a sword, Tristan?"

He frowned. "Yes, I have had proper training."

"Good," she replied. "You're about to use it."

"Why?" he said beginning to panic. "What is happening?"

She pointed up at the bird circling the caravan again. "Mehtian pirates." She looked to the head of the caravan. They were coming up to a path along the cliffs. She cursed when she saw it.

The path winded along a cliff face. One side of the path dropped a hundred feet into the ocean below while the other edged along a thirty-foot cliff wall. Many men have fallen to their death on this narrow trail. The caravan faced sudden and certain difficulty at this change in terrain. It was the perfect place for an attack.

The Tigress scanned along the cliff towering over the path and noticed large boulders by the edge. Boulders large enough to hide behind. Large enough to block their path if they were to fall.

She pointed to them. "There!" she proclaimed. "They are going to jump us from there." She pulled on her reigns again, causing her horse to spin in a circle. "Warn the guards at the front! Don't let them make it to the cliffs! They will charge everyone either forcing them to the water below or crushing them with the boulders."

She raced back toward some of the guards that were undercover and told them of the impeding danger. Some of them went to form a tighter grouping around the princess while the others rode off toward the cliffs. A guard offered her his shield which she gratefully took, racing back to where Tristan was following her directions.

She saw Tristan trying to tell the people of the caravan to make ready, but it was already too late for the people in the front. A quarter of the caravan had already passed through the cliffs and The Tigress watched as the pirates jumped up from the rocks—archers pointing their arrows down.

She pulled her own bow off of her back and dug her heels into her horse and screamed trying to get closer. The cries and shouts from the people that were being rained on by arrows filled the air. The Tigress readied her bow and pulled back releasing an arrow toward the pirates. She cursed when she saw that it missed; she was too far away. She galloped harder and aimed. The second arrow hit one of the pirates in the arm bringing attention and arrows her way.

She lifted the shield up and ducked behind it, her heart skipping a beat with every arrow that bounced off of it. The sounds of galloping horses joined her, more guards finally taking charge.

She aimed her bow again, this time striking a man in the chest. She held the shield up once more for a second wave of arrows sent her way. She let out a grunt when an arrow nicked her thigh.

When she got to the second rise of the cliff, several of the pirates slid down the slope and she jumped off her horse. Two men charged her. She threw one of her knives at one of them, hitting the man in the throat. The second man lifted his sword and swung down onto the raised shield and The Tigress crouched sweeping the man's feet from under him bringing the edge of the shield down on his face.

The clanging of swords and shouts of men surrounded her as the battle escalated. She ran to pull her knife from the throat of the first man when another pirate lunged at her causing her to tumble out of the way. He snarled at her saying something sounding unpleasant in Mehtian as he tossed his sword from one hand to another.

She narrowed her eyes at him and threw the knife she had retrieved but he hit it away with his sword. He laughed at her, shouting more Mehtian insults. She stood waiting, reading the muscle movements of his body, trying to predict what he was going to do. She watched as the man turned slightly sideways holding the flat part of his sword on his forearm, aiming it at her.

She faced him head on and waited until he lunged forward and slashed at her with a back hand. Anticipating this, she blocked the sword with her shield and maneuvered herself so she could stab him in the back. She then, for good measure, slit his throat.

She quickly wiped her knife clean and scanned the scene. Dead bodies littered the sandy road, blood puddling along the path.

A short distance away from her, she caught sight of Tristan falling to the ground and rolling out of the way of a sword that a pirate was trying to bring down on him. She ran full speed toward him jumping over the bodies scattered on the ground and thrust her knife into the back of the man's ribcage and into his lungs.

The pirate dropped his sword and fell to his knees, gasping for air. She looked down at Tristan who was panting on the ground. His eyes grew wide and he opened his mouth to tell her to duck just as another Mehtian swung his sword. She moved just in time, feeling the wind of the sword moving the hair on top of her head. Crouching, she then swung behind her stabbing the man in the leg. He screamed and she turned still crouched in time to block the man from bringing the sword down on her.

Dropping the shield, she grabbed onto his wrist with one hand and thrust with the other against his elbow, the sound of his arm breaking being heard over the battle. He dropped the sword he had been holding in that hand but grabbed a handful of her hair in the other. He pulled her up and threw her down onto the ground kicking her hard with his good leg.

She grunted placing her hand on the ribs he had kicked. The man then yanked the knife that she had lodged into his leg with his good hand and straddled her. He raised the knife bringing it down just missing her face as she moved out of the way. He raised the knife again. The Tigress brought her hands up blocking him at the wrist stopping the blade just inches above her nose.

The man yelled and spit in her face pushing against her. Even with both of her hands pushing against his one, the knife slowly made its way closer to her face. She grunted and with all her strength threw her hip up, throwing him off of her. She then crawled to her feet and kicked the man in the face just as he was trying to stand. He fell backwards dazed as Tristan brought a sword down on him.

The Tigress collapsed to her knees for a moment pressing a hand gingerly to her side. Tristan held out a hand for her to take and pulled her back onto her feet. She grimaced and grabbed her side once again. She picked her knife back up and was about ready to turn to go back into to battle when a horn blew in the air resounding off the walls of the cliff.

From around the bend of the cliff, the royal army of Thren charged into the battle on their large horses adorned with the gold and blue colors of Thren, their gold-plated armor glinting in the sun.

The battle was soon over as, in a matter of minutes, the rest of the pirates retreated as Thren's army pushed them back into the sea.

The Tigress winced as she walked hoping that one of her ribs was not cracked. Tristan gave her his arm for support, but she shook her head.

"I am all right," she said almost breathlessly.

The horn sounded again as a line of horses approached them.

"I am Prince Castuhl of Thren," said a young man looking at the people strewn about the ravaged caravan. He was pleasant looking with golden hair and broad shoulders. "My army and I have come to escort my betrothed and her caravan the rest of the way to the capitol. Where might I find her?" he asked looking down at the pair of them, a sense of panic in his pale eyes.

The Tigress gave a small bow. "Thank you, your highness, for coming when you did," she said trying to grit away her pain. "The princess is being guarded down the line in her carrier. That is where you shall find her. If you will allow me a moment to get on my horse I can bring you to the right one."

The prince gave a sigh of relief and nodded.

The Tigress called for her horse who immediately made its way over to her. She grabbed the saddle and took a deep breath, gritting her teeth as she jumped up and swung her leg over. She led the prince down the line of the caravan where the camouflaged carrier was surrounded by the guards and prince Mohrr whom she nodded to.

The two princes greeted each other as she slowly got off of her horse and knocked on the carrier door.

The princess opened the window and peered out. She breathed a sigh of relief when she saw the assassin. "Is it over?" she asked.

The Tigress nodded. "Yes, your highness. We were saved by the royal army of Thren," she replied. "In short, we were saved by your betrothed."

The princess shrunk back into her carrier.

"He is here," she nudged. "He wants to take you the rest of the way to Harpren."

The princess did not respond but the door to her carrier opened.

The Tigress entered the carrier, grimacing as she bent over to get in.

"You are hurt," the princess said. She pulled a handkerchief out and wiped away the blood that had dripped down her cheek from a small cut on her face.

"Nothing I haven't experienced before," she explained. "He is waiting for you out there, princess."

Princess Rain sat back into her seat and bowed her head. "What am I to do?" she asked.

"Get out and meet with him, your highness," The Tigress replied. "You cannot hide in here forever."

The princess remained silent.

"He seems very gallant, your highness. He rides his horse very well and his hair is the color of gold," The Tigress said trying to get the princess interested enough to see him for herself.

It worked because the princess met her eye. "Hair like gold?" she repeated curiously. "I have only seen one person with golden hair before. She was my cousin's handmaid," she smiled. "I remember being jealous of how her hair glowed in the sun." She pursed her lips. "What of his eyes?" she asked almost shyly after a brief silence.

The Tigress held in an amused smile. "I only caught a glimpse of them, but I believe they are as blue as a clear summer sky."

The princess smiled. "Then he is handsome."

The Tigress nodded.

"But is he a gentle kind of man?" she asked timidly.

She gave a short nod. "He seemed generally concerned about your safety, your highness. And he was very polite, not at all too demanding," she added. "I think he is a gentle man. But you will never know if you don't take that step and meet him."

The princess still did not move.

"Do not let him think you ill bred by keeping him waiting, your highness. He did save us."

The princess nodded. "Do not leave me yet," she said.

"I promised I would see you through to Harpren and I shall keep my word."

The princess nodded again taking a deep breath and letting it out slowly. "I am ready," she resolved.

The Tigress made her way back out of the carrier to find the prince still on his horse waiting, looking almost nervous. She bowed to him and stepped aside allowing the princess room to finally step out of her carrier.

When the princess' head emerged at last, the prince jumped from his horse and helped her out. When she placed her hand in his and their eyes met they both gave a shy smile.

"Princess Rain," he said almost breathlessly. "I am Castuhl."

The princess smiled and gave him a curtsey. "My prince," she sighed, her eyes wide.

The Tigress watched as the prince ordered the horse he had bought for his future wife to be brought through the crowd and helped her onto it. The princess did not even look back as the two of them began their way to Harpren.

"It is strange," Mohrr said coming up to The Tigress. "My little sister leaving with her betrothed. Married before I am. A queen before I am king perhaps."

The Tigress looked at him. "Do I sense regret in your voice?" she asked.

He smiled. "No," he replied. "It was I who made the decision about Castuhl. I had met him once before and thought that their tempers were much alike. My sister deserves someone like that. Just as sweet and nice as she is."

The Tigress gave him a small smile.

"My father almost signed a treaty with a prince from a different realm," he continued. "One across the Dormant Sea, beyond Meht."

"Ganavan?" The Tigress asked.

The prince nodded. "Yes," he replied. "But I couldn't see my sister shipped so far away."

"Ah," The Tigress replied. "Ganavan is wonderful though. I spent a couple of months there last year. The hot springs are delightful and the land beautiful. The streets smell of spices and herbs."

He smiled at her. "Still," he told her. "My sister deserved better than that. She deserves a man like Castuhl."

The Tigress didn't argue. She turned and tried to get up on her horse but lost her footing, holding in a shout of pain.

"You're injured!" Mohrr said sounding concerned. "Please allow me to help." He held out his hand and helped to push her back on her horse.

"Thank you, your highness," she said taking a deep breath and wincing.

"There are great healers in Harpren," the prince said grabbing the reigns of her horse and riding next to her. "I will make sure you get the care that you need."

The Tigress once again felt the heat rise in her cheeks as she looked at Prince Mohrr. It was strange. She had this want to be around him and, yet, she couldn't shake the feeling that this man was keeping something from her.

CHAPTER 8

THE TIGRESS SLOWLY INCHED HERSELF INTO THE WARM WATER OF THE royal bath house of Harpren and let out a sigh of relief. She looked down at the bruise on her ribs and gently touched it with the tips of her fingers. She winced but was glad that the injury wasn't as bad as she had originally thought it was.

She was lucky that her only injuries were two small cuts and bruised ribs. She wasn't trained for a battle like that and she knew it. She was trained for stealth, quick kills, and quick escapes. None of that included prolonged fighting.

She had already been recuperating in the city for the past few days, the luxuries of the palace open to her. She felt relaxed; the healers were doing wonders for her.

Tomorrow, she would continue her journey with Tristan beyond the Stronghold Mountains in Bornnen in search of the secret armory, but right now The Tigress was using this time to regain her focus.

When she rose back out of the steamy waters, servants were there to help her dry and a nurse helped bandage up her ribs again.

"Your cuts are healing quite nicely," she said applying a medicinal paste to her cheek and thigh.

She thanked them all when they had finished dressing her and fixing her hair. She made her way back to the room Prince Castuhl had graciously lent her when she was met by the princess in the hall; a large smile adorned her face.

The Tigress bowed. "Your highness," she said.

"How are you healing?" the princess asked.

"Very well, thank you," she replied. "I'm quite satisfied with the healers here."

The princess turned to walk with her. "Are you really to leave so soon?" she asked her after a moment.

She nodded. "I still have business to attend to for your father."

The princess frowned. "Meaning you have someone left to kill," she added.

"I was not raised to be a farmer, nor was I born into money, at least not to my knowledge."

"Can you not stay for the wedding?" the princess asked looking hopeful. "You must stay for that. It is only in a week."

"Forgive me, but I cannot. I have already stayed here longer than I had planned. Another delay from my journey would be inexcusable."

The princess gave a small smile. "I thought as much," she said. "I have also come to apologize for my harsh words the other day. They were the words of a child who refused to grow up. How silly it all seems now."

"And what do you think of your betrothed now, your highness, if you do not mind me asking?"

The princess blushed. "I am only now ashamed of what I had asked you to do," she replied. She turned to look at The Tigress. "He is a wonderful man. Smart, kind and gentle. He is everything that I could ask for."

"I am happy for you, princess."

"I am having a care package prepared for you and Tristan," she said as they reached The Tigress' door. "But I wanted to give you this as well." The princess handed her a small book. "It was in the royal library."

The Tigress took it in her hand and looked down at it.

"Can you read?" the princess asked hesitantly.

The Tigress nodded, suppressing a laugh. "A History of Family Seals?" she said looking up.

"I recognized your necklace from somewhere," the princess said. "I just couldn't remember until I saw this book." She flipped the book open to where a page was marked.

The Tigress gasped and placed her hand over her necklace as she looked down at its image, the name of the seal ripped from the page. She turned the pages to look for information about the seal but the next several pages of the book had been torn out as well. She looked up at the princess

"Where is the rest of it?" she asked.

The princess shrugged. "The one in my father's library is like that as well. But I wanted to show you that you are more than an assassin, that you came from somewhere. Normal families do not have family seals."

The Tigress smiled. "Thank you," she said never meaning the word more than she did at that moment.

The princess smiled back. "I shall pray for a safe journey for the two of you," she said. "Good-bye."

The Tigress bowed, and the princess curtsied before they went their separate ways.

When she entered her bed chambers Prince Mohrr was waiting inside for her. She immediately blushed and took a step back. "What are you doing in here?" she asked in surprise.

"Forgive me," he said getting up from her bed where he was sitting. "I was just looking to talk. I did not mean anything by just appearing in your bedchambers. I was not going to wait, but I heard footsteps and did not want to be caught slipping out of your room." He gave a soft smile. "That is how rumors are started."

She nodded.

He walked over to her. "I was just wanting to see you before you left real civilization. Bornnen is a little different from the lush capitol of Thren."

She nodded. "Yes, I agree," she said taking a couple more steps into the room. "But I have been there several times before. I am no stranger to the barren lands and the mines or the harsh principles of the people."

The prince nodded stopping right in front of her. "I am sorry that I have not had the time to talk with you more during your recovery here," he said brushing back a lock of her hair.

She turned her head slightly. "We had a nice walk by the beach with your sister the other day." Her cheeks flushed from him being so close and her breathing quickened as confusion about her reaction spread over her once again.

He nodded again. "Yes, but Tristan was there as well."

"We also dined together a few times."

"Yes, true."

"And yesterday we had lunch in the garden."

The prince took her hand and gave it a light squeeze. "Yes, but all of those were spent in the company of other people as well. I meant spending time with just you and me."

She felt a strange shiver crawl up her spine. She looked back up at him. "What is your design with me, your highness?" she said slowly taking her hand back and moving toward the window, looking out into the torch lit courtyard down below.

"My design?" he repeated sounding slightly offended. "I don't believe I have a *design*. Do you think I am trying to take advantage of you?"

She gave a small laugh. "I have not been taken advantage of by a boy in a long time," she replied. "And the last one to do so did not fair too well."

His smile only broadened. "A woman like you, I can only imagine."

She considered a moment and softly smiled back. "It might be best if you did not."

He took a deep breath and let it out slowly taking a few more steps toward her. "I find you very alluring," he said gently placing his hands on her arms. "I wish I could convince you to maybe stay, but I know that you wouldn't."

She blushed again, her heart mildly racing. She didn't quite understand what was happening. "I have," she started shakily, "business."

He nodded. "Yes, you will be traveling with Tristan," he said letting her go. "I am a little envious."

She shook her head. "I would not be," she said. "This journey will be the most aggravating of my life. He really does not take a hint to stay quiet."

He laughed. "I meant I was envious of Tristan."

She nodded. "I know."

"Perhaps, one day, we could journey on our own."

The Tigress suppressed a laugh. "And where would we go?"

Mohrr shook his head. "It wouldn't matter to me as long as you were there too."

He brushed her cheek with his finger tips, his other hand on her lower back pushing her closer to him. He leaned in close until their lips were almost touching. She could feel the heat from his skin and smell the wine on his breath. She trembled under him.

She trembled not because she was scared of him, but because she was uncertain of herself. She was not one for fawning or feelings and, yet, she couldn't deny there was something about him she found alluring.

"I should prepare for bed," she whispered breathlessly.

"Yes, you should," he replied not budging. He hovered there for a few more moments before lightly brushing her lips with his but not fully pressing them together. "Have a safe journey," he whispered. "I shall think of you often."

He pulled away, brushing her hair back once more before he walked out of the room leaving her standing there, her cheeks flushed and heart pounding.

"HOW LONG IS THIS TREK SUPPOSED TO TAKE?" TRISTAN ASKED, looking back at the gleaming city of Harpren, knocking The Tigress from her thoughts of the night before.

"If we are not stopped or distracted it could take us at least two weeks," she replied looking down at the map the prince of Thren had drawn up for them to distract her from her thoughts.

He groaned. "Two weeks?" he said.

She shot him a side glance. "Does that cut into your busy schedule?" she asked him.

"Not necessarily, but I would prefer not to be traveling my entire life," he replied. "Nor do I really want to be spending more time than necessary in Bornnen." He let out a sigh. "But I think I can handle being back in Harpren in two weeks. You were right. It is a beautiful city." He smiled. "There are plenty of beautiful women to be had there."

"When I said it would take two weeks, I meant that it would take us two weeks just to get to where we're going, not for us to get there and back."

The smile fell from his face. "A month?" he asked loudly. "A whole month on the road?"

She let out an annoyed sigh. "You don't have to come," she said. "If the journey is going to be too much for your delicate soul then you can stay back in Harpren with all of those 'beautiful women to be had'. I can make my way on my own."

"If I let you go by yourself you have no cover to get you through the Stronghold Mountains and on to Mahk Lake."

"Priestesses make religious journeys by themselves all the time," she said.

"Yes, but who is going to protect you if you were to get into trouble?" he asked.

She scoffed. "Do you really think I have never travelled on my own before?" she retorted.

"Honestly, I truly don't really know how you have survived by yourself however many years you have been on your own," he replied. "I mean the way you fought the other day with those pirates, I was ashamed for you."

"You are quite serious?" she asked incredulously.

"Unimpressed, really."

The Tigress took a deep breath to calm herself, knowing he was just trying to get under her skin.

"I did save your life, Dahlen."

She all but gawked at him. "My life?" she repeated. "You saved my life?"

Tristan nodded. "I killed that Mehtian pirate that was attacking you."

She shook her head. "You killed him after I threw him off of me," she replied. "Had you not been there, I would have done the job myself." She held her hands up. "And all of that was after I saved your life," she added getting heated. "Actually, had I not noticed the red-winged eagle there would have been several more casualties than there were."

"Yes, I have been thinking about that. What is it about the eagle?" he asked coolly changing the subject.

She shook her head and let out an annoyed sigh. "Eagles are used as scouting birds. Red-winged eagles are native to Meht and Meht is known for its pirates. I put two and two together and came to the conclusion that there was an ambush waiting for us."

"The coven taught you this?"

She nodded. "Despite the fact that people think we assassins are nothing but ignorant, bloodthirsty thieves, we are actually among the most educated people you will ever meet." The Tigress's horse shook its head to keep away the flies and she patted its neck to comfort it. "We are fluent in the shared language, Ganavanese, Mehtian, and even a couple of languages of the Lost Tribes." She looked over at him. "We read, we write. We are taught history, herbology, toxicology, warfare, survival skills. There is not much we are not taught."

"Do you sing and dance as well?" he jested with a grin.

She lifted an eyebrow at him. "Laugh all you want but I have an education that even the son of a lord could boast of," she replied. "We are versed in all the major religions of Skahrr, Bornnen, Thren, and Meht. Though they are basically the same they do worship a little differently and pay more patronage to one or more of the gods or goddesses or both depending on where you are from. We know several of their important customs as well and we are equipped with the knowledge of how to kill quickly and swiftly without being caught or seen."

Tristan shrugged. "I suppose those are very necessary skills if you are to be traveling as much as you do." He stretched his arms. "But it still goes to say that you were extremely sloppy out there in the battlefield."

She glared at the road ahead and took a deep long breath letting it out slowly to calm her. She had never met anyone who aggravated her like the man riding next to her. "I was built for speed, agility, and stealth as well as cunning. I was not built for strength. I am not a six-foot-tall, bulky woman that can hurl a sword around like any man. I am a slender woman of average height who knows how to dodge a sword and use her enemies' strength against them. That was, more or less, my first actual battle."

Tristan nodded. "Mine as well," he said. "I cannot say there is much of that going on in The Hills. Unless you count trying to catch a squealing piglet a battle. It is certainly difficult. Slippery little bastards."

She stared at him skeptically. "Is this your first voyage away from home?" she asked him.

His cheeks flushed a bit. "Hardly," he said.

"Away from Skahrr, then?"

He looked at her.

"Gods be blessed! It is!" she said incredulously. "The man who has vowed to help me find out about my past has never left his homeland before?" she groaned. "How are you supposed to help me find what I need if you don't know anything about the world beyond The Hills?" she asked.

"I know plenty about the world!" he shot back at her.

"Are you truly a bounty hunter or 'finder of things'?" she asked him. "Or is it just a stupid title like The Tigress is to me?"

He didn't answer right away. "A bit of both," he finally said.

She cursed. "What does that mean, 'a bit of both'?" she almost yelled at him.

"The 'finder of things' was just something my father used to say because I would run around the manor finding things that he or one of the servants misplaced. When I got older I started to do it for the people of the surrounding village." He paused. "Then the king hired me a few times and now here I am."

She stared at him for a moment. "Clearly, you are not ready for a journey like this," she finally said. "I think that you should go back to Harpren."

"I promised that I would help you and I mean to follow through on that promise. If there is one thing I take pride in it is that I never break a promise."

"You have no experience in anything!" she said. "Your ignorance could get us both killed."

"I have experience in battle," he insisted plainly.

"One battle does not make you an expert," she retorted.

"It is better than no experience at all."

She pursed her lips to keep from screaming. "I have never met someone who makes me so ridiculously angry more than you do," she said after regaining a bit of her composure.

"Must be love, I imagine."

She shot him a scowl. "Do not flatter yourself."

"Well, it doesn't matter anyways," he said frowning. "Our papers say we are on a religious voyage and you can't make it without me. The papers say two people, so you need me to be the second."

"Or I could just find someone who might actually be useful to me."

His frown deepened. "Like Prince Mohrr?" he asked. "Where was he when the pirates raided the caravan? Nowhere that I saw. You seem to forget that I did in fact save your life. I would classify that as being very useful." He scoffed. "I didn't go hide behind a bunch of guards and pray that they protect me."

"First off," The Tigress started bitterly, "you did not save my life. If what you did were to be classified as anything, it would be an assist. You assisted me. Secondly," she continued, "the prince did not hide behind the guards. He went to protect his sister as an older brother, I assume, is supposed to do."

"Sure he did," Tristan replied rolling his eyes. "What is it about him anyways?" he asked her. "Every time he walks by, you all but swoon over him. It is enough to make any man sick."

"I do not swoon!" she replied defensively.

"You swoon!" he said back. "Your face gets as red as a drunkard's and you can barely even look at him!"

She shot him a murderous glare. "I will not go as far to say you are jealous, Tristan, but, whatever it may be, it does not look well on you," she retorted. The Tigress then tapped her heels into her horse to speed up just enough so she didn't have to look at him. She didn't want to hear what he had to say, but it was true. The prince did have some strange effect on her.

She twitched uncomfortably in her saddle as she thought of it. It was not as if she had never been around attractive men before. She has actually killed men better looking than the prince without a second thought. So why was he different?

The rest of the day's ride was spent in angry silence except for Tristan whistling the occasional tune. When night was not far off they made camp only speaking when necessary.

"Is the rest of the journey going to be this pleasant?" he finally asked when she made her bed for the night.

She shot him a glance before she lied down and rolled over, turning her back to him.

CHAPTER 9

THERE SHE WAS AGAIN, SHE THOUGHT, LOOKING BACK INTO THE familiar green eyes of that woman smiling down at her. She had such a pretty smile. A small child's hand reached up to touch the woman's face and she kissed it, her dark curls bouncing around her.

The hand then reached for the shiny necklace dangling down as the woman leaned over her, but she gently grabbed the hand before its fingers could wrap around it. The woman spoke in a soft, smooth voice but she couldn't understand what she was saying.

Suddenly the woman's eyes grew wide in fear and she stood erect.

The necklace, she thought! She could see *her* necklace! That woman was wearing *her* necklace.

The sound of someone banging on the door brought the woman into a panic and she reached down to pick up the child, holding her close. She ran to the far side of the room and lifted a hatch hiding a secret passage. The woman grabbed a candle and held closely to the child as she ran down the stairs and through a long passage. She turned down a corner, the child still pressed closely to her chest. The child made a whining noise but was quickly and softly shushed by her mother.

Was that her? Was she the child?

Finally, they emerged from the stable, the smell of horses strong in her nose. Shouting was heard outside, all around them. She looked out through a crack in the wall and saw men cutting down those around them, their yellow robes glowing in the dimming sun.

The woman let out a small cry as a yellow and orange banner flickered in the wind, a black bird in midflight in the middle of it.

The woman hugged *her*, the child, close and kissed her forehead. "I love you, An—"

"Are you alright?"

The Tigress sat up, blindly grabbing the throat of the man that awoke her and pressing a knife against his ribs.

"Calm down!" Tristan croaked. "It's just me!"

The Tigress panted as if she had been running. "I was dreaming," she said through gritted teeth releasing her grip.

"Well, it sounded like you were being attacked," Tristan replied rubbing his throat.

She looked up at the sky just starting to turn pink and orange as the sun rose. "What's that smell?" she asked her nose slightly turned up.

"I was trying to make a stew for breakfast but I walked away for a moment and it burned."

She let out a sigh. "There is a small inn just up that hill a few miles or so," she said getting up and gathering her things. "We can get something to eat there."

"An inn?" he said. "Why didn't we just sleep there last night instead of sleeping outside in the grass?"

"Forgive me, my lord, I did not realize that sleeping under the stars was beneath you. We did just that on our way to Harpren."

He opened his mouth to respond but stopped himself. "I am not going to start another argument with you," he said. "If we are supposed to be traveling together for four weeks I would prefer that those four weeks are as pleasant as possible. I don't need to waste my precious time being miserable just because you are."

Tristan kept to his word the rest of the day and filled the silence between them with songs and exclamations about the countryside as they rode along. She, on the other hand, was so wrapped up in the dream she had that night she was less inclined to speak than she normally was. Even when Tristan would make jokes at her expense she did no more than shoot him annoyed looks.

They reached the Vron woods around midday a few days later and The Tigress had them stop for more supplies before they entered. The shop that was right at the woods' edge was a good place to stock up so the pair of them tied up their horses and went inside. They were met with a scraggly, plump looking man who greeted them warmly.

Tristan avoided the man's one-eyed stare, but she was not shaken by his appearance. She greeted him back.

"A nun and a monk?" he said. "I get a few of those uh year. Makin' your religious trek to all the godly places, I take it?" he asked.

"Yes, sir," she replied. "We are hoping to make it to Vremir's Rest by tonight if the travelling is good."

"Do ya know thu path?" he asked.

"We were told that following the line of the forest is easiest."

"That it 'tis," he said getting them the things that she asked for. "Is your monk there useful wit' thu sword?"

Tristan made a quick glance over to him.

"Neither of us are useful, I am afraid."

"Then ya should be afraid," he said almost shouting. "Them woods hold uh lot o' mystery," he continued. "Plenty of people go in but not so many come out again."

"Bandits?"

He shrugged. "From what I hear, thu woods are infested wit' man-like bears that will gut ya before ya can scream."

She regarded him for a moment. "Is that how you lost your eye?" she finally asked.

He laughed. "No, sister," he replied. "I was in thu Five Years War forever ago. When I was not much older than this here monk," he motioned toward Tristan again. "No one has ever lived to tell about their encounters wit' the man-like bears," he continued.

"No one has lived?" The Tigress said. "Then how is it you know they exist?"

The man laughed. "Ya can hear them callin' tuh each other. Ya can see flashes o' fur runnin' through thu trees."

She paid the man and bowed. "Thank you, sir, for your business and your knowledge of the woods."

"Thank *you*, sister," he said taking her money. "Please be careful. Keep your eyes and ears opened." He pointed to his missing eye and shot her a smile chuckling at his own joke.

"There was something wrong with that man. I think he was crazy," Tristan said as he strapped their new goods to his horse.

"I think there is something wrong with you," she replied as she mounted. "The whole day you don't shut up once and we get in there and you don't say one word!"

They led their horses back onto the road.

"The man made me uneasy," he explained. "He had this crazy look about him and he kept staring at me with his one eye."

She laughed at him. "How else is he going to look at you?"

"And what was that deal with the man-like bears?" he asked. "I have never heard of them before."

She shrugged. "Folklore, local legend, Tristan," she said. "They don't exist."

"The man seemed pretty adamant about them."

"You just said that the man was crazy and, yet, you believe him about the man-like bears?" The Tigress asked.

"Crazy people can still speak the truth from time to time."

She shook her head.

"Have you ever been to these woods?" he asked her as the trees enveloped them.

She shook her head. "No, at least not coming from this side," she replied.

They fell into silence and Tristan shivered as they went further into the woods.

"Tell me about Dead Man's Rest," he said in an interested tone.

She ducked to avoid a low hanging branch. "If I have to tell you about it, you shouldn't know."

"Is your whole life really shrouded in mystery?" he asked arching an eyebrow.

"Yes," she replied. "I cannot tell you anything about where the coven resides other than what you already know."

"And what is that? That Dead Man's Rest borders Bornnen and Thren because that is about all I know about it." He swatted a fly away. "Would you take me there?"

"No," she replied incredulously. "The coven of The Nameless does not take kindly to outsiders and chances are as soon as your foot crosses that border you will be killed."

"All you assassins are nothing but business, I suppose."

There was a brief pause.

"How does one hire an assassin anyways?" Tristan asked, a pensive look on his face.

The Tigress lifted a brow at him. "Why? Are you looking to hire one?" she replied. "Perhaps to get rid of your stepmother."

He blushed. "No," he quickly responded. "I wouldn't do that to my brothers and sister. I was just curious."

She nodded. "There are a few ways," she started. "The least recommended being asking around for one. Obviously, you don't want word to get around that you are trying to hire an assassin to kill someone, especially if that word were to get back to the person you're trying to have killed."

Tristan nodded.

"Another way is to get ahold of one of the coven attorneys and they can help direct you to one."

Tristan laughed. "Wait! The coven has lawyers?"

The Tigress narrowed her eyes at him. "Of course, we have lawyers. People hire us to do their dirty work. Our lawyers, who are also the coven liaisons between the rest of the realm, make sure that if there is an issue, our contracts are air-tight. Contracts made between assassin and employer are legally binding. The assassin is only doing their job. It is the employer that is held legally responsible for the mark's death. They can be prosecuted, not us."

"Huh," Tristan replied. "What if I cannot find one of these lawyer-liaisons?" he asked after a moment. "How do I go about finding an assassin?"

She nodded. "You can send a message to the coven requesting one and they send messages out to their assassins. First assassin there gets the contract."

"Interesting," he said in reply. "Now, are contracts actually written up?"

She gave another nod. "Of course!" she answered. "A contract of the job is written up by the two parties and then signed by both. Then, two copies are made, one for each side of the party. The original is sealed with the assassin's stamp and sent to the coven."

"So, they read it?"

She shook her head. "Every contract is confidential," she told him. "An assassin does not divulge who her employer is or their mark. The contract is sent merely for legal purposes if an issue were to arise."

He lifted his eyebrows and nodded. "A way to cover your asses," he said.

"Exactly."

"So, how did King Breht go about hiring you to kill King Ahlenwei?"

She shook her head. "It annoys me that that is such common knowledge," she replied. "King Breht cannot keep a secret. Our first contract was a sham; he only stuck to it through force," she grumbled. "Anyways even if King Breht is so open with that information, I will not be."

He sighed. "Of course not."

She smiled deviously. "I can, however, tell you something that would change the way you look at prostitutes. I know how much you love them and all but," she said with a strange half smile on her face.

He laughed. "Good luck with that."

"The easiest way to get to a male politician, or male in general, is to pose as a prostitute. I must have used that trick at least half of the times I have made a kill. Men are by far the easiest creatures to trick. All you have to do is show a little skin and act like you are willing and the work is done for you. They practically fall on the knives themselves."

He blinked at her. "You have done it again," he said. "You have taken something truly beautiful to me and just distorted it to make it scary and grotesque."

She shrugged. "It could save your life one day. People are the most vulnerable when they believe they are in complete control. That is why men are so easy to kill. They just do not think to check a whore for weapons because they believe they are wielding the only one." She chuckled at her own joke.

"Yeah, that's real cute." He shook his head. "You are a terrible person to say things like that to me." He yawned and stretched his arms out. "Will we stop and rest when we reach the next tavern?" he asked after a moment. "I was spoiled while we were in Harpren and would kill for a bed. Though I doubt I could ever find one half as soft as the ones in the palace."

She gave him a strange look. "This is a forest, Tristan," she answered. "A sacred wood. Building here would be considered sacrilegious."

"I don't really buy into all of this religious hysteria. No one has ever seen these gods, so how do we truly know they exist?"

"Have you ever seen the wind, Tristan? Or the air you breathe?"

He opened his mouth to comment but then shut it again to think. "No," he finally said. "But they make their presence known."

"Well, some people believe that the gods do too in their own way. You just have to know where to look."

As if she had planned the speech and timing herself, the two of them emerged from the trees into a clearing where a pristine lake surrounded by a plethora of wildflowers laid shimmering in the sun.

Several deer had their heads lowered to the water, peacefully drinking as a gentle wind sent tiny ripples throughout.

"Gorgeous," Tristan said breathlessly.

The Tigress took in a deep breath of the fresh, lightly sweet-scented air. "The Oasis," she said with a smile.

"Will we be camping here for the night then?" he asked getting off of his horse without waiting for an answer.

She looked up at the brilliance of colors telling her that the sun would be starting to set soon. "We have made pretty good time," she said. "We are here half a day earlier than I expected." She slid off her horse as well and led it to the cool waters of the lake. "I have always heard of the serene beauty of this place, but I never imagined it would be everything that people said it would."

The two of them found a used campsite and set up before they had a look around; both of them feeling more refreshed and happy than they had in a while.

"Tell me about the gods again," Tristan asked as he peeled off his boots and socks. "We are on a 'pilgrimage' so I feel like I need to have some more background knowledge just in case I am asked a question."

"The beauty of you being a monk is we can always pretend that you have taken a vow of silence," she replied slipping her feet into the water.

"I'm being serious. I want to know what this pilgrimage signifies."

She furrowed her brows pensively at him. "Do you really not know?" she asked him. "I thought your father paid for your education?"

"He did, but was never big on religion. My stepmother who is from Ganavan, however, is monotheistic and would not have anyone in her household worshipping differently, even her husband's bastard. So, I know little about the fallen gods."

The Tigress reached down and traced the water with the tips of her fingers, holding her hair back from falling in the water with her other hand. "You have truly never heard of Vron, Vremir, Gher, Behr, and Mahk?"

"I have truly never heard of their stories. I have heard of the gods and goddesses themselves."

She nodded. "Well," she started, "thousands of years ago when the world was as barren as the desert and as dark as a moonless night, four of the gods and goddesses in the sky decided to create man. But before they could make man, they had to make the world hospitable. So, the twin goddesses of earth, Gher and Behr made the land fertile with the fruit of their loins."

Tristan made a strange face. "Fruit of their loins?" he repeated.

"I didn't come up with the story," she said. "They made the land fertile while the gods, Vron of water and Mahk of wind, carved out the land with their mighty sword and hammer laying down the sweet waters of the lakes and rivers. When the land was shaped to their liking they populated it with the animals so that man could have something to eat. When they were satisfied that man would not starve and would have a safe place to live Vron and Gher and Mahk and Behr consummated their relationships and gave birth to the children of the land. When they finished making their children together, they switched partners to bring about different kinds of people. Vron and Gher made the Skahrrians. Vron and Behr made the Threnians. And Mahk, Gher and Behr made the Bornnenians."

"What about the people of Meht?" Tristan asked. "I know they are not often thought of in the greater scheme of things, but they are part of our realm."

She held up a hand. "I am getting there," she continued. "There was a fifth god that the others had left out of their plan and he became jealous that he was not included in the making of the realm, so he set out to destroy what they had created.

"Vremir, god of fire, younger brother to Vron, used the power of fire to destroy the lush land; sending his fire out as he moved across the realm of men. Though the men fought to save their home they were no match for the strength of Vremir. Everything he touched turned to dust and sand. He wreaked havoc, killing the men and ravishing the women. Finally, the people of the land prayed to the four gods and goddesses of creation to save them.

"Mahk and the twins knew that they were no match for Vremir's fire so they gave what strength they could to Vron and he sent out to defeat his brother."

Tristan looked at her. "Is that it?" he asked when she didn't continue.

She shrugged. "Basically, yes."

He blinked at her.

"Do I really have to tell you that Vron won?" she asked. "He made this Oasis that stopped the fire from spreading anymore and buried Vremir at the edge of the lake and the desert. The strange grass that grows between the desert and the oasis is known as Vremir's Rest." She pointed across the lake to the horizon where the lake stretched out, the sun beginning to sink behind it.

"You still didn't tell me about the people of Meht and how they came into being," he said.

"The women that Vremir ravished all sent themselves away to take care of their fatherless children, their skin blackened by the fiery blood of their father."

"So, the legend of the gods and goddesses makes the people of Meht bastards? No wonder they hate us," Tristan mumbled. "Doesn't seem fair."

She shrugged. "No, I suppose it doesn't. But again, I did not come up with the story myself."

"And why do people go to Vremir's Rest if Vremir was the one that wanted to destroy everything?"

"They don't go there to worship Vremir; they go there to remember and to thank Vron and the other gods for their protection."

Tristan shrugged. "Still seems strange that people would believe something as farfetched as that," he said beginning to remove his shirt.

The Tigress took a step back. "What are you doing?" she asked.

He gave her a strange look. "I'm going to go for a swim," he replied throwing his shirt onto the pebbly shore of the lake. "Join me?" he asked untying his trousers.

"I cannot," she replied backing out onto the shore.

"What, you can't swim?"

She shook her head. "I can swim. I just can't swim with you."

He frowned at her. "Should I be offended?" he asked.

She shook her head. "I am forbidden to be in any vulnerable situation with any man," she replied.

"You will pose as a prostitute in order to kill a man and, yet, you cannot go swimming with one?"

"It is not the same," she explained.

"You claim to be a free woman, yet, you are forbidden from giving into the body's desire? I am not saying that anything would happen if you were to join me for a swim, but, in general, are you not allowed to have sex?"

She shuddered as the memory of an older boy's hand ran across her body. "We are encouraged not to engage in such acts, yes."

"Even if you were to marry?" he asked her.

She shook her head.

"Are you going to tell me that you cannot have sex with a man even if you marry him?"

"I am saying that those of the coven do not marry."

He looked at her incredulously. "You are not really free at all, are you?" he asked. "The coven seems to control everything that you do."

She didn't say anything but averted her eyes and walked away as he began to remove the rest of his clothes.

She was lighting a fire just a few yards from the lake when Tristan, clothed once again, walked back up to her in the last dwindling light of the sun.

"I found some kind of berry bushes just in the tree line over there," he said.

"What kind of berries?" she asked striking the flint rocks together.

Tristan shrugged. "I don't know but they smell pungently sweet and are a delightful purple color," he replied picking one up between his fingers and looking at it. "I can only imagine they taste as sweet as they smell."

The Tigress looked up just as he was about to put one in his mouth and screamed knocking them out of his hand causing berries to fly everywhere.

"What the hell was that for?" he asked looking at the scattered bits of purple all over the ground.

"Those are Dragon's Bane berries, you idiot," she replied.

He lifted an eyebrow and put his hands up.

"They're poisonous," she said. "They send an extreme burning sensation throughout your body, give you convulsions, make you vomit and if the toxicity is high enough can cause death. Also, if you get it in your eyes it can cause blindness. And in some cases, an extreme rash if you get the juice on your skin."

Tristan looked down at his hands and then scowled at her. "You could have just told me that instead of yelling and scaring the hell out of me."

She ignored him picking the berries back up off of the ground, gathering them in the beds of her skirt.

"If they are so poisonous, why are you picking them back up?" he asked.

She sneered. "They are great for lacing your knives and arrows in. You grind them down into a nice little paste and use something to spread it over the blades and arrow tips and you have a very effective weapon," she replied. "It is also useful as just a poison. I once killed a man using only these. I posed as a barmaid, got my target drunk and then poured crushed berries in his drink. And when he hit the floor all I did was walk away."

Tristan looked down at the small, and, what some people might think, fragile-looking girl picking up berries and shivered.

"You are not allowed to prepare food for me this entire journey," he said.

She looked up at him and smiled. "I think I can live with that."

CHAPTER 10

THE TIGRESS WOKE JUST BEFORE DAWN IN A PANIC. SHE SAT UP IN HER bed, her knives ready. When she noticed that nothing had truly woken her, she breathed a sigh of relief and wiped the sweat from her brow.

It was that dream again. The one about the woman, her mother. Even without being woken by Tristan she did not get much further in the dream. She still could not hear what her mother was saying, but this time they got further than the barn.

She lied on her back staring up at the sky. She saw that strange banner again, too. Seeing it brought fear to her mother, but she had never seen it before, didn't know what land it belonged to. She tried to conjure up the image of the banner, yellow and orange, almost like the rising of the sun, with that great bird in the middle. She sighed, as the image of the banner continued to fade, as most dreams do when you wake.

Was the banner even real? Or was it just a dream? Were any of her dreams real? They felt real. The fear in her mother's eyes, the sounds of death in the background, the smell of blood and fire. Everything felt real.

The Tigress gave a sigh as she sat up. The morning was cool, but she was hot, so she walked to the edge of the lake and removed her clothes. She entered the cool waters of the lake and gave a small shiver. She dove in, letting the water wash away the dirt and dust from her hair and body and smiled to herself.

She looked across the lake at the peaceful sight and sounds of the woods. She could hear the distant chirping of birds and could see on the far side of the lake a small group of people making their way to, perhaps, Vremir's Rest which she could just barely make out from where she was treading water.

The Tigress could feel a strange calm come over her as she immersed herself in the almost sweet water of the Oasis. She did not believe in the gods or goddesses or the supernatural, but she almost felt like she could feel a bit of magic sweep through her as she bathed. It warmed and comforted her like nothing else she had ever felt before. It was no wonder that people voyaged for weeks just to get here.

She looked about her as a bird cried in the distance. She frowned, and a cold chill ran down her spine. She had never heard such a bird.

TRISTAN AWOKE TO FIND THE TIGRESS MISSING AND CRAWLED OUT OF bed to find her. He rubbed his bare arms in the brisk morning air as he walked along the lake's shore. He found the pile of clothes that she had left behind and looked out into the lake to see her standing waist deep in the water, her skin glowing in the rising sun. He was going to shout out to her but decided that it would be better if he remained unnoticed by the shore.

As she moved her hair off of her back, he noticed a long scar starting at the back of her right shoulder down to the left side of her hip. The scar was a strange pink against her tanned skin and he was taken aback by the sight of it. Surrounding that scar were smaller ones littering her back.

Tristan tried not to gape at the horror of her back, but it was hard for him to avert his eyes. Curiosity stirred his imagination. How could someone so young be littered with so many scars? His heart went out to her, pitying her pain but at the same time he respected her and found in her a new sense of courage.

The Tigress turned to come back out and Tristan darted behind a tree, so she wouldn't know he had seen her.

THE TWO OF THEM GLANCED BEHIND THEM AS THEY RODE BACK INTO the trees, leaving the peace and serenity the lake had shared in their wake. They both sighed as the scene vanished from their eyes.

The Tigress pulled out the map and glanced down at it as her horse trotted along the path. "We should be reaching Vron Wood today," she said. "Once we get there, the Stronghold Mountains won't be that far off, maybe another day or two. The forest actually lines the edge of the mountains." She moved a branch out of her way with her hand. "There is an iron mine there blocking the way we want to go but if we wait until night fall, the mine should be empty and when can just travel around it."

Tristan didn't comment. He just rode in silence next to her.

"The king's secret armory should be in the valley between the mountains and the Mahk River or along the mountain itself, per King Breht's spy's information." She looked down at the map in thought-filled silence for a moment. "Once we figure out the set up, we can plan our attack. Actually, my attack." She put the map away and directed her attention on the road again. "You're very silent today," she said not looking over at him.

"You never fail to remind me that I talk too much, now you point out that I am not talking at all," his voice was a little distant.

Somewhere in the forest a bird let out a strange cry; similar, yet, more alien than the one she heard earlier that morning.

"Do as you please, I guess," she replied looking at the trees around them.

They fell into silence once again until Tristan's curiosity got the best of him and he had to ask. "Those scars on your back," he started making her quickly turn her head and glare at him, "how did you get them?"

"Were you watching me this morning?" she asked.

He didn't respond.

"I gave you the common courtesy to walk away when you were bathing in the lake and you have the audacity to watch me while I—"

"I realize you are probably upset," he said, holding up his hands. "But that was all I saw. I left before I could see anything. The rest of your body is still unknown to me."

She took a deep breath and let it out slowly. "Forget it. I am not worried about you anyways."

He creased his brows. "Not worried about me?"

"You are a clumsy fool, stumbling around this world like you own it," she replied visibly disgruntled. "You are about as worthless as an infant screaming for its mother."

He pulled his horse in front of hers. "You have a lot of right to talk," he retorted. "You are just as self-righteous as anyone I have ever met. You think that you are so different, so special! But you are just as pretentious as the rest of them!" he yelled.

She shook her head and maneuvered her horse around his.

"I ask a simple question and you get all upset and start yelling at me. I just wanted to know what has happened to you."

"It is none of your business!" She spat the words over her shoulder. "Every detail of my life is not for you to know or understand so I would appreciate it if you—" she paused and looked around, hearing the same bird call from earlier, "stayed out of my business," she finished trailing off.

"Just like the whole bastard thing wasn't any of your business but I told you anyways."

"What are you, a child?" she asked, listening for a noise in the distance. "That is a very petty argument for a man of however old you are."

"You are never too old to get your feelings hurt," he replied.

"I'll be sure to apologize," she said looking around her, only half listening to Tristan.

"Not that you'll mean it."

She saw movement out of the corner of her eye. There was something large and fast in the woods.

"We need to keep moving," she said to him, her voice slightly calm.

"You are all about yourself. Everything that you do. I mean, granted, you kill people for a living, but in your personal life I think you could afford to be a little nicer," he continued not paying attention to her.

That ominous bird call continued to ring out in the trees louder and closer to them.

"Tristan," she said trying to keep her voice level, "we cannot stop here. You can continue to yell at me as long as we keep moving."

He waved his hand in the air dismissing her, but turned his horse along the path. He continued to yell at her, calling her out on her lack of empathy and her stubbornness, all of which she paid little to no attention to. She was focused on the bird calls, one answering another from either side of them.

"Tristan," she whispered harshly, "we need to move faster. Something is not right."

Tristan ignored her, still focused on his rant. "And not that you care or anything, but I did not appreciate that—"

All of a sudden, an arrow whizzed past him making a loud 'thunk' in a tree. They both gave a quick look at each other before they dug their heels into their horses hightailing it down the path.

"I am not prepared for this!" Tristan yelled.

"Shut up and ride!" she yelled back. She ducked her head and leaned into her horse hearing and feeling the air of the arrows as they flew past her. She whipped the reigns trying to will her horse to go faster, taking small glances behind her to make sure that Tristan was still following.

She looked into the woods and saw the hairy creatures on either side of the path with rope waiting for them. "Duck!" she yelled as they pulled the rope taught. "What the hell are they?" she thought as she felt the rope brush the back of her clothes as she moved out of its way. Tristan, however, did not heed her warning and she heard him shout out as he fell to the ground, his horse whinnying in surprise.

She cursed as she pulled out her bow and arrow, turning her horse back around. The two creatures that had pulled the rope were already on him and The Tigress released a bow into one of their backs causing the other creature to stop and help the other one back into the woods, both of them grunting bulks of fur.

She jumped off her horse and helped pull Tristan back up off of the ground. "Are you alright?" she asked.

He nodded, a hand on his chest trying to regain his breath. "I'm alive," he said breathlessly. "That hurt like hell though." He rubbed his chest where the rope had caught him.

"There is no time to assess damage," she told him. "We need to get out of here before those things come back. Can you still ride?"

Tristan nodded. "Yes," he replied hopping back up.

"Good. Ride and ride fast," she told him.

They began to ride again, the sound of the bird calls filling the forest air. The horses gave all they could jumping over fallen trees and avoiding low-hanging branches. They ran until they heard the bird calls off in the distance and then they ran a little more until the calls could no longer be heard.

The Tigress slowed down first, patting her horse. "I think we are safe for now," she said. "Are you alright?"

Tristan nodded. "You came back for me," he said.

She slowly nodded. "Yes, I did."

"When I fell and I saw you riding away, I swore I was a goner. Another victim for the man-like bears."

"They were not man-like bears," she replied.

"Then what would you call them?" he asked pointing in the direction that they came from.

"I don't know," she said. "But we cannot let the fear of what just happened get the best of us. Chances are, there are more of those creatures or men or whatever they are somewhere. And I don't know how comfortable I feel sleeping in these woods again not knowing where their territory ends."

"How much longer until we reach the end of the woods all together?"

"Another two days at least."

"A lot could happen between now and then."

CHapteR 11

"AnnJella."

The Tigress opened her eyes to see that dawn had not yet come. She winced as she got up; the tree she was sleeping against was hard on her back, and her ribs, though healing, were still sore. She looked over to find Tristan still snoring softly in front of the tree next to her. She let him continue sleeping while she got their things together.

She began to secure their belongings onto the horses as they licked the morning dew from the leaves scattered over the ground. She was just about to secure the last piece when she heard a twig snap. She froze and listened. She heard a rustling noise. She turned her head slowly and caught movement out of the corner of her eye.

She grabbed two of her knives in her hands and ran over to Tristan to wake him up but just as she was opening her mouth to speak, one of the creatures from the woods tackled her to the ground. The Tigress fell onto the wet leaves and twigs of the forest with a grunt. She looked up to see the mad eyes of the creature staring down at her.

She struggled to get up, but the creature's weight was bearing down on her.

It leaned its grey colored face close to hers and said something she didn't understand and showed its mangled teeth.

The Tigress laughed. "You are no creature," she said finally gaining a position where she could drive her knife into its thigh. "You are just a man playing dress up."

Despite what The Tigress said, the man gave an animal-like howl into the air as he fell off her. She rolled away from him but as she stood, he grabbed at her nun's habit causing her to be pulled back and shout out in surprise. She turned and slashed at the man's hand making him release it before she brought the knife down into his chest.

She then looked to find Tristan being dragged away by two more of the heavily furred men. She ran full speed as she jumped and landed on the back of the man that had a hold of Tristan's hair and slit his throat. The second man turned and growled at her, his face barely visible behind his hooded face. He reached for a sword that was on his hilt but before he could retrieve it, she hurled a knife at him, hitting him in the face. He fell to the ground, leaves crunching under his bulk.

She then hurriedly cut the ropes around Tristan's hands.

"Well, this has been a pleasant morning," he said removing his gag and the ropes around his feet.

She picked up the sword that the man she just killed had on his waist and gave it to Tristan. "This is a Bornnenian sword," she said, a little surprised.

"We are near Bornnen now, aren't we?" Tristan asked, inspecting the sword.

"Yes, but that is a sword of the royal guard," she replied. "These men are just bandits using the tale of man-like bears to scare everyone."

"Are you sure that's not what they were?"

"They had teeth like you or me."

"Again, man-like bears," Tristan said. "Man-like, meaning 'has characteristics of man.'"

She shook her head. "Not important," she said. "Let's just go."

But as they turned to move back toward their horses three more men jumped them. One grabbed The Tigress from behind and squeezed her lifting her into the air. She struggled for a second in surprise before she kicked back with her heels as hard as she could, hitting the man in the groin. He grunted and dropped her, giving her time to turn and jab him in the back of his neck with a knife as he was already bent over in pain. She turned to help Tristan as the third man, twice as big as the other two, grabbed her by the hair and threw her against a tree.

He pinned her there and smiled flashing another set of grotesque teeth. "Pretty," he said in a strange accent she had never heard before. She then heard the sounds of a belt being loosened and she struggled and pushed against him in a panic. Her eyes went wide as the flashbacks of that older boy ran through her head. The pain, the panic, the shame all came back to her at once.

She headbutted the man who took a few steps back in surprise. She then lunged at him with her knives but he was more agile than he appeared to be and he was able to move out of the way of her attack and grab her by the wrist lifting her in the air. He laughed and dangled her there, reaching again for her dress.

With her free hand, she slashed at the arm holding her, the hulk of a man howling as he dropped her to the ground with a thud.

He bellowed at her, backhanding her as she stood, sending her flying to the ground again. He then grabbed her by the throat and re-pinned her to the tree, resuming his unwanted advances.

She froze in panic, realizing that she was once again powerless to stop this nightmare when the man caught sight of her necklace.

He let go of her throat and picked the silver wing up in his hand, staring down at it before looking back at her.

"Where?" he asked her, a confused look on his face.

She didn't understand as she coughed and tried to catch her breath.

"This!" he yelled at her, pulling at her necklace. "Where?"

She didn't have time to answer before the silence was filled by an awful 'thunk' and the man fell to the ground. Tristan stood in front of her holding a club of some sort in his hand. He threw it to the ground.

"Are you alright?" Tristan asked, approaching her.

She gave a long blink but didn't respond.

"Dahlen," he said, "are you alright?"

She finally looked up at him and swallowed hard trying to regain her bearings. She nodded after a moment.

He reached out to touch her, but she immediately recoiled. After a moment, she shook away her feelings of helplessness and resumed a pretense of calmness.

"We should leave before more come," The Tigress said, quickly placing the saddle on her horse and mounting it.

THEY RODE IN SILENCE, TROTTING ALONG THE TRAIL. BOTH OF THEM kept their ears opened for that strange bird call. Any other noise coming from the forest got their attention as well, putting them into high alert. Every now and then Tristan would look over at her, a question lingering in his mind, but he knew that he should remain silent.

She seemed to be afraid of him earlier, after the attack. He had only reached out his hand to help her and she jumped from him. She had not reacted in such a way after the Mehtian Pirates attacked them. Perhaps, there was something different about the last attack.

He looked at her tattered dress and knew what that man had in mind. The fear that littered her eyes was easy to see, but it was also apparent to him that she was not just scared of what had happened. Instead, she was scared of what had happened before.

She made a glance over at him and caught him looking at her. He quickly turned his head back to the road.

"Thirty-six men," she said after a moment, her voice as distant as her look.

He looked at her. "What?" he replied.

"That is how many men I have killed under contract," she said. "Men all together, including guards and self defense and those men in the woods, I do not know, but I do know that I have killed at least thirty-six men."

"What happened to you?" he asked after a moment's pause. "Those scars on your back and the way you reacted to that man. It was not something I would have expected from you."

She shook her head. "The scars are from training and missions and being disciplined. I have been hurt so many times I can't even tell you where each scar comes from, most of them anyways. The physical scars are not what matter sometimes," she explained. "They are not the ones that keep you up at night or wake you from a deep sleep. The physical scars, the ones you can see, remind you that you survived, but it's the nightmares that remind you how weak you truly are."

Tristan didn't know what to say or whether or not a comment would be welcomed, so he remained silent.

"I was still really young when he first came to me," she said. "When he first forced himself on me." She shook her head. "He was one of the older boys, well liked. A favorite among The Teachers. Some nights I can still feel his hands on me, can still see his eyes boring into mine." She paused. "It went on for months until he got tired of me, I guess. And then one night a year or two later I found him with another young girl. I heard her crying and for a moment I thought that girl was me. I saw that girl as me." She took in a shaky breath and let it out. "You want to know what it was like growing up in the coven?" she asked finally looking at him.

Again, Tristan remained silent.

"It was hell," she said, "because when you screamed for help, no one was allowed to save you. If you couldn't fight for yourself, then you weren't worth saving. You're taught to walk away because if you are always helping the ones that need help, they will never learn how to fight for themselves."

Tristan could hear the anger and passion rising in her voice.

"When I saw him with on top of that girl, I taught him a lesson worth learning. I taught him that if you go around sticking your business in places it does not belong, then you might just lose it." She turned to look at him. "Some of those scars on my back are from the lashing I received for helping that girl." She laughed. "It wasn't because I castrated that boy. They blamed him for his actions. His behavior is not welcome at the coven and it does go punished, but it can't go punished if no one says anything." She looked back at the road. "It is difficult for me to realize when I need help because no one has ever truly helped me before. Not even Marten helped me. By then, he had earned his title and was on missions. I wrote to him about the boy, but he could do nothing. It was months until he probably received my letters. The Master perhaps would have spoken out, too, but I was too scared to tell him. So, if I do not automatically say, 'Thank you,' please do not assume that I am ungrateful."

"You're welcome," was all Tristan said in response. For the first time he saw her the same way that he saw himself. Vulnerable and human. Before, he only saw her as a drone, just going day by day as ordered. But now she seemed a little more real. She fought just like everybody else to survive. She had feelings, pain and regret. She felt just as alone as everyone else. Just as alone as he felt. It somehow made her seem more beautiful.

It was going to make his job a lot more difficult.

THEY REACHED THE END OF THE VRON WOOD AND BORNNEN'S SIDE of the Stronghold Mountains just before sunset the next day, the iron mine just visible below. They stopped their horses just inside the trees and watched the miners from a distance.

"We can rest here until the miners leave and then we will make a pass for that small valley," The Tigress said pointing to the path they were going to take. "Once we are far enough out of view of the mine, we can make camp."

Tristan nodded.

They led their horses to a little brook and let them drink from it while they waited. When the sun finally set, the two of them watched silently as all of the miners left for the day. They waited another half an hour to make sure that the mine was clear before they rode as swiftly and as silently as possible. They made it to the small valley and continued riding until they got to a path that led up the mountain.

Once they made it a little ways up, they looked out across the valley just making out the Mahk River. Several small lights glowed in the night along the river lining its banks.

Tristan pointed off to the north. "The map showed this road as the pilgrimage route," he said. "So, the armory must be up that way."

She nodded. "Travelling will be easier tomorrow when we resume our ruse. As long as we stay incognito, we shouldn't be questioned."

"How much further do you think it is?"

"It took us about eight days to make it here," she calculated. "We might be able to make it there in another three or four. We have been making very good time."

He nodded. "How are we going to make it back to Thren? I would suggest a different path back than the one we took to get here."

"Agreed," she said getting off of her horse. "We can follow the river south until we come to the end of the Stronghold Mountains on Thren's side and then take the main road there back to Harpren." She took a bundle of sticks off of her horse and threw them into a pile arranging them so she could start a fire.

"I am guessing that will make our journey a little longer?"

She nodded as she prepared her bed for the night. "It will add another two weeks, possibly, but the countryside of Thren is normally very safe. And I am not willing to go through the woods again just to shorten our trip."

Tristan let out a sigh and got off his horse as well. "Safe is good with me." He sat down on the dust trail and propped himself up on a rock.

"And you will be able to see the border of Dead Man's Rest if we take that route. You have been asking so much about it the past few days it might interest you to see it. Though you cannot go any closer than Thren's side of the river. That is as close as you will be able to get."

Tristan nodded. "A land of mystery," he said. The mountain winds blew and he let out a shiver. He glanced over at her. "Are you going to be able sleep tonight?" he asked her cautiously.

She looked back at him. "Why shouldn't I?" she answered.

"I just thought that after the other morning you might not be able to sleep as well as you normally would have. I mean, I know I didn't sleep well last night."

She blinked at him, her green eyes dancing and glowing in the fire. "What makes you think I ever sleep well?" She shrugged. "I have seen many horrors in my life," she said. "I have somehow learned to adapt to them all."

He shrugged too. "I was just asking in case you wanted to sleep a little closer to me."

He saw the anger begin to rise in her eyes.

He put his hands up. "Wait a minute!" he said. "I was not trying to make a move on you. I was merely saying it out of concern. In case you wanted to fall asleep with a sense of security."

She stifled a laugh.

He frowned. "Really? Do you have to be so demeaning all the time? I was hoping that yesterday morning's conversation would open a door to, perhaps, a friendship." He shivered again.

She pursed her lips. "I don't trust people enough to make friends," she replied. "But that's my fault, not yours."

"Well, then maybe for my own sense of security we could sleep a little closer tonight," he said after a few moments.

She gave him a serious look.

"Plus, it is colder up here in the mountains and I have very thin skin, I am told. I am terrible during the winter months. I suffer like no one else you have ever seen. The cold just seeps into my bones."

She raised an eyebrow.

"I am not kidding. I will whine and complain all night if you leave me to freeze by myself. Sleeping close together will be beneficial to the both of us," he continued. "We will both feel safer and warmer throughout the night."

She let out a sigh. "I get it," she said finally allowing him to set up his bed next to hers. "Just remember that I sleep with my knives and I am a very light sleeper. So, if you value all of your body parts, keep them to yourself."

He placed a hand over his heart and raised the other in the air. "I swear on the honor of my father Drakus Stahrs, I will not touch you inappropriately throughout the night if I can help it."

She gave him a look.

"I move in my sleep," he said.

"Just *go* to sleep," she replied. "We have just as long of a day tomorrow as we have had the last few days."

CHAPTER 12

There was the woman again. The warm smile that she usually had on her face was replaced with a look of panic. The Tigress could feel the pressure of her hand on hers as she pulled her along.

There was a strange shouting or screaming noise behind them.

"Don't look back," the woman said.

She tripped, stumbling over her feet unable to keep up with the quick strides of the woman, so she was picked up off of the gound. The woman ran with her, the child, in her arms through the woods pressing her head close to her chest to protect her from the low hanging branches.

"I'm scared," she, the child, whimpered.

"Shh!" the woman said pressing on. "Stay strong."

The shouting became louder behind them, increasing the woman's fear. Unable to run any further with the child, the woman spotted a large tree with a suitable hole in the trunk. She placed the child inside telling her to stay put and to keep quiet.

The woman gave her a sad smile before planting a kiss on her head.

"I love you," she whispered and ran off further into the woods.

After the woman had vanished, a scream broke through the silent woods.

The Tigress sat up in full alert searching around her, expecting to find someone standing over her; a feeling that woke her most nights and mornings. The cold morning air made her shiver and she could see her breath. Tristan stirred next to her inching closer to her, mumbling in his sleep.

She stood up and checked the area. She climbed up a boulder and checked again, squinting in the early morning light. She listened, waiting for a sign that something or someone was there. She shook her head, trying to shake the feeling that someone was there watching them.

"You know, my whole life I have heard that Bornnen is nothing but a barren wasteland," Tristan said as they rode along the mountain side later that day. "But looking around this valley, I have to say that other than the Oasis I have never seen a more beautiful view. I don't think I have ever seen grass this green before and the mountain air is very refreshing."

"Most of Bornnen is a wasteland," The Tigress replied. "But you are right. The valley is beautiful, peaceful. The people even seem nice. If I had not known better, I would have thought we were in Thren."

"Can I ask you a question?" Tristan asked.

Her eyes grew a little wide. "Something tells me I am not going to want to answer."

"If growing up in the coven was so terrible, why didn't you leave?"

She regarded him for a moment. "It was not all terrible," she finally replied. "I learned more than I ever could living in the coven. I learned how to take care of myself. Women raised outside of the coven are seen as weak. They are not expected to contribute more than children to a marriage. That thought process does not exist in the coven. Women are expected to pull the same amount of weight as the men are, figuratively speaking, of course. Take a look at me," she said motioning to herself. "I hunt, I work and I live for myself. I do not have to worry about how I am going to live. Scrambling to find myself a husband so that I might be taken care of is something that does not concern me like it does most women." She nodded. "I have the coven to thank for that."

"You can certainly handle yourself," Tristan agreed.

There was a brief pause in their conversation.

The Tigress shrugged. "But even had I wanted to leave, which part of me always thought I belonged somewhere else, I don't think that I would have."

"Why not?" Tristan asked.

"Why didn't you leave if your stepmother was so terrible?" she responded.

He thought for a second and nodded. "We stayed because we had nowhere to go," he said. "We are kind of alike, you and I."

"How so?"

"We are both looking for a place where we truly belong."

She looked at him, truly looked at him, and knew that he was right. "Maybe we don't really belong anywhere," she said with a sigh.

Tristan shrugged. "Or maybe we just haven't found where we belong yet."

Down the road they came to a tavern where they stopped to eat and replenish their supplies. The owner's wife, an older, skinny little woman, was polite and obliging talking up a storm about their pilgrimage.

"If ya don't mind muh askin,'" the elder lady said, "but whar's yar nun's veil?"

The Tigress put her hands on her head and gasped. "We got into a scuffle with some bandits in Vron Wood. We barely escaped with our lives. I did not even realize that it was missing," she said. "What am I to do?" she asked to no one in particular, pretending to be in alarm. "I am not fit to enter into any of the temples."

The woman waved a hand at her. "Thar's uh very nice shop just down tha way whar ya can buy new clothes free o' stains and rips." She motioned to Tristan's robes. "They also sell othar religious materials."

The Tigress thanked her and was about to turn to walk out when the woman called after her again.

"I'd be carrful on yar way tuh tha lake," she said. "Thar's guards everywhar."

"What for?" The Tigress asked in a curious tone.

"They haven' really esplained it tuh anyone. They jus' showed up uh few days 'go and began askin' ev'ryone fer therr papers. Tha guards ha' been mighty 'spicious of ev'ryone since the king's death. Though 'tween you an' me that king ne'er did us no good alive."

"I'm sorry to hear that," The Tigress replied. "I wish the next may treat you better."

The woman shrugged. "I doubt the next'll be any beh'er," she replied. "Be carrful."

"Thank you, ma'am," The Tigress said again. "May the gods and goddesses of creation bless you forevermore."

She walked out of the tavern with Tristan right behind her.

"Did you hear what she said?" The Tigress asked in a low voice.

"Absolutely not," he replied. "Nothing that came out of her mouth was discernable."

She pulled him over to the horses. "She said that Bornnenian guards are everywhere and have been asking everyone for their papers," she whispered.

Tristan shook his head. "Yeah, that is not what I heard at all." He gave a shrug. "All of our papers are in order, though. We shouldn't have an issue with travelling."

She raised an eyebrow at him. "Yes, but with a heavier presence of guards, my mark will be more difficult to get to than we had originally thought," she said.

"Right," he said nodding. "That is a big problem."

"Yes," she agreed in a bland tone, "it is." She sighed. "If the guards are to pull us over or if we come into contact with any of the other pilgrims, which we most likely will, you have to pretend that you are taking your vow of silence."

"We both know how almost impossible that is," he said lifting an eyebrow at her.

"Your life actually depends on this, Tristan," she said. "Both of our lives do."

He nodded after a moment. "Alright, Dahlen. I will keep my mouth shut."

"Good," she said. "Now, we need to make haste, but the woman was right. We need to buy new clothes before we continue. We cannot be seen in clothes like this." She motioned toward both of their torn and dirt stained clothes.

"When did she- how did you understand anything that she said? Seriously, all I heard was noise."

She laughed, a true laugh that actually shook her and rang out. She put her hands over her mouth almost in alarm.

Tristan gave her a funny look. "I almost didn't think you were capable of laughter," he said. "I have heard you give a little snort or a soft chuckle, but the sound of you enjoying yourself is refreshing."

The Tigress shrugged. "Maybe it's the mountain air," she mused, leading her horse down the road to where the woman said the shop was.

Tristan followed after her, watching her move along the road, not realizing that he was smiling the entire time.

THE TWO OF THEM TROTTED ALONG THE TRAIL, COMING ACROSS SEV-eral monks, nuns, and priestesses on their pilgrimages. When it came time to set up camp, they shared a site with a large group of monks who were singing songs of praise over their wine and roasted boar.

One of the older monks was handing out mugs of beer and when he got to Tristan The Tigress waved the mug away.

"He is taking his vows, brother," she said.

Tristan frowned at her.

He nodded and took a seat near them. "Where are the two of you from?" the older monk asked between bites of boar and sips of wine.

"Our temple resides in Boutowen," The Tigress replied before Tristan could say anything. "It is a fishing village."

"In Thren," the monk added. "Yes, I have been there. Beautiful place. Quiet little fishing village just south of Behr Wood where Mahk River opens to the Dormant Sea. Behr is your main goddess there, is she not?" he asked.

The Tigress nodded. "Where are you from?" she questioned.

"Ah, our main goddess is yours' twin, Gher in northern Skahrr a few miles south of the border of Bornnen and west of the Desert of Vremir," he replied. "That is actually where we started our journey. From there to Mahk Lake where we will take the river down to your temple and then make our way to the oasis and Vremir's Rest and back home again."

She nodded again. "Mahk Lake is our last stop. We will head home via the river afterwards."

"How long has your friend left on his vow of silence?" the same monk asked.

She looked over at Tristan, a pensive look on her face. "It has been perhaps eight months since he has begun, so another four or so to go."

He nodded. "It is a weird feeling once you find your voice again," he said filling his cup up with more wine. "But it was a spiritual journey I would no sooner give up than my right arm."

"And he's left handed," the monk to his left said sending them into drunken laugher.

The Tigress smiled.

"Seriously, young brother," the first monk started again, "my mind had never been more open, my ears had never heard more clearly, my eyes had never experienced such colors as when I was taking my year's vow of silence. Your world expands if you just shut up a moment just to look and listen."

The Tigress elbowed Tristan lightly and smiled at him.

"You are quite young, the both of you," another monk asked. "Is this both of your first pilgrimages?"

"It is his first ever and my first full one. I made a partial journey but was struck sick with mountain fever and I was urged to stay behind," The Tigress said.

A few of the older priestesses, nuns and monks nodded their heads.

Tristan shot The Tigress a strange look.

"A terrible time, mountain fever is," one of the priestesses said. "I have had it at least twice."

"How is the lake area?" The Tigress asked the first monk who said they had just come from that way. "I heard that there are a lot of guards in the area. It is not dangerous, is it?"

The monk took a sip of his wine and shook his head. "No, they seem to take a more careful look at your papers, but other than that, I did not come across any problem and considering the hard feelings they have toward people from Skahrr, we did not have any trouble." He took another sip of wine. "Coming from Thren you should be fine though. They might make the usual prejudicial gesture or joke but nothing more."

The Tigress gave a nod to Tristan.

The conversation went on like that for the remainder of the night until the fires finally burned down, and no one really had the energy to keep building them back up, and, like the fires, everyone settled down for the night.

THE TIGRESS WOKE UP HEARING THE SOUNDS OF STIRRING AROUND her. She sat up and smiled greetings to the monks that had gotten up to pray and joined them. They prayed facing north for the goddess Gher, they prayed east for the god Mahk, they prayed south for the goddess Behr and finally they prayed west for the god Vron. They even prayed facing the mountains citing their scripture. And when The Tigress looked up at the rocks, her arms lifted toward the sky in praise, she saw a flash of movement—a dark figure ducking behind one of the large rocks.

She paused in her prayer, waiting to see if she could catch a glimpse of what she thought she saw, but nothing emerged. An animal, perhaps, she thought.

Before all of the monks went on their way, The Tigress warned them about the dangers of the Vron wood.

"Once we left the Oasis," she started, "I think we entered the territory of vicious bandits. They don't discriminate against their victims. They did not seem to care that we were adorned in religious garb. And since you will be entering the way we came out, you will have to be on your guard right away. I would avoid that path altogether and enter the Oasis from Vremir's Rest."

They bowed to her. "Thank you, sister," they said. "We shall heed your warning. May the gods and goddesses bless you and keep you safe on the rest of your journey."

She bowed and repeated the blessing to them.

The next couple of days they crossed the paths of several other pilgrims coming and going on their religious journeys. All of them had their own stories to tell and news to report about the guards.

The second day they were stopped by three guards patrolling the mountain side, their blood-red capes whipping around in the wind.

"Whar yur papers?" one of them said holding his hand out for them.

The Tigress gave a small bow in greeting as she produced their papers from one of her bags.

The guards snarled down at it for what seemed like a longer time than necessary before they shoved them back at her.

"Keep off tha mountain pass. If ya stay on tha valley road ya'll be fine." The guards walked off grunting to each other in the opposite direction and The Tigress and Tristan went on their way again.

By the third day they finally reached Mahk Lake where hundreds of others were gathered around the waters drinking from the lake and pouring the water over their heads. And just up the mountain, surrounded by guards and adorned with ornamental flags was a small castle.

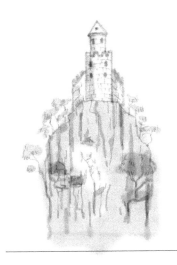

CHAPTER 13

"ARE YOU READY FOR THIS?" SHE WHISPERED TO TRISTAN AS SHE TIED up her hair and wrapped a black veil around her head.

"Can we go over the plan again?" he asked, looking uneasy.

She laughed through her nose and shook her head. "I am going into the castle, searching for the armory, taking whatever blueprints there might be for the weapon, killing the weapon makers and getting the hell out of there."

"Do I actually have to follow you into the castle?" he replied. "My whole job was just to be part of your cover, right? Your whole part of the job was to sneak into the castle and do the killing."

She smiled. "I don't need you up there. I need you down here to man the horses. When I get back, we will need to make a run for it to a different camp further down the road. Keep our things close enough together so you can just throw them on the horses if need be. Wait just off the mountain path and when you hear me call," she made a soft whistling noise, "bring them to the edge of the path and we can ride off into the night."

"And then our job is done," he said in a distant tone.

"And then *my* job is done. Your job after this one is to find where I came from, remember?" she reminded him.

He nodded, his heart dropping a bit. "True, I did promise that I would do that for you. I cannot promise immediate results," he said. "It might take me a year or so, but I will do what I can."

She reached out and gently grabbed him by the arm, her eyes sparkling in the moonlight as she smiled, her face almost happy. "Thank you," she said.

He felt the heat rise in his cheeks and he nodded somewhat speechless, a lump caught in his throat.

"This should not take too long," she said turning away.

"I will be waiting right here," he replied emotionless.

Suddenly, she turned back around and looked him square in the eyes, her face lit up with a smile. "You have given me hope," she told him. "Which is something that I have not felt in a long time, if ever. I am not sure how I will be able to repay you for that."

Tristan nodded. "Don't mention it," he replied trying to smile back.

"You know," The Tigress started, "you're not so bad once one gets used to you." She gave a small laugh before pulling her veil up to cover her mouth and nose. "Keep your eyes and ears open. I am counting on you for a fast escape."

With that, The Tigress turned and began her trek up the mountain.

Tristan stood, his heart racing and cheeks flushed as the full effect of her words sank in. She had shown him a sign of trust and friendship, a sign of loyalty. He slowly ran his hands through his hair and sighed in defeat.

"What have I done?"

THE TIGRESS RAN UP THE MOUNTAIN, SILENT AND SUREFOOTED IN THE dark of the night. She hid behind rocks to avoid detection from the guards and waited in their shadows until it was safe for her to continue. She ran along the mountain path parallel to the castle until she found a blind point of entry and began her ascent.

She clung to the face of the cliff the castle was built on, ignoring the sweat that began to roll down from her brow. When she finally reached the outer walls of the castle, she used her knives, shoving them in the cracks and then pulling herself up. The work was slow and painstaking but nothing she hadn't done before.

When she finally reached a window, she was breathing heavily and her arms shook from the effort. She rested inside the windowsill scanning the room that she had pulled herself up into. The room appeared to have been a chapel. The ceiling had several buttresses shaping and supporting the roof in which she crawled onto and rested for a few minutes.

The chapel was indeed empty. There were a few torches up on the alter that cast small shadows throughout the room, but other than that, there was nothing.

After rubbing her arms and giving her a few moments to regain her bearing, she silently jumped down and made her way to the door. She slowly opened the door to the chapel and peered outside, slipping into the hall when she saw that it was empty.

Odd, she thought, as she crept through the empty halls.

When she and Tristan scouted the area during the day, he came to the conclusion that the room the armory was in was most likely to be in the room that had the best ventilation.

"The spies said that the substance had a strange smell," she said to him when she agreed with his suggestion. "A room with more windows would allow for fresh air and for them to work into the night without the use of fire which would surely be dangerous."

He pointed to a large square tower. "There makes sense."

The tigress had nodded. "That would allow for the best lighting with windows on either side of it."

Tristan's assumption appeared to be right when she turned the bend of the castle and saw the guards standing in front of the door leading to the tower they had agreed on. She ducked back around the corner keeping the view of the guards in her mind.

She closed her eyes and counted. Four guards in total. Two down the hall, two at the door. If she could take them on one at a time silently, she could make it inside that door. But they were not spread far enough apart for sneak attacks on them all.

The hall was dark enough, even with the torches blazing away there were plenty of shadows to hide in. She thought for a moment on how to distract them and poked her head around the corner for another look.

She smiled when she saw the blood red banners of Bornnen lining the halls. She took out one of her knives and cut out a small piece of cloth from her garbs wrapping it around one of her arrows. She then loaded her bow and took a deep breath before she whipped around the corner lighting her arrow in the torch closest to her and firing it down the hall hitting one of the banners.

Catching the banner on fire got the reaction that she wanted. Three of the guards ran to douse the flames leaving a lone guard at the door, his back turned to her. She quickly crouched up behind him and slit the man's throat before she threw three knives at the others, hitting her targets. She then retrieved her knives and slipped through the door, climbing the winding stairs up the tower, emerging silently into the room.

The room was darker than the chapel; there was no fire, as she had predicted. The only light was from the moon that shown in from the west-facing window. She scanned the mostly empty room until she saw a man by a window hovered over a table in a dark corner. She moved toward him before she froze a moment. Something wasn't right. Her skin prickled in a cold sweat as the realization hit her.

"We've been expectin' ya,'" a gruff familiar voice said.

She turned to see the towering shape of the Bornnenian guard that had captured her when she posed as the princess of Skahrr.

She did a full circle of the room and saw that she was in fact surrounded. Five men twice her size and heavily armed emerged from the darkness sneering and laughing at her.

"Put tha knife down, dove," the guard said. "Thar's no gettin' out o' here," he laughed.

Just then the door swung open and more guards carrying torches, lighting up the room, filtered in escorting a man whose head was bowed, his brown locks of hair bouncing as he walked.

"Thanks tuh our friend here, we war able tuh catch ya," he laughed again slapping the man on the back.

Tristan lifted his head and shook his head violently. "I didn't—"

The guard squeezed Tristan's cheek with his hand. "Oh, don't be lyin' now. Thar's no point," he said. "Tell her how ya led her right to us. That ya set her up tuh be caught."

The Tigress looked at Tristan in disbelief, but he refused to meet her eye.

"Best thing was, we didn't even haff tuh pay him too much," the guard continued. "Just a bit o' gold and his own estate somewhar in Bornnen of his choosin'." The guards all chuckled.

She shook her head. "No," she said breathlessly. She stepped toward the table and pushed over the man, her heart sinking when a dummy hit the floor.

The guards laughed at her, the obnoxious noise reverberating off of the stone walls of the room.

She whirled back around and glared at Tristan. "You son of a bitch," she hissed.

The head guard laughed harder and approached her. "Thar's no escaping now," he said backhanding her across the face.

The Tigress felt a sharp pain in her face just before her head hit the edge of the table and the world went black.

CHAPTER 14

SHE HEARD A SCREAM AND WHIMPERED, TRYING TO SINK DEEPER INTO the hole of the tree. Where had her mother gone, she wondered? Why had she left her here all alone? After a few minutes, she began to hear voices approaching and the sounds of twigs snapping as they were trod on.

Was it mother?

She let out a small cry and moved to leave her hiding spot when a strange warmth enveloped her.

Don't be afraid, came a voice. *You are safe where you are.*

THE TIGRESS GROANED AS SHE AWOKE, HER HEAD THROBBING. SHE tried to lift a hand to rub it, but they were both bound behind her. She heard the squeaking of a wagon as it pulled along, tiny streaks of light shone in through cracks or holes in the fabric that covered the wagon, the sound of horses' hooves clopping on the ground.

They were on the move.

She tried to sit up but grimaced as pain shot through her head again and decided that it was best to just lie down.

"You're finally awake," a sheepish voice said from the other end of the dark wagon.

She scowled and said nothing as anger and hatred rose within her when the events from the night before came rushing back. She began to breathe heavily in and out through her nose to try and control her emotions.

The wagon rocked slightly, throwing her about and she winced again.

"I know how much you might hate me right now," Tristan started, "but I just want to let you know—"

"You have now idea how I feel," she said yelling over him and immediately regretting it. She closed her eyes to keep the pain at bay. "You have betrayed me, made me look like a fool. You took what little faith I might have stowed away deep inside of me and threw it on the ground for all and everyone to stomp upon," she said.

He bowed his head.

"But hear me, whoever you truly may be, that before I die, I vow that I will kill you," she said, her voice sharp. "I will rip your eyes from their sockets and rip your lying tongue from its mouth all before I peel the flesh from your worthless bones. I will then tear your beating heart out of your chest and feed it to the crows before I burn what may be left of your tainted remains. I will kill you," she repeated, "but not before I make you suffer."

"Dahlen, please allow me to explain," he started again.

"Do not talk to me!" she yelled interrupting him again. "Haven't I suffered enough in my life without your unnecessary, incessant babbling?"

He could hear the anger and the pain in her voice as it shook when she spoke and he once again bowed his head and remained silent.

So many thoughts ran through both of their minds, one wanting so much to speak, the other replaying the last two weeks in her mind, kicking herself for not realizing that he was a spy for the other side. All of the questions that he kept asking about the coven should have been an obvious sign, but she was so distracted by his stupid, clumsy act that it had never occurred to her. How could she have been so blind?

After a while, the silence was too much for Tristan and he finally got the nerve to break it again. "I'm sorry," he said. "I know that you might not believe me or think that I mean it, but I do."

She gave an annoyed groan. "Is that it then?" she asked, the anger once again rising in her voice. "You just apologize and that makes it all better? Do you expect me to just forgive you? You're sorry! How wonderful!" she said sardonically. "I am so relieved! Now we can put this whole thing behind us and start where we left off!" She huffed. "If you're so sorry, then untie me, so I can escape."

"I can't do that," he replied. "There are too many men and if I release you, you will try to kill them all and get yourself killed."

"Or, I could just kill you," she retorted.

"Also, a good reason not to untie you," Tristan replied.

She shook her head. "Untie me, Tristan."

"I won't untie you just to watch you die."

"I would rather die fighting than on the executioner's block," she growled through her teeth. "Why am I even here? I shouldn't even be in this situation. I am protected by the coven. I did not murder their king. My contract to kill him was legal. If they want to take it up with anyone, it is the person who hired me for the contract."

Tristan blinked at her. "I don't know what they want with you."

"Shouldn't you know?" she asked annoyed. "You're one of them."

He sighed. "Again, I *am sorry*."

"Yes, you certainly are sorry," she replied in a more bitter tone. She shook her head. "How could I have been so stupid?" She gave an exasperated sigh. "I know better than to trust anyone and yet, against that judgment, here I am. You're not even charming! That is the ridiculous part of it all. You are a silly boy incapable of the most mundane tasks and, yet, you somehow got me to trust you."

"If you would just listen to what I have to say, then—"

"Would me hearing you out change the fact that I am tied up in the back of a Bornnenian wagon?" she asked.

He didn't respond.

"Then once again, do me the pleasure of shutting up."

"You are not the least bit curious why?" he asked getting a little annoyed that she wouldn't let him finish a sentence.

"Again, would it change the current situation?" she retorted. "If the answer is, 'no' then, no, I am not curious as to why you stabbed me in the back like the coward that you truly are," she said. "And it will most certainly not change me wanting to kill you, so why waste your breath?"

"Because maybe I feel guilty and explaining my side of things will make me feel better."

"You think I care how you feel?" she asked. "This may come as news to you, Tristan, if that truly is your name, but I could not care less about how guilty you feel. If you feel bad about your actions, then good. I only wish you felt worse." She huffed. "Why are you even in here with me?" she asked. "Shouldn't you be out there on a giant Bornnenian horse riding in all of your traitorous glory?"

"No," he said a little angrily.

"Were your gentle lordling legs too soft for the rough saddle-less riding of the Bornnenians? I am sorry for that."

"No," he said again a little louder.

"Then please!" she said. "Bore me with the details! Why did you choose to ride with me only making my embarrassment worse?"

He huffed and shook his head. "Because the men wanted to take turns with you. And I told them to leave you alone."

She didn't say anything for a few moments. "And they just listened to you?" she asked. "Seems very unlikely."

He took a deep breath and let it out loudly. "I offered them my reward money if they promised not to touch you," he said. "And then I set up in here to make sure they kept their promise."

She wasn't sure how to react, so she remained quiet.

"I know it may not change how you might feel. It doesn't make what I did less wrong. But you are right. You have suffered enough in your life."

"Just say your piece and be done with it," she said in a bland tone.

He looked at her lying on her side motionless, except for the swaying of the wagon that rocked her body gently back and forth. "I was a nobody before," he started. "I still am. The bastard of a lord. No one lets you forget that. I was tired of people writing me off before they even got a chance to know that I am more than just a bastard. You at least wrote me off before you knew I was a bastard."

She huffed.

Tristan shook his head trying to stay on point. "A few weeks ago, I met a guy in a tavern that offered me a chance to break free from the restraints of being a bastard. He told me that I could be my own lord."

She laughed out of her nose.

"He somehow knew that I had a rapport with the King of Skahrr or at least that my father and him are known friends, my father's sister being the late wife of the king, and that I could get close enough to him to find you."

"You are the King's nephew?" she asked incredulously.

He nodded. "It is a fact he likes to forget."

"Who is this man that hired you?"

Tristan shrugged. "I don't know, I had never seen him before. At least, I am pretty sure I never have."

"You don't even know that?" The Tigress scoffed.

Tristan sighed impatiently. "He wore a hood and hid his face from me. He didn't even give me a name or a way to reach him. He just told me that he would be able to contact me if he wanted."

"So you have no way of identifying this man?" she asked skeptically.

Tristan thought for a moment, nodding pensively. "He had a curved scar running from the base of his middle finger to the base of his thumb."

"Wonderful," she mumbled. "All we have to do is check every man's hands for that specific scar and we have him."

"I wasn't really thinking further than the money when I met him."

"Is the man who hired you the same one who hired The Shadow to kill King Breht?" she asked.

Tristan shook his head. "As far as I know, killing King Breht was not part of the plan. Not part of any plan that I heard, at least," he explained.

"Then who hired The Shadow to kill King Breht?" she asked slightly shifting in her spot on the floor.

"I don't know."

"Okay," she said a little annoyed. "Tell me something that you do know, like, if no one in Bornnen hired anyone to kill the king then why are they capturing me?" she asked. "The king hired me to kill Ahlenwei."

He shook his head. "I don't know that either."

She huffed. "Were you actually apart of this plan or what?"

"Listen," he started, "all I was supposed to do was deliver you to them."

"Are those weapons real?" she asked. "The one the king sent us to steal?"

"No," he replied. "I don't believe they are. Ohtt, the captain of the Bornnenian guard, now leader, until Ahlenwei's heir comes of age, told me they paid off King Breht's spies to lie. I was then supposed to lead you to the castle overlooking Mahk Lake, luring you to a trap. But the truth is, Dahlen, I did not expect you and I to," he paused to think.

"To what?" The Tigress interrupted, annoyed.

"Connect," he finished.

She made a scoffing sound and laughed again. "Connect? Do not make me laugh, Tristan," she said with disdain. "It hurts enough to think."

"What?" he said getting heated. "Am I not good enough for you?" he asked. "Am I not fit enough to be with you?"

"Gods be blessed, you are an idiot, Tristan," she said hissing through her teeth.

"I know you were at least starting to care for me," he continued.

"You are mad if you think that."

"As a friend, not as anything else, but you regarded me as a companion, someone in whom you could trust."

"Hmm. I guess you've ruined that now, haven't you?"

"Dahlen," Tristan started. "I am so sorry. I wish that I could take it all back. That I could start over from the beginning and somehow come to my senses just before I agreed to work with Ohtt."

"How did you find me that day?" she asked him. "The day we met?"

Tristan sniffed and cleared his throat. "The man who hired me handed me a letter," he replied. "I don't know how, but the letter described you to me. Not just you though, but the day, the time and atmosphere of the place I was to find you." He paused. "The man who handed it to me told me to tell King Breht that I could find you and bring you back to him. So, I did and on the day the letter told me to be at the tavern I was, and so were you."

The Tigress took a moment to understand what he told her. "You got a letter telling you where I was going to be?"

"Yes," Tristan said with a nod.

"That doesn't make sense."

"Listen," he replied, "it didn't make sense to me either, but it was right. I found you wearing exactly what the letter said you would be wearing with the person the letter said you would be with."

"And you did all of this to become a lord?" The Tigress guffawed. "How could you betray your country like that?"

Tristan took a deep breath and let it out slowly. "It was the day that my father died," he replied after a moment. "And my stepmother threw me out of that house that morning. I guess in a drunken stupor his offer sounded appealing and," he paused, "so I took it."

"I didn't know men were so weak to let their emotions guide them," The Tigress said in a scowl.

"You have a lot of nerve judging me!" Tristan yelled. "You kill people for a living, yet, I am the bad guy."

"I kill rapists and murderers!" The Tigress yelled back. "I don't kill innocent people. I choose my contracts carefully; I find out who I am being hired to kill and why before I even accept a contract. I do *not* just kill people for a living. I have the freedom to choose, the free will to take what contract I want." She paused. "And if I don't agree with why my employer wants someone dead, I walk away."

Tristan laughed. "An assassin with a conscience," he said. "That's a funny concept."

"It's better than making friends with someone just to stab them in the back."

Tristan sighed in defeat. "So, we are friends, admit it."

"Let us go back to being silent," The Tigress said. "I am tired of this conversation."

The sounds of the wagon and the men outside engulfed the two of them in their silence. The Tigress glared at the wooden frame until she finally fell back into a restless sleep.

SOMEWHERE IN THE DEAD OF THE NIGHT THE SOUND OF SHOUTING woke her. The wagon was still but she could hear horses running around her. She stirred, trying to prop herself up as the sounds of shouting and fighting became louder.

"Tristan," she whispered, "what is going on?"

"There was an ambush," he said scrambling around in the dark. "I don't know by whom." He was now right by her in the wagon. He placed his hand on her and she flinched.

"What do you think you are doing?" she hissed.

"Calm down," he said untying her legs. "I just thought that maybe—"

Before he could finish his sentence, she kicked him in the face and then slipped her legs through her tied arms and chewed off the ropes.

Tristan groaned and sat up. "Wait a minute. Before you—"

She lunged at him, pressing both hands around his throat and forcing him onto the floor of the wagon. "Where are my knives?" she asked.

"Let me go," he choked out barely fighting against her. "Please, don't do this."

She could feel the anger well up inside of her as she stared down into Tristan's face. She could make out the large whites of his eyes growing larger as she continued to squeeze.

"Why?" she said glaring down into his eyes. "Give me one good reason why I shouldn't just end your pathetic life right now."

"I'm sorry," he said his lips turning blue.

She squeezed harder, her nails beginning to dig into his flesh.

Tears came to Tristan's eyes and he closed them as if to accept his fate to die at her hands.

She let out a scream of frustration as she released his throat, sending him into a coughing fit. She slid off of him and sat staring at him coughing and gasping for air.

"Where are my weapons?" she finally said when the sound of the fighting became louder and closer.

He pointed to the chest at the far end of the wagon and she scrambled to it, flipping open the lid and letting out a sigh of relief. She pulled out her belt of knives and placed them back on her person.

She paused in her movements and held her breath when she realized it was silent outside. She looked up to see the bouncing light of torches glowing through the holes of the wagon's cover. Whoever started the ambush was getting closer to the wagon.

"We should go," Tristan croaked, finally catching his breath again, noticing what she had just noticed.

"We?" she said venomously, turning back around. "There is no 'we,'" she told him putting her bow and arrows on her back.

He shook his head. "I know I messed up and that you might never fully trust me ever again, but you have to believe that I wanted to turn back. I wanted to tell you that it was a trap, but I couldn't." He rolled over onto his knees and slowly stood up.

"Yes, I imagine the loss of your Lordship would have had something to do with it," she replied half standing in the wagon.

"If you allow me to, I swear I will spend the rest of my life making it up to you," he said.

"The rest of your life will not be very long if you think you are wanting to follow me after this."

"Will you not even give me a chance?" he pleaded.

Before she could respond the cloth that was covering the wagon was ripped to shreds from several directions. The two of them stood back to back. She took the bow off her back and shot arrows where the blades of swords were sticking through. Shouting came from outside of the wagon. Unsure if the arrows made their marks, she shot until she ran out before moving onto her knives. By then the wagon's cover was tattered and they could hear more men swarming around them.

Looking through the tattered canvas, The Tigress saw a man approaching. "I do no care what happens to you after this," she said. "Once we make it out of here, we will go our separate ways." She didn't give him enough time to respond before yelling, "Get ready to run!"

Before Tristan had time to react, she jumped landing on the approaching man, her knees making contact with his chest. He fell and let out a quick grunt before she stabbed him in the throat. She then jumped up and ran looking behind her only to see if Tristan had followed her out of the wagon. When she saw that he had made it out she focused all that she had on running.

She ran blindly through the foreign country, unsure of which direction was the way she wanted to go. There were no trees or anything to hide in. She had made it about a hundred yards when she heard the sound of running horses gaining on her. Tristan screamed somewhere behind her and she knew that it wouldn't be long before they got her too.

No sooner had she thought it, a strange whirring sound came from behind her and she felt something wrap around her legs causing her to trip. She fell, sliding in the dead grass, putting her arms up just in time to save her face from the impact of the ground.

She pushed herself off of the ground and began cutting the ropes around her legs. But just as she freed herself a man on horseback pulled her up onto the saddle kicking and screaming taking her back in the direction that they had both come from.

The man dropped The Tigress down on the ground in the middle of a circle of the other men. The Tigress groaned and rubbed her side. When she looked up at the men that ambushed them, she saw the same kind of men that had attacked them in Vron Wood. She stood and pulled out two of her knives, ready for an attack, turning around and looking at the men. None of them moved. They just sat on their horses or stood staring at her, torches in most of their hands.

"What are you waiting for?" she yelled glaring at them all.

None of them answered, but a few horses moved, making a gap. Coming through the gap was a tall, broad man on a large, dark horse. He was wearing the same kinds of furs as the other men but the way he held himself and the way they moved out of his way made her think that he was someone of importance to them.

"Enough," he said slowly riding up to her.

She took a step back as he stopped his horse and slid off. She brought her knives up, ready to fight.

The man put his hands up to show that he wasn't armed. "I will not hurt you," he said in a steady accent. "Please, put away your weapons."

She hesitated, but knowing that killing this man would have meant her own sudden death, she reluctantly obeyed and put her knives away.

The man snapped his fingers and one of his men with a torch ran over. "My eyes are getting old," the man said with a smile. "I can no longer see by the moon alone."

The man stepped closer to The Tigress, the man with the torch right by him. He reached out and picked up one of her dark curls, feeling the texture of it between his fingers. He then put his hand under her chin and gently lifted her face toward him, turning her head so that he could inspect her face.

"You look just like her," the man said in a soft voice.

The man then moved his hand down the line of the neck, causing The Tigress to flinch.

"You do not have to be scared of me, love," he said finding her necklace and pulling it out from under her clothes.

The man motioned for the other man with the torch to step closer and he gave a small relieved laugh as he looked down at the silver wing that hung from her neck. He continued to laugh as he put his hand on The Tigress's cheek and looked into her eyes. Confusion swept over her when she saw tears glistening back at her.

The man fell to his knees in front of her and grabbing her hands he kissed them. "I thought that I had lost you all those years ago," he said through his tears. "I thank Vremir for this."

The Tigress even more confused and a little alarmed ripped her hands away from the man kneeling in front of her. "What is going on?" she asked.

The man slowly stood once again, unashamedly wiping away his tears. "You do not remember me?"

She gave him a blank stare.

He stood back up and put his hand on her arm giving it a light squeeze. "Of course not, AnnJella," he said, "it has been so long. And you had been so young."

The Tigress creased her brows. "What did you call me?" she asked almost in a whisper.

"I called you by your name," he replied stepping toward her again, his accent strange and unfamiliar. "AnnJella."

She gave a ragged breath. "The woman in my dreams called me that," she thought to herself. "AnnJella," she repeated slowly.

He put his hand on her cheek again, his eyes glistening with tears. "I thought I would never see you again, but now, you can finally come home." The man pulled her to him in an embrace, the smell of musty fur filling her nose.

She struggled against him. "Hold on," she said breaking free of his grasp. "What is going on here?" she asked. "I don't understand. Who are you?"

"I know you don't recognize me," he explained sounding a little hurt. He shook his head almost immediately. "No, I would not expect you to. You were so young the last I saw you." He gave her a soft smile. "My name is Vorce Brahn. I am your guardian."

The Tigress blinked at him in confusion. "My guardian?" she repeated. "I don't understand."

"Your parents trusted me to keep you safe," he told her.

The Tigress's mouth gaped slightly. "You knew my parents?" she asked softly.

He nodded. "Your father and I were great friends and your mother—" he stopped himself. "Your mother was a very kind woman."

"Are they dead?" she asked him in almost a whisper.

He paused for a moment, choosing his words. "It is, perhaps, a very long story and we have a long ride ahead of us. We should get going," he said looking around the wreck of a caravan, dead Bornnennian soldiers on the ground. "We can talk while we ride. We do not want to be here when the rest of their men come looking for them."

He turned and looked at another one of the men and said something to him in a harsh, gruff sounding language she didn't understand. Moments later a horse was brought to her and she was urged to get on.

"We need to make it back to the Vron Wood," the strange man said to her, helping her to get on the horse. "We will seek refuge in the mountains again laying low. Your friend is welcome as well."

"Friend?" she thought to herself before scowling. "That man is not my friend," she said when she realized they meant Tristan. She then thought for a moment about what Tristan had said the Bornnenian soldiers wanted to do to her and how he saved her from several more shameful moments. "But he is not necessarily my enemy," she sighed. "He can ride with us, but I would feel safer if he were tied up."

Vorce shouted an order at a couple of other men who nodded. He then turned back to The Tigress. "Come," he said motioning for her to follow him as he got on his horse. "Ride with me."

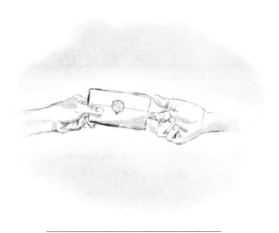

CHAPTER 15

THE TIGRESS TRIED NOT TO STARE AT THE MAN WHO RODE NEXT TO her. She tried not to look for the truth in what he had told her. She tried not to hope that this man was who he said he was, that he was connected to her past. She tried not to hope too much for an answer to her questions.

She had spent half the night before staring up into the night sky thinking about the possibility of this man being the key to unlocking everything she wanted to know about where she came from, who she was. Despite his offer to talk while they rode, she was too confused to think straight. She needed another day to gather her thoughts. She kept trying to add everything together. The coven had never really told her where she had come from. And those that she tried to ask would immediately get her off of the subject. She had always had a feeling that they were hiding something from her, but she had never imagined that it would be this.

She had wanted to find out where she had come from, who her family was and what happened to them ever since she could remember. But could she really have just stumbled upon her past this easily?

She looked at the man trying to see if she recognized him in any way when he turned and caught her staring.

"You look like your mother," he said as if he knew what she was thinking. "The same dark hair and green eyes."

"Is she dead?" she asked.

He nodded, squinting in the sun. "She died trying to protect you, I imagine," he replied.

"Why?" she asked. "Why did she need to protect me?"

He gave her a somber look and sighed. "Is it true that you do not know who you are? Who your family is?"

The Tigress did not respond as a feeling of resentment washed over her.

"Where have you been all these years?" he asked her.

The Tigress pulled a bug from her horse's mane and threw it to the ground below. "I have been at Dead Man's Rest for the most part," she replied blandly. "I was never told of my past. If they know anything about it, then they have made a huge secret of who I am and how I came to be there. They hardly ever answer my questions."

"You are of the coven?" Vorce asked. "A spy or assassin even?"

"Assassin," she replied.

"Then he must know—" he stopped himself again. "No, I will not." Vorce looked deep in thought, his brows furrowed, and his lips pursed. "Then it must have been for your own protection," he finally said breaking his own silence. "There must be a reason."

The Tigress watched him curiously.

Finally, Vorce shook his head. "All in good time," he all but muttered to himself.

"Vorce," The Tigress said breaking his thoughts.

He looked at her, a sharp, quick turn of the head that made it seem like he had almost forgotten she was there.

"What happened the day my mother died?" she finally asked. "If you were my guardian, why weren't you there to protect me?"

He looked off into the distance watching the road, letting the memories that haunted him every night resurface. She could see that his failure to be there in their time of need affected him deeply.

"I had received a message from your father, or rather, a message I thought was from your father. I later learned that it was only sent to bring me away. The note said that he was on a mission and needed my help."

"Mission?"

He sighed looking at her. "It was during the war," he started. "He was on a mission to kill a Bornnenian diplomat that was helping to fund their cause for war. For centuries, the kings of Bornnen have tried to fight for a piece of coastline to open up a cheaper way to trade throughout the realms. They have lakes and parts of rivers but no sea to move about from realm to realm without being taxed by other countries like Thren and Skahrr." He paused for a moment. "Over thirty years ago, King Bahlen, king before Ahlenwei, waged war on a group of tax collectors on the Mahk River."

The Tigress nodded. "Yes," she said. "He refused to pay the tax so that he could use the river to get to the Dormant Sea."

He nodded. "King Bahlen had thrown his money away for so many years that he had nearly bankrupted the crown. He believed that his only hope was to finally gain control of a seaport. His rampage started with the tax collectors but as he made his way down, he burned villages and even some of the sacred Behr wood. And a few days later another attack from Bornnen began on Skahrr starting down the Gher River. Thren and Skahrr were beating them back, winning the war when out from the sea came the Mehtian pirates splitting the Skahrrian and Threnian forces in half, weakening them.

"The war waged for five years before we figured out how they were paying the pirates to fight for them. When the other nations finally found out where the money was coming from, your father was employed by King Ehrman, father of King Breht of Skahrr, and King Mahst, father of King Caston of Thren, to find the diplomat that was paying the pirates and to take him out."

Vorce took a moment to collect his thoughts. "I had received a letter from your father informing me of this mission. It described the difficulty he was having finding this man and he needed my skills as a tracker to help find him."

He shook his head. "I did not know until I made it to the place I was supposed to meet your father that it was false information." He looked down gravely. "The mission was not a real thing, you must know, but," he paused. "I was a fool. By the time I returned, your mother was dead, and you were missing."

She glanced over at him feeling the pain he was going through. "You said that my father was sent on a mission," she said. "The way that you talk about Bornnen, Skahrr and Thren makes it sound like you are not of any of these places."

He met her gaze. "That is because I am not." He thought for moment. "Like you, I was of the coven."

The Tigress was taken aback. "You are one of The Nameless?" she asked incredulously.

Vorce nodded. "And so is your father," he said looking back at the road ahead. "I had been a mercenary while your father was an assassin, like you."

"And he broke his vows to the coven?" she asked even more incredulously.

He nodded, his slightly unkempt hair moving freely about his head. "Yes," he replied distantly.

They rode in silence for a few minutes.

"What happened?" she finally asked.

He took in a deep breath. "When I realized the letter from your father was a fake, I rushed back as soon as I could, but it was too late. The village was burned to the ground and you and your mother were nowhere to be seen. I thought the worst," he said shaking his head. "I thought, perhaps, you were sold into slavery. Taken by Mehtian pirates and shipped off to the other realms. I searched for you tirelessly."

He paused a moment and sniffed. "It was not until a few years later that I ran into a survivor of the attack. I recognized him from the village. He told me that he could not be for certain who attacked them. Their banners were like none he had ever seen. Yellow and orange with a great black bird in flight."

The Tigress took in a small gasp. He was describing the banners from her dream.

"When I asked if he knew about you and your mother, he frowned. He said that he did not know what had become of you, but he saw your mother's body. He said he helped bury her."

The Tigress stared off into the distance.

He took in a ragged breath. "I should have been there."

"You blame yourself for what happened?"

He gave another nod. "How could I not?" he replied. "It was I who foolishly ran off after receiving that letter."

She rubbed her lips together, almost at a loss for words. "How could you have known it was fake?" she asked not sure how to feel. "I cannot blame you for what you cannot control. It is not your fault what happened."

"If only I could see it that way as well."

"Even if you were there, perhaps their forces were too strong and you would have been overpowered. You could have died yourself."

"It would have been an easier fate than to live without your mother."

The Tigress looked at him pensively. "You were in love with her, weren't you?"

Vorce met her gaze and nodded. "Yes," he replied softly unable to avoid the question. "I love her still."

The Tigress blinked and returned her gaze back to the road trying to process what Vorce was saying.

They continued to ride along in silence, the sounds of the horses and wagons surrounding them.

"What was your title?" she asked after a few minutes trying to break the awkwardness of the moment.

"The Bear," he replied sitting up straighter in his seat as if proud of his title.

She gave a soft smile at his large frame and bulk. "The name certainly suits you," she replied. "It would also explain why you choose to dress like one."

He gave a small laugh. "What is your title?"

"The Tigress."

He gave a soft smile. "Then you have grown up fierce," he replied.

The Tigress's attention was caught for a moment by a burst of laughter coming from the other men in the caravan. "You said my father was of the coven, an assassin," she continued. "What was his title?"

Vorce rubbed his mouth for a moment, thinking. "In time, I am sure you will find out, but I do not believe I should be the one to tell you."

"What do you mean?" she asked disappointed. "If not you, then who would be the one to tell me who my father is?"

"There must be a reason you have not been told. He has always had a purpose for everything he does," Vorce replied. "Forgive me, but I cannot reason away his decision not to tell you." He saw the disappointment on her face. "All in good time, my dear. All in good time."

The Tigress nodded and bit her tongue, remembering that this man had just saved her life.

"How did you find me now?" she asked after another silence.

"Your necklace," he replied. "We found one of my men still clinging to life and he described that necklace to us, knowing its importance. We found your trail and then followed you for a few days. When we saw that you had been captured, we sprung into action."

The Tigress thought for a moment and recalled the strange reaction the man who had slammed her against the tree had when he saw her necklace and scowled. "Your men need to learn some manners," she said bitterly. "One of your men tried to force himself on me."

He blushed, ashamed, or was it anger? "Forgive my men for such behavior," he said clearing his throat. "I do not condone it, but I cannot monitor all of them all of the time." He frowned, bringing deep lines to his brow. "We do not have a lot of women on our grounds," he said. "The men get lonely."

She huffed, disgustedly. "Yes, as long as they are lonely, it is alright," she retorted sardonically.

"We are all animals, AnnJella."

The Tigress seethed. "Men are animals, Vorce," she replied. "Women seem to be the prey."

"The behavior does not go unpunished. I do not stand for it."

"And what is to be done to the man who made an attempt on me?"

"Nothing," Vorce replied. "He died not long after he told me about you. But it would have been severe had he lived. Banishment, even death."

She huffed again and looked away. "What about my necklace, then?" she asked changing the subject, trying to calm down. She took the cool metal object in her hand and squeezed it reassuringly. "What is so important about it?"

"It was you mother's," he responded. "Whoever found you must have taken it off of her body and given it to you."

"What does it mean? Where did the seal come from?" She pulled out the little book of seals that Princess Rain had given her and showed him the missing pages. "Why is there no information about it?"

He nodded. "That necklace you have around your neck," he started, "it represents the ancient family line that you came from. A special kind of family line."

She rubbed the wing between her fingers and looked at him waiting for him to continue. "Is this where you tell me that I am actually a princess?" she asked half laughing when he didn't go on.

He smiled. "No," he replied. "Your mother was a direct descendant of Strahm Mahrkai."

"The original prophet?" she asked a little confused. "The man who supposedly predicted Vremir's coming and urged the people to pray for protection before it was too late?"

Vorce nodded. "Yes," he said. "The seal is his. But that is not his true story. A lot has been lost and changed over time. Vron has changed the true story to fit his liking."

The Tigress blinked at him. "Right. "Wasn't Strahm Mahrkai also some kind of warlock or wizard?" she asked.

Vorce gave a small laugh. "Not necessarily," he replied. "That is an exaggeration. He just spoke to the gods and was able to discern their messages to the people."

She pursed her lips and lifted an eyebrow. "So why is all the information about the seal ripped out?" she asked. "The princess of Skahrr told me that even the book like this in her library back home has the pages ripped out. Why would someone try to erase the Strahm Mahrkai seal from existence?"

"You have much to learn, AnnJella," he replied. "More than I can tell you in a few days' ride."

After a moment's pause in the conversation, one of his men rode up beside him and said something to him in their language; his voice was gruff and irritated.

Vorce laughed in response. "It seems that your friend is very popular with my men. They can't seem to get him to stop talking."

She gave a half smile and huffed. "Yes, he is not really the silent kind. Our entire journey I had to threaten his life just so I could get a few moments' peace. And even that didn't work."

Vorce laughed. "Seems violence is not always the key to solving one's problems," he replied.

The Tigress smirked. "Nor is silence."

He flashed her a knowing look but ignored what she was inferring to. "You were on a mission when you were caught?" he asked purposefully avoiding the subject.

She frowned. "Yes, and he betrayed me," she replied a little heated. "He led me right into a Bornnenian trap. He played me for a fool the entire time that I have known him."

"And you did not kill him?" Vorce asked, a look of anger and confusion rising on his face.

She sighed. "He showed me a small act of gallantry pertaining to the Bornnenian soldiers," she replied. "This has bought him a reprieve."

"Ah," Vorce replied. "I understand." He shot Tristan a glance. "He is not of the coven, is he?"

"Oh, gods, no!" The Tigress replied. "He would not have survived the first week of training."

Vorce smiled. "I was about to say, with you as an exception, they don't make them like they used to."

CHAPTER 16

THE NEXT AFTERNOON THE GROUP OF RUFFIANS AND BANDITS MADE IT back to the Vron Wood and The Tigress noticed an immediate change in atmosphere among the men. There was a sense of ease that seemed to spread around. The men began to laugh the closer they got to where they were going and by the time the sun began to set, they reached a thick part of wood, where the trees were so dense, you could barely see ten feet in front you. The men gave a hooting noise like an owl that traveled down the line of them.

The Tigress looked around her in surprise when the calls were answered on the other side of the thick trees. A strange rumbling then shook the trees and ground causing some of the horses to stomp and neigh in a subtle alarm. She watched in mild amazement and confusion as two of the thickest trees began to slowly fall back into the thick brush letting out a muffled thump when they hit the ground.

The men moved their horses toward the gaps, jumping over and onto the fallen trees entering the thick brush.

The Tigress followed them slowly, cautiously. When the entire group entered through the gap she turned and watched the trees slowly move back up.

"Come, AnnJella," Vorce said to her. "There is much to see."

As she was turning with him, she caught a glimpse of Tristan on his horse, his shoulders slumped, a frown set on his face. He slowly looked up and made eye contact with her immediately trying to straighten his back. He opened his mouth to speak but she turned away before he could say anything to her.

Vorce Brahn led her to a low-lying land where an ancient lake had left an impression on the earth. Dozens of wooden houses lined where the coast of the lake would have been. On the far side of the makeshift village there were climbing walls and firing ranges, training grounds for Vorce's men.

"This," Vorce said spreading his arm out, "is home."

She nodded. "Looks familiar," she replied.

Vorce's mouth curled into a smile and he nodded. "I might have been inspired by the coven somewhat. Their methods seemed to have worked quite well."

"This is where you train your men to murder those they come across in the woods?" she asked.

Vorce waived his hand in dismissal. "We do not murder," he corrected. "We rob. On occasion there may be a casualty or two, but we do not kill unnecessarily." He pressed his hand to his heart. "I still live by many of the coven's rules, though I no longer live bound by my vows. All of those stories about murders in the wood, they are greatly exaggerated."

She regarded him for a moment. "How were you released?" she asked him.

He bowed his head. "I was tired of fighting in wars that I had no interest in, so I faked my own death."

She looked at him wide eyed. "But how? The coven does not just accept someone's death without proof." She thought of what she had to do to prove The Shadow's death.

He took a deep breath and let it out slowly as he pulled back his long hair to reveal his right ear was missing.

She nodded, mildly astonished. "Who helped you?" she asked.

He smiled at her. "Your father."

They rode further down the slope to the grounds of the village where men and women were working on the land, growing their own food and raising their own livestock.

"Where do you get your water?" she asked looking out across the dry lake bed.

"We have a well system," he replied. "The lake that shaped the land seeped back into the earth and the rain replenishes it. We are very self-sustaining here," Vron responded as they rode by.

She nodded again. "The coven has truly left its mark on you."

"How could it be otherwise?" he asked almost in a whisper. "And after what happened to your mother, I wanted those around me prepared to fight, prepared to defend those who cannot defend themselves." He looked over at her and gave her a sad smile. "He never wanted that life for you," he said. "He wanted what was best for you, but I cannot change what has already been done. All I can do is apologize for the horrors you must have seen while you were there."

"Horrors." She nodded. "You learn to adapt," she said. "I certainly did." She paused. "I do not necessarily regret my life at the coven, it has made me strong and independent, I just regret not knowing who I could have been."

"Come," he said after a break in the conversation. "There is something that I want to show you."

He led her around to the far side of the lakebed where a modest house was slightly hidden away. To the right of the house was a beautiful garden of colors surrounding a small pond and a statue of a winged woman sitting on a bench, smiling down at a small child sitting on her lap.

The Tigress rode up to the garden and hopped off of her horse walking the stone path to the bench, taking a closer look at the woman and child. She turned around and looked at Vorce.

"You built us a memorial?" she asked.

He nodded following her up the path

The Tigress reached out her hand and touched her mother's face. "Tell me about her," she said softly.

"Her name was Mirabelle," he continued, "Mirabelle was the most giving, kind and loving person that I will ever know." His voice shook as he spoke. "She loved you more than anything. You were her world. It was the greatest joy seeing you together."

The Tigress looked at him intently. "What was the extent of your relationship with my mother?" she asked. "Were you lovers?"

Vorce shifted where he stood. "It was not our intention," he replied after a long pause. "Your father had left me in charge during his missions. He was there so sparingly that you never knew him when he returned. At first, I tried to keep my distance. By then, I had already faked my death, but your father was duty bound to return. He had to keep his wife and you a secret and in return for helping me leave the coven, I promised I would help him."

The Tigress nodded.

"It started out as just a friendship. Your mother was lonely and sad at your father always being away. I was someone she could talk to, depend upon. At first, when our feelings became something more, we resisted, but there was no use. We just," he paused thinking for a moment, "fell into each other."

"Did my father know?" she asked causing him to slightly flinch.

"Yes," he nodded. "He knew. He came back, surprising us one day. He caught us in an embrace." He shook his head. "It hurt him, I know, but he understood, forgave us. Gave us his blessing knowing that he could not give you the stable life he wished for you." He paused a moment.

She shook her head. "Why would he not just fake his death, too?" she asked. "Why not break away as you did?"

Vorce rubbed his beard. "It is different for an assassin than it is for a soldier for hire," he replied. "There is the hierarchy. Spies are lowest, then mercenaries, with assassins at the top. Assassins are held with more esteem than the others; it is why all of The Leaders are assassins. It is an untold truth, but spies and mercenaries are less respected. If a spy or mercenary dies, then the coven needs but a little token to prove it. But if an assassin dies—"

"The coven wants to see the body," The Tigress finished with a nod.

He nodded too. "So, he could not fake his death as I could."

"What happened after he found out about you and my mother?"

He shook his head. "He made me promise him that I would continue to protect you both, raise you as my own, but that you would always know who your father was."

She gave him a slight glare. "If you promised I would always know who he is, why won't you tell me now?"

He shook his head again. "No, I cannot. It is not the time," he replied. "It is not for me to do so now."

She shook her head as well, frustrated. "And if he is of the coven, *still* of the coven, I must know him."

Vorce did not reply. He merely nodded.

"And what of my mother's family?" she asked with a sigh. "You say I am related to Strahm Mahrkai. Why do I feel as though this has more to do with the story? What else are you not telling me?"

He took a deep breath and let it out slowly. "Before your father and I met your mother, the coven was propositioned to send a group of assassins to kill someone who was raising questions about the temple, claiming to be a new prophet. The prophet was beginning to stir things up among the different temples, talking about a second coming of Vremir and that we should prepare ourselves, saying that when the grass in Vremir's Rest withers away and dies, the power that Vron gave to imprison him will fade and Vremir will rid this realm of the wicked, restoring it to its former glory."

"Why is that any of the coven's business?" she asked. "They never seemed to care about the temple."

He looked at her in surprise. "The temple used to invest a lot of money, believe it or not, into the coven. It is one of the reasons why the coven can live as cheaply as it does, that and the free labor that the trainees provide. We have performed a lot of jobs for them."

"So, the temple paid the coven to find this prophet and kill him?"

He shook his head. "Not just the prophet but the entire family."

"The entire family?" she repeated disbelievingly.

He nodded again. "Yes, but that is not the way of the coven. We have never wiped out an entire bloodline. We do not believe in it. So, instead we went on a mission to save them, against the temple. I was a part of the escort travelling with you father. We travelled for weeks until we came across the estate. We thought we would find no opposition when we arrived, but we were wrong."

She looked at him intently.

"They were already under attack," he continued. "The walls of the estate were starting to burn. I led my men in, taking down those hostile to our cause. They fought like men I had never seen before. Quick, strong and unrelenting. Their swords were oddly curved but highly effective. I took a hit to my side. Had I not been wearing my fur over my leathers, I would have been killed that night."

"And this is where you found my mother?" she asked. "Amongst the battle?"

He shook his head. "Your father discovered her," he replied. "She had taken refuge in the gardens. She had woken before the attack and was walking the grounds when it started. It saved her life."

The Tigress sighed, thinking. "Who were the men that were sent in the coven's place?" she asked after a moment. "Did you ever find out?"

Vorce shook his head. "No, but I remember their banners," he said with a scowl. "Yellow and orange with a great black bird in flight."

"The same banners carried by the men who killed my mother," she said.

Vorce nodded.

"And the same ones from my dream," she thought to herself.

"You will have many questions during your time here," Vorce said placing a strong, yet, loving hand on her shoulder. "Do not hesitate to ask." He squeezed her shoulder gently. "I am glad you are home." He smiled and his eyes misted.

The Tigress smiled back. "Thank you," she replied softly. "For everything."

He bowed deeply.

"I do have another question though that has been on my mind."

He lifted a quizzical brow.

"Where did all of these men come from?"

He shrugged. "All over the realms. Men and women who heard and believed the word of the prophet. Though most of them are from the Lost Tribes, some of them have been with me since your mother was alive, and others have joined us along the way."

"If these people are from all over the realms then what language are you speaking?" she asked him. "I have never heard such a language before."

He gave a small, almost sad, laugh. "Vremerian," Vorce replied. "Thought to have been lost long ago, but revived once again by the prophet."

"Vremerian?" she repeated confused. "Revived by the prophet the temple wanted dead?"

He nodded. "It is a shame you do not remember," he added. "It was your first language."

THE NEXT NIGHT IN THE DYING LIGHT OF THE SUN, TRISTAN finally found the courage to approach The Tigress, He found her sitting alone on a side bench next to the shrine Vron had built.

"You have been freed, I thought?" she said hearing him before he said anything. "Why are you still here?"

"I haven't technically been freed," he replied coming up to her. "I am free to roam the grounds, but they have not permitted me to leave them. They do not want me to be able to find my way back. They blindfolded me as soon as we got to the woods," he continued.

"How terrible for you," she said sarcastically not looking up. "If they had gagged you as well, I am sure it would have been your own personal hell."

"I just came to talk," he said.

"Of course, you did. It is one of the two things you are actually good at." She turned to finally meet his gaze. "Talking and betrayal."

He closed his eyes and pursed his lips, ashamed. "Dahlen, I wish that I—"

Before he could finish she had jumped from her seat and had a knife pressed against his throat. "What?" she said. "What do you wish, Tristan? That it could have been different? That you could have gotten paid in advance?" She spit to the side. "You make me sick!" she said.

He glared back into her eyes, his face slightly red. "Then just kill me!" he yelled back. "If I am truly so disgusting to you, then just do it!"

They stood glaring at each other for several seconds before The Tigress huffed and grabbing his wrist gave him a swift, small cut with her knife.

"You aren't worth the effort or the clean up," she said starting to walk away.

Tristan looked down at the cut on his wrist just deep enough to allow a few drops of blood to trickle out. "Really?" he said. "That's it? A little cut and—" He looked back down at his wrist as a burning sensation began to take over his arm. "Ow," he said. "Ow!" he yelled as the burning sensation grew. "Oh, my gods," he said. "What the hell did you do to me?" he screamed after her, grasping his wrist in his other hand.

"My knives are lined with dragon's bane," she said calling back. "It won't kill you, a small dose like that, but it will hurt like a fiery hell for a few hours."

He screamed squeezing his wrist where the cut was. "How do you make it stop?" he yelled trying to run after her.

She turned back around and lifted her knife at him again. "There is no antidote," she replied. "And if you think you are going to follow me the rest of the night you are wrong. I will slice you again."

He stopped, the sweat on his brow glistening in the remaining light. He groaned and clenched his teeth to keep him from screaming. "Granted, I deserve some sort of punishment," he said his eyes beginning to water, "but I really think this is excessive." He fell to his knees and held in another scream. "Ah! How can anything hurt this much?" he yelled in agony.

She huffed and continued to walk away. "Obviously you have never been stabbed in the back by someone you thought you could trust."

She continued to walk back toward the village where a bonfire was being made, leaving Tristan whimpering and screaming on his own.

THE TIGRESS, THOUGH SHE STAYED WITH VORCE AND HIS TRIBE OF ruffians for a week, could not obtain from him any further information about her father. He told her stories from when she was a child, his eyes smiling as he remembered, but nothing more.

And, though it was clear that the other men and women in the village regarded her with respect and awe, they kept their distance. Even Tristan was absent. Most of her time, therefore, was spent in reflective thought. Most mornings she walked the grounds watching the villagers as they went about their normal tasks—taking care of their farms, returning from hunts, and training.

But one of the most curious things that she observed was the prayers. She had not seen anyone worship the way these people did. They built pyres and danced around them, and though she could not understand what they were saying, she swore they were calling out the name of Vremir.

None of the known religions in the realm based their worship on Vremir. Vremir was the god who destroys, so why would they be worshipping him? What did that prophet mean by Vremir would restore the realm to its former glory?

She was missing something and, though Vorce had been helpful in revealing certain details of her past, there was only one place she would be able to truly find the answers she was looking for.

By the fifth day of her arrival, she decided that she needed to return to the coven.

CHAPTER 17

"YOU ARE SURE YOU MUST GO?" VORCE ASKED THE TIGRESS AS SHE packed up the horse he had given her. "You are welcome to stay as long as you like."

She gave him a soft smile. "I know," she replied. "But I have questions that need answering."

Vorce gave her a sad look. "I wish for answers as well," he told her. "But they can always wait another day. I have waited this long to find you, it saddens me to see you leave so soon."

She took his hand in hers and squeezed it affectionately. "Thank you," she said with feeling. "I cannot remember before the coven, but I know from what you have told me and how you have treated me this past week that you have loved me as your daughter."

Vorce gently pulled her to him and kissed her forehead. "And I will continue to do so," he told her in reply.

After a moment, Tristan's voice was heard approaching them and The Tigress suppressed a groan.

"I still do not see why you are just letting Tristan go," she said frowning over at him. "I do not think it wise. I don't trust him."

"Open your heart, AnnJella," Vorce told her softly. "Forgiveness will set your soul free."

The Tigress twitched at her name, still finding it unsettling. "This man almost got me killed, Vorce," she replied. "There is nothing to open my heart to."

He gave a small smile. "That is where you are wrong," he told her. "We shall meet again soon. I will be watching out for you."

She nodded. "Yes," she said. "But until then, I am going to go to the library at the coven and find those banners you have spoken of. They must be acknowledged or written down somewhere."

Vorce nodded.

"I will find them and send you word."

"Be careful," he said patting her horse's neck. "Keep heading a steady southeast and you should reach Dead Man's Rest in three or four days."

Tristan, once again blindfolded, shifted on his horse and gave a shout as he almost fell, his bound hands catching the reigns just in time.

The Tigress held in a snort.

Vorce laughed. "He is only with you until you reach the end of Behr Wood in Thren and then you can let him go on his merry way. Or," he said pausing, "you could just kill him. It would make no difference to me either way."

She lifted a brow. "What about your speech about forgiveness," she smirked. "Killing him is a long cry from that."

"That is because I know you are not the kind to just kill someone. I trust you are more than that."

She huffed. "Has the bird been sent to Skahrr telling the king of his spies' betrayal?" she asked.

He nodded. "Yes, the bird was sent a few days ago."

"Good, then I guess I am ready to go." The Tigress gave him a small smile before getting on her horse.

"Be safe, AnnJella, my daughter," he said. "I will be eagerly awaiting your return."

She gave him a small nod and turned her horse to leave when

she stopped. "Vorce," she called to him. "How do you have a name?" she asked.

He lifted a brow.

"I only know of one other person of the coven that has a name. He was old enough to remember it," she continued. "But how did you get yours?"

He smiled. "Your mother gave it to me."

The Tigress' cheeks slightly blushed and she nodded turning her horse to leave.

"May your travels be prosperous," Vorce called after her. "I shall see you again soon."

She looked over her shoulder and sighed but did not respond as she led her horse and Tristan's back out into the forest.

"Would it be possible for you to remove my blindfold?" he asked her after they were an hour out. "I am sure I have no idea where it is we have come from."

She remained silent.

"Dahlen," he said trying to get her to answer him.

"That is not my name," she answered in a bland tone, pulling on the reigns of his horse.

"Yes, I have heard," he said. "Your name is AnnJella. How do you like having a name?" he asked her. "Does it fulfill you more than you had hoped?"

She gave him a side glance. She hadn't really thought about how figuring out her past had made her feel. She had found out every-thing that she had wanted to know, other than who her father was and without that, nothing else seemed to matter.

"The name doesn't suit you," he continued when he didn't get an answer. "I am not saying that you are not of an angel, or angel-like, which your name implies, but I *am* saying that at the same time."

She slowly let a breath out of her nose, mildly annoyed.

"I just think that Dahlen describes you a little bit more than AnnJella."

"Are you quite done?" she asked.

He stopped talking for a moment. "You know, the other day when you poisoned me, I had a lot of time to think. Actually, it was difficult to think when so much pain was coursing through my body, but something did seem to happen to me while I was lying there crying like a baby." He waited for her to respond. "Well," he started back up when she again didn't say anything, "I had a vision, or an epiphany, or something."

"Could you get to the point, Tristan," she said irritated.

"Point is," he said turning his head in the direction he heard her voice, "that I have changed. I have seen the error of my ways and I want to correct my wrongs and—"

She laughed. "Yes, it sure sounds like you have changed. Your talking has clued me into that."

"Not," he huffed annoyed with her sarcastic attitude, "the way that I act just the way that I think and feel," he said.

"Oh, please, do go on," The Tigress said sardonically. "Inform me of your great transformation."

"I see you have not changed," he said. "I guess having a name didn't give you a new outlook on life or leave you less bitter than before."

"Neither have you, Tristan."

"No!" he exclaimed trying to sit up better in the saddle. "I have! I have learned a lot living among those men and women. They live off of the land and help one another out when necessary. They don't worry about money or stupid titles," he said. "They care about each other."

She gave him a strange look even though he couldn't see her. "Tristan, those men are ruffians who rape and steal from people that happen to walk into the wrong part of the wood."

He shrugged his shoulders. "But don't you remember when they knocked me off of my horse when we first crossed through Vron Wood?" he asked. "You shot one of them and the other man stopped what he was doing to help take that man to safety," he said. "That man is still alive because of the other man's selflessness. I mean, he could have just left him and ran off to save himself, but he didn't. He actually came up and talked to me the other day. Decent man." He cleared his throat. "Anyways, the village is like a large family unit where they are loyal to each other and offer each other help."

"Yes, Tristan," she said. "People helping each other. What a strange concept."

"You are obviously still bitter, Dahlen, about the other day," he said. "And maybe you should be, but I just want you to know that I no longer care about a lordship or enormous amounts of money. I care about my life and the people in my life."

"You changed that much in a week?" she asked.

He nodded. "I was talking to a monk that was in that village. A different monk, not like the ones that we ran into on our trek to Mahk Lake," he said. "He told me that Vremir could come back and once again try to destroy the wicked with his wild fire and gift us all with the knowledge we seek."

"Have you found the gods and goddesses then?" she chortled. "I am happy for you," she said blandly. "Perhaps it could give you purpose."

"It made me think about my priorities. Made me think about where I want to be years from now and who I want to spend it with."

"I am happy that you have somehow figured a small piece of yourself out, but future good deeds do not erase past grievances."

They fell into silence for a few minutes.

"Will you be alright going to Dead Man's Rest alone?" he asked.

"Are you offering me your protective services?" she said lifting an eyebrow.

"I have been training this past week with the men," he replied. "Perhaps I will be a little handier with a sword than I was before."

"A week's worth of special training against hordes of people who have been training their entire lives? The scales would not likely tip in your favor."

He shrugged. "Perhaps," Tristan replied. "But I meant more emotionally will you be alright?"

"Are you worried that I would have a break down?" she asked. "You did tell me once that I was a stonewall of emotion or something of the sort. I am sure I can handle keeping my emotions at bay all on my own."

He didn't answer, only nodded his head in response.

AROUND AFTERNOON THE NEXT DAY, THE TWO OF THEM EMERGED OUT of the Behr Wood and, as promised, The Tigress cut the rope that bound his hands and removed the blindfold from his eyes.

Tristan massaged his wrists, rubbed red from the ropes. "Finally," he said smiling. "I am a free man." He squinted in the dying light. "Seems bright out for sunset."

"Harpren is that way," she said pointing west. "You might be able to make it there in a day or two."

He gave her a small nod. "Come with me," he said after a few moments.

"What?" she said incredulously.

"Come with me," he repeated.

She frowned. "I heard what you said," she replied. "I am just confused as to why you think I would ever consider coming with you after what you have already done to me."

"I told you that I would make it up to you," he said. "You just have to give me the chance."

She shook her head. "I am going to Dead Man's Rest; I am going to figure out who killed my mother and I am going to avenge her death. I do not have time to play around with you."

He gave her a sad look. "Revenge will get you nothing," he said. "If you take revenge on those that killed your mother, who is to say that someone will not do the same thing to you for killing that person? Revenge is a vicious cycle that never ends. If you do not stop it, then soon the whole realm will be caught up in it. An eye for an eye leaves everyone blind."

She stared at him. "It won't," she started, "if I just kill them all."

Tristan sighed. "My biggest regret will be what I have done to you," he told her. "I hope it doesn't stop you from trusting others in the future."

She blinked at him.

He took a deep breath and then let it out slowly. "I hope that you one day find peace. May the wisdom and strength of Vremir guide you on your way."

She frowned at him. "Playing a monk for a week does not make you a monk," she said. "And if I recall you did not even know the story of the gods and goddesses until I told you about them. Do not preach to me."

He gave her another sad look and nodded. "Good-bye, Dahlen," he said turning his horse in the direction that she had pointed. "I will pray for you and I will pray that we will one day meet again."

She huffed out of her nose. "For your sake, pray that we don't." She clicked at her horse, speeding away in the opposite direction.

The Tigress rode fast until just after dark, when the line of Behr Wood was just in view on the horizon. She stopped her horse and patted it as she led it to a grassy patch next to the road, taking refuge behind a few trees and bushes. She then started a small fire and settled herself for the night, falling asleep staring into the warm glow of the fire.

Part 2

THE SECOND
COMING

CHAPTER 18

THE TIGRESS AWOKE TO THE SOUND OF HORSES THUNDERING PAST her. She quickly, and quietly knelt from her hidden position, obscured by thick underbrush. She grabbed her horse's reigns to steady it and rubbed its nose to keep it quiet as she watched from the bushes at the small band of men and women on horseback that flew past her. She looked in the direction they came from. They were coming from the direction of the wood. Assassins from Dead Man's Rest perhaps.

She counted at least twenty as they rode by her. It has been over a month since the summer solstice, she thought. Perhaps they are leaving for the first time, going out on their first missions. Newly titled.

She waited a few minutes after they had disappeared from sight to pack up her belongings and continue her ride, waiting only long enough for her and her horse to eat before she charged through another leg of the trip.

She reached Behr wood, making it about halfway through before she found a camp of men sitting and laughing around a fire. The Tigress slowly got off of her horse as soon as she saw its glow. She left her horse to chew on what twigs and small brush were available while she crept in closer to the campsite.

She silently moved across the forest floor following the glow of the fire and the sounds of the men echoing out through the trees.

Getting close enough to observe, she crouched behind a bush, listening.

"War is coming, boys," the oldest looking of the group said. He flashed a gap-toothed smile.

"He must be one of The Trainers," she thought. She counted three trainees and two trainers and another one trying to sleep. The trainees she did not recognize but she thought the trainers looked familiar.

"I can feel the warm vibrations of tension between the kingdoms stirring things up."

"Doesn't mean much for us," a built-up boy said swigging something from a canteen. He wiped his mouth with the back of his hand and passed it on to the next one. "We don't fight like the rest of the realm."

"Would be nice to see a real battle," a second boy with dark hair said taking the canteen from the third.

One of the trainers laughed. "Get your first kill on the job first and then you can start worrying about getting yourself on the battlefield."

The sixth one, off to the side was curled into a ball. He grunted and waved his hand angrily at the others as if to hush them.

They all laughed at him in hushed voices.

"Who would we fight for if a war broke out?" the third boy asked, trying to whisper as he took another sip of the canteen.

"The coven tries not to get into political affairs from the rest of the realm, but we tend to fight for the side whose cause we most believe in," the second trainer explained. "But we don't get involved right away. We wait and see."

"Wait? That's boring" the boulder-like boy said with a frown. "Where's all the action? That's what we want."

"Patience, child, patience," the first trainer told him. "Those who rush into battle without a plan tend to be the first slain."

"Pft," replied the boy. "I am sure I could hold my own."

The others in the group laughed.

The boy scowled, obviously offended.

"Do not be so eager to lose your head, child," the first trainer warned him. "You still have much to learn."

Seeing this as her entrance, The Tigress stood and approached the fire. "He is right," she replied walking up to them, her hands open, palms up showing she was not armed.

The men and boys jumped in surprise.

"The battlefield is less glory and more gore than you think," she continued.

"Spying now, are we?" the gap-toothed trainer snarled, picking up his sword.

She kept her hands up.

"Do you know what we do to spies in Dead Man's Rest, pretty?" one of the older boys asked her.

"We throw a party," another of the boys said. "But only after we roast you alive."

The Tigress sighed and smiled.

"Brothers," she said lifting up her sleeve to reveal her tattoo. "Do not fret. I am no spy."

"A sister?" the dark-haired boy breathed.

"What were you doing not announcing yourself, love?" said the man with the sword.

"I was not sure whether or not *you* were spies. I had to be careful. If you were spies I would have had to kill you myself." She lifted a brow and smirked at them.

They laughed at her joke.

"I should have recognized you if it were not for the dark," the second trainer exclaimed. "You're The Tigress.

She gave a small bow. "It is good to see you again The Eagle, The Sword."

The trainers laughed.

"Yes, of course!" The gap-toothed trainer known as The Sword proclaimed. "Take off your veil and join us!"

"Yes, come, come. Let us warm you by the fire. The woods get quite cold at night," The Eagle urged. He introduced her to the three trainees. "These three have not yet earned their titles," he added, tilting his head toward the boys. "Maybe in a year or so, if they continue to do as well as they have been."

She took off her cover and shook out her hair before she whistled for her horse who came trotting after her.

"Are you all returning from a training expedition or are you starting one?" she asked.

"Returning," The Sword responded. "We were just taking the young ones out for a few days of survival training."

She nodded. "I am returning from a long journey. Perhaps I can join you. It might be nice to have some company for awhile," she said. "I have not seen a brother for quite some time now."

They all walked to the fire where the other man was still sleeping off to the side, his back turned to them.

"Have your travels been prosperous?" The Eagle asked her as they all sat down.

She gave a small nod. "They have been quite prosperous," she replied.

They nodded.

"Where are you coming from?" The Sword asked.

"A job in Bornnen," she said shaking her head to the canteen of what could have been wine. "Soldiers have been littering the countryside since the death of their king."

The Sword nodded. "Yes, at the hands of an imposter princess, I hear." He laughed and nudged one of the boys next to him. "Have you been playing royal dress up lately, The Tigress?" he asked laughing again.

She smiled and bowed her head a bit. "I am sure I do not know what you are talking about."

"The Tigress," the more muscular of the two boys said. "I have heard of that name."

They all looked at him.

"I heard of the boy whose manhood you took from him."

The elder men laughed while the other boys' eyes grew wide.

"It's still much talked about at The Rest," the boy continued. "Is it true?"

She lifted an eyebrow at him. "Is that a question you really want to know the answer to?"

The boy didn't respond.

The Eagle gave him a slap on the back and laughed. "I remember the story you mean, boy, and I believe that it was The Tigress here, but that was before she gained her title," he said. "I shared a room with that boy, if I recall." He made a pensive face. "How long ago was that?" he asked.

"It was about ten years ago," she replied. "It was right before he was to receive his title."

"Did he ever end up receiving it?" the boulder of a boy asked.

The Tigress shook her head. "No," she replied. "He died of shock a few days later."

The boys looked at her in awe.

"How is it you didn't get in trouble for killing him?" another boy asked. "Is that not against the rules?"

"Oh, the boy deserved it," The Eagle said. "He was messing around with the girls, touching them and taking them without their consent. Something we don't approve of."

The Sword nodded. "He got what he deserved."

"Was that your first kill?" the smaller of the three asked.

She nodded.

"How old were you?" the other boy asked.

She shrugged. "No older than ten years old, I imagine."

"Ten?" the sleeping figure said stirring. "She was closer to twelve or thirteen, I believe."

The Tigress felt her heart drop at the sound of the voice. She turned slowly to see Marten propping himself up where he lay.

"Marten," she said trying to keep her surprise at bay. "What are you doing here?" she asked.

"It is strange how we keep meeting up like this, isn't it?" he said. He smiled at her, a nicety she did not return. "You just missed the induction last week. The titling of the deserving boys and girls."

"I passed them on my way in," she replied. "Really they passed me." Marten nodded.

"Do you know The Tigress?" The Eagle asked.

Marten nodded again and gave a small yawn. "T and I go way back," he said lifting his canteen to her before taking a swig. "I helped to mentor her. She was just a wee little thing when she was brought to us. The poor orphan that she was."

The Tigress could feel her face twitch. "Are not we all orphans when we come here?" she asked trying not to let her voice shake with the anger she felt. "Abandoned, lost, discarded children all found and saved by the coven." She looked at the trainees. "Do you know where you are from?" she asked him.

The smaller boy thought for a moment. "I believe I am from Thren. They tell me that I was found wandering one of their almond orchards crying and covered in blood. They say that there was a farm house a ways down the road burnt to the ground with a few dead bodies in it." He shrugged. "That could have been my family."

She nodded. "They told you that?" she asked. "You do not remember it?"

He pursed his lips thinking. "I kind of remember hearing screaming and running. I also remember the fire." He pulled up his shirt to reveal a burn mark going from his hip to his ribs. "I remember the pain, too."

"How old were you?"

"Four almost five, I believe," he responded. "I have a strange memory of a woman telling me that I was going to turn five. I was born just after the harvest season, she said."

The Tigress nodded. "And you," she said turning to the other boy, "do you know where you have come from?"

He shook his head. "I was younger than him," he said motioning toward the other boy, "when they brought me here. I don't remember much of anything before the coven and they never told me about it when I got there." He shrugged. "But if I had to guess, I would say Skahrr."

"And why is that?" she asked.

He gave another shrug. "I look like another boy who they say came from there."

She gave a soft smile. "That is a good assumption." She turned to the last boy, the one built like a rock. "And you?"

He shook his head. "I was dropped off at a monastery in Bornnen when I was an infant. The coven brought me here a few years later."

"The Tigress, what about you?" one of the other boys asked.

She heard Marten take a deep breath and let it out as a long sigh.

"I have no recollection of what little life I lived before the coven," she replied. "And like you, they never told me. There was not much to tell." She looked off into the fire. "But I am grateful for what they have given me, the coven. They housed me, fed me, educated me, and trained me. They have taught me loyalty and respect." She let out a small sigh. "And though I am unable to tell you about where I came from and who my family was by blood, I can tell you that the coven took in a scared, small little girl and grew her into an independent, self sufficient woman. The coven is my family, our family." She smiled. "Our own family of misfits."

The lot of them cheered and drank to her words.

Marten gave her a strange look but said nothing.

"The Tigress," the younger of the two boys said. "What made you," he paused, "you know, do that to that one guy?"

Her smile deepened. "I didn't like the way he looked at me."

The boys' faces turned red and they immediately looked away from her. The men laughed and raised their canteens in her honor.

CHAPTER 19

"You seem changed," Marten said riding alongside The Tigress the next day. "All that talk about the coven being your family, it doesn't sound like you."

She nodded. "I learned something new on my last little voyage across the realm," she replied.

He looked at her and smiled. "Oh?" he said. "And what is that? Could it possibly be that you now realize everything that I have been telling you over the years is true?"

She laughed. "Oh, gods, no," she replied. She turned and looked at him. "I have merely learned that the truth does not necessarily set you free." She set her face in a cold stare. "It merely opens the door to a different kind of hell."

Marten started at her words but did not respond. He watched, half confused and a little unsettled as she sped up her horse just enough to get ahead of him.

"What could she have meant by that?" he thought. He watched her sitting on her horse almost triumphantly, haughtily. "She could not have found out about her family. All possible proof had been destroyed."

He didn't talk to her the rest of the journey.

The Tigress and the six others arrived at Dead Man's Rest a few hours later crossing the bridge over the turbulent waters of the Mahk River as it made its way to the Dormant Sea. The land was still the same as when she left it after she earned her title. The horses kicked up small clouds of dust in the semi-arid land until they reached the grove of trees that lined the path the rest of the way to the village.

She took in a deep breath and gave a small smile as the scent of ripe fruit hit her nose forgetting, for almost a moment, why she was there in the first place. She shook the expression from her face as the tan stones of the village came into view.

The men and two boys of the group seemed somewhat chatty, but she was not in the mood to talk anymore. She had a mission to complete.

When they reached the edge of the village the watchers on duty asked them to show their tattoos before letting them pass. Those titled, obliged.

"Welcome back, brothers and sister," the dark-skinned watcher said to them standing erect and placing his fist over his heart.

The others did the same before they continued on into the heart of the village. Before they got far, they reached the barn where they all got off and placed their horses in empty stalls.

"Well," The Eagle said turning to The Tigress, "it was nice seeing you again though I do not think we ever really had the pleasure before. I received my title a few years or so before you."

She nodded. "Yes, I remember. You are The Eagle because of your sharp vision."

They shook hands and the rest said their good-byes as they parted ways, all except for Marten who regarded The Tigress somewhat carefully.

"What have you come back for?" he asked watching her brush her horse. "I have already brought back your contribution for the year and I did not hear anything of you being called to duty around here. So, I just wonder as to why you have returned. It is unlike you."

She didn't look up from what she was doing. "I came back to visit," she replied blandly with a shrug.

Marten laughed. "One does not come back to Dead Man's Rest simply for a 'visit,'" he retorted. "Why are you lying to me, T?"

"Why are you still here, then?" she asked.

He made a sucking noise with his teeth. "I have been asked to help train the trainees."

"Really?" she asked half surprised. "That does not sound like something you would do," she said. "And what are you teaching them? How to be masters of deception?"

He narrowed his eyes at her. "No," he said a little annoyed. "I am teaching them religion."

She scoffed.

"It is temporary," he replied. He took a step closer to her. "I am also partly here to clean up a mess you have made."

"I have made?" she said looking up, a scowl on her face.

"Yes," he said. "You have started a war taking that job from the king of Skahrr and killing King Ahlenwei," he almost shouted.

She could feel her face becoming hot as her anger escalated. "I saved the princess of Skahrr's reputation and very likely her life. Whether I killed Ahlenwei or not, a war would have been started. Breht would not have stood for the violation of his daughter."

He huffed through his nose. "It doesn't matter. We do not mix in the affairs of kings and queens of the realms," he said.

"Bullshit!" she yelled at him. "We stick our nose and meddle wherever the hell we like because the only allegiance we truly have is for ourselves!"

"Saving a reputation of a princess is not the means of starting a war," he said a little more quietly but still visibly angry.

She glared at him. "No," she said, "of course not. No one's innocence or reputation is something that deserves to be saved."

"Gods be blessed!" He met her glare with one of his own. "You still blame me for that then?" he asked her incredulously. He shook his head trying to find the words. "You know if I had the means to do so, I would have done something. But I did not receive your letter until after you castrated him," he told her. "I had been travelling to the other realms on my missions. By the time I read your letter, another one had been sent to me saying the boy was dead. What could I have done?"

She nodded continuously as the anger swam inside of her. She knew that incident was not Marten's fault. It was not even that issue she was angry with him for. The incident was just fresh in her mind.

"You will never understand how much I resent you, Marten," she said.

"Resent me?" he asked. "I have done nothing but help you since you were first brought here all those years ago."

"No!" she said pointing an angry finger at him. "You have done nothing except give me half answers and half-guided advice. You have never gone out of your way or lifted a hand to truly help me out. So, do not look at me with those disgusting eyes and tell me that you are my friend when you have been nothing but a vulture. Picking at the remains of what is left of people." She put the horse brush back in the hanging bucket and began to storm away when he caught her by the arm.

"Did it ever occur to you that I don't have all the answers?" he shot back at her. "Or that I have been forbidden to repeat anything about it? That perhaps you knowing is dangerous."

She wrenched her arm from his grip. "You're just full of excuses," she told him, a disgusted look on her face. "You have one for everything."

"What has come over you, T?" he asked with feeling. "Is it that man I saw you with on the road to Harpren?" he asked. "I know he was not trustworthy."

"Trustworthy?" she asked, saying the word as if it were a bitter taste in her mouth. "I do not believe you know the meaning of the word," she said. "I don't believe anyone does anymore. Its meaning died a long time ago with loyalty and truth."

She turned to storm off again.

"Why are you here, T?" he called after her.

"The Monk should mind his business," she said, contempt apparent in her voice.

He was taken aback. She had never called him by his title before. He shivered as he watched her walk away, a tell that something bad was going to happen.

The Tigress stormed out of the barn and into the streets where she grew up. She walked the main street, taking in the familiar sites. The only difference were the trainees. There were children of all ages, shapes, sizes and colors carrying on chores that were given to them by The Teachers or perhaps their overseers.

Some of the kids were laughing, playing small jokes on each other, others were reading, eating or just talking. But in the far corner of two buildings she heard shouting. She turned to see what the commotion was when she saw a circle of boys laughing and shouting at a smaller child in the middle of the circle. She made her way over to find a group of children throwing rocks at and pushing a smaller child around.

"And what are we up to here?" she asked approaching them.

The four boys no older than twelve all stopped and looked at her.

"We're teaching this little rat a lesson," one of them said, the obvious leader of the group.

The others agreed cheering.

"Oh, I see," The Tigress replied in a fake interested voice. "And what lesson would that be?" she asked looking down at the small little boy who stood defiantly against the other children.

The kid gave her a look up and down, curious as to who she was and why she would want to know. "He made me look like a fool during our teachings today. So, I am teaching him that he is the fool for messing with me."

She nodded. "And what an important lesson to teach someone," she said. "What lesson was it by chance that he made you look like a fool in?"

He lifted an eyebrow. "Herbology," he said scoffed.

The Tigress nodded. "Herbology is an important class," she told him.

"I know all I care and need to know about that stupid class."

"Is that so?" She nodded. "You must be exceptionally smart to already know so much about Herbology at such a young age," she said. "If you're so smart, can you tell me why a boy younger than you is in your class?"

"The rat isn't in an older class," another one of the boys from the group said. "He's in the rat's class."

The Tigress looked at the main boy who was scowling at his friend. "You're a few classes behind, then?" she asked.

The boy scoffed again. "Like I said, I know all I need to know."

The Tigress nodded. "Can you by chance tell me what dragon's bane is?" she asked.

He gave her a funny look. "No," he replied annoyed. "But it sounds like a stupid name for a pretty flower."

"Oh, it is a very important plant," she said. "Something that you will find useful when you receive your title. Just a small amount of it can be used to cripple your enemies by causing a severe burning reaction and," she paused and smiled. "How about I just give some to you and let you try it on your own?"

His eyes brightened. "That would be awesome," he said.

"Just hold out your hand," she said.

The boy readily obeyed, a strange, triumphant smirk on his face.

The Tigress gently took the boy's hand in hers and smiled as she quickly and swiftly scratched his hand with the knife she was hiding behind her back.

The boy's eyes grew wide and looked down at the small cut she made in his hand. "What did you do that for?" he asked frowning.

The Tigress let go of his hand and took a step back. "To teach you a lesson," she replied, one eyebrow lifted waiting.

The boy's hand began to shake and a strange crying noise began to escape his mouth.

"Maybe you should pay more attention during your lessons," she continued as the boy fell to his knees and began screaming in pain.

She looked up at the other three boys in the group all with terrified looks on their faces. "Would you like me to teach you how dragon's bane works as well?" she asked holding up the knife.

They all silently and quickly shook their heads, mouths hanging open.

"Get," she said pointing her thumb in the opposite direction.

The boys immediately ran off leaving their friend to cry by himself on the ground.

The smaller boy they had been bullying shot her a small smile, his lip busted and one of his eyes swollen shut. For a few seconds the two of them stared at each other, a strange understanding between them.

"You should get that looked at," The Tigress said and walked away.

"WONDERS NEVER CEASE!" SAID THE TALL, AGING, YET, STILL MUSCU-lar man opening his arms out to The Tigress.

"The Master," she replied putting her fist over her heart and giving a slight bow.

"You have returned," The Master said placing his hands on her arms and giving them a slight squeeze. "Have your travels been prosperous?" he asked.

She gave a deep nod. "Yes, sir," she responded with a slight smile. "Full of surprises."

He nodded. "I remember my first few years away from the coven. No amount of training can prepare you for some circumstances."

She gave a small laugh. She wanted to ask him about her past, to see if there was anything he said that matched what Vorce had told her, but she thought she should wait.

"Come! Come!" he goaded, ushering her further into his house. "Let us talk over a drink."

She followed him through the halls of his house to his study.

"So, what brings you here?" The Master finally asked breaking the silence. "The Monk brought your tribute for the year, I thought?"

She nodded. "He did," she affirmed. "But I decided that I wanted to come back for a brief rest between jobs."

He nodded, understanding.

"How are the trainees doing?" The Tigress asked.

"Ah, the little ones," he said taking a step back and pouring them a couple of drinks. "Some are as they have always been. Rude, lazy, thinking they deserve more than they actually do, not working hard enough for what they want. But then there are a select few who fight for what they believe in, are eager to learn, eager to survive." He looked over at her. "Ones like you," he said. "They do not make many like that anymore but when they find their way here," he smiled at her. "Well, I do not have to explain, just look at you."

She gave a small smile. "Thank you, sir," she replied.

"So," he began handing her a drink, "not that I am not glad to see you, but what truly brings you back home?"

"Home," she repeated softly, placing the drink on the table next to her. "I guess I cannot hide anything from you, can I?"

He raised a brow at her. "Were you trying?"

She gave a small laugh. "Not well enough, apparently."

"So?" he asked taking a sip of his drink.

She took a deep breath. "I came to use the library."

"Oh?" The Master said. "What for?"

The Tigress cleared her throat. "To find a book," she told him.

He regarded her for a moment before nodding. "Anything particular?" he asked taking another sip. "Perhaps I can help?"

The Tigress opened her mouth to speak but closed it, smiling. "I think I can manage," she replied.

He nodded. "If you cannot find what you need in the library, I have a collection myself," he told her motioning to the shelves along the wall. "Though the coven's library is quite vast. I don't believe there is a book it does not have." He motioned to his own collection. "These are only some of my personal favorites, but they are at your disposal."

"Thank you," she told him.

The Master nodded smiling at her. "Of course. How long do you think you will stay?"

"No more than a week or two, I suppose."

"You wouldn't want to help train for a while, would you?"

She lifted her eyebrows. "I am not exactly patient enough to teach children. My methods would be," she paused thinking of what to say, "a little unorthodox." She suppressed a smile thinking of the bully from earlier.

He laughed. "I would not doubt that, but I would trust that you would be fair in your discipline."

She gave a small bow. "There is another matter, something of importance, I must discuss with you," she hesitated. "While on a job in Bornnen, I was betrayed."

The Master's facial expression grew dark.

"My client," she took a deep breath and let it out slowly, "whose name I would not normally divulge, but given the circumstances, I must."

The Master crossed his arms. "My gods, this must be serious."

"My client, King Breht, hired me for a specific job, a job that was based on information that his spies had related to him. This information was false and almost cost me my life. They were paid to lie to the king."

The Master's face turned red with anger. "Do we know who his spies are?" he asked in a shaky voice.

She shook her head. "No, sir," she responded. "But I know that, whomever they are, they deserve to be punished."

He nodded pensively, almost aggressively. "This is an utter disregard of our vows," he mumbled rubbing his mouth. "We will find these spies out and, if they are ours, make sure they are punished to the full extent of our law."

She gave another bow.

He tried to smile at her. "I am certainly glad you are safe," he told her. "Is there anything else I can do for you, my child?"

"For now, I think all I will ask for is a place to stay for a short time," she said.

His face softened. "Anything for you," he replied. "My most loved student." He took a few steps closer toward her and gave her a kiss on her cheek. "I have never been prouder of anyone in my life."

Her cheeks flushed at the compliment and wondered. This man had always seemed to take an interest in her, watched out for her.

"Thank you," she said. "You have always been kind to me, sir."

"I was the one who found you, you know?" he said turning back to his drink, draining the glass.

Her heart dropped, and she could feel her cheeks flush again. "You have never told me that before, sir," she replied.

He nodded pouring himself another drink. "You were so young and trusting back then, but smart. Not much of a crier. You attached yourself quite quickly to me."

"Where did you find me?" she asked finally moving about The Master's study, wondering what he was about to tell her.

"Haven't I told you this before?" he asked smirking and taking another swig. He then looked up, staring at the ceiling as if he was recalling a memory. "You were found in the Gehr woods in Skahrr, left behind after a gang of bandits raided a nearby village. They raided as far up as the Bornnenian border. You were the only one left after the slaughter."

She nodded. It was a bit longer than the version that she was usually told but just as vague. The only thing new that she learned was that The Master has been the one to find her.

"And what were you doing around that way? Patrolling the woods?" she asked.

The Master started. "We were, uh," he cleared his throat obviously not sure what to say, "scouting for children actually. You know the coven gets a lot of the children from such tragedies. Others we save from the sex trade."

Like Marten, she thought.

"We saw the smoke from the fires that they set to your little village and rode there to find only the remains. We would have left but I heard a soft crying from the woods and there I saw you clinging to your mother." He stopped and cleared his throat.

"Is that when you took the necklace from her neck and gave it to me?" she asked fingering the silver wing around her neck.

He started. "I didn't give you the necklace until a couple years later," he replied cautiously. "How did you know that it came from her?"

She shrugged. "I always assumed it was my mother's," she told him. "I can't imagine any other way it would have come into my possession."

He nodded. "Yes, of course."

"Why do you think I was spared?" she asked, watching his face.

He laughed somewhat nervously. "Why these questions all of a sudden? You have never asked anything like this before."

She smiled. "You are the one that brought it up, sir," she replied, gently jesting. "I thought that was an open invitation to ask what I wanted."

He swirled his glass and looked down into it, smiling softly. "I did bring it up, didn't I?"

She gauged his body language; he seemed tenser than he usually did.

He walked back over to her and placed his hand on her cheek. "You need not concern yourself with the past," he told her. "I cannot tell you a lot about your past life except that you were loved. It was easy to tell that because you were clean and well fed and dressed in nice clothes." He leaned in and gave her another kiss on the forehead. "Forget the past, my dear. What matters now is today."

She huffed, a half laugh, out of her nose. "You have not changed," she said looking up at him.

He patted her cheek. "I shall find you a room in my house," he said holding his arm out. "Come. There is a room upstairs and down the hall fit for any Skahrrian princess."

She started before giving another small laugh.

He smirked at her. "You did not expect me to know," he said, "but nothing gets past me, my dear."

She nodded and stopped just before the door to the room he had led her to. "I have another question, sir," she said.

"Yes?"

"On my way in, I met with a group of men, including The Monk, and a couple of trainees. I overheard them saying something about a war."

He nodded. "Yes," he replied. "There has been a lot of talk of war recently. But, yet, there is always talk of such things. Bornnen is a sensitive country always trying to prove that they are bigger and better than the rest."

"So, they are just rumors so far?" she hoped. "Have any of our spies brought back any reports?"

He smiled. "Our spies have brought us back the normal reports of tension and unrest between the countries in the realm," he replied. "I see no cause for concern just yet."

She sighed. "Thank you for letting me room here, sir," she said after a moment.

"Anything for you," he replied giving her a smile. "I have missed you these long years," he said holding her gaze for a moment. "For now, I will leave you to rest. I know your journeys must be long." He gave her a small bow before turning away.

The Tigress smiled softly as she turned into the room The Master provided for her. Perhaps, she thought, he is my father.

CHAPTER 20

THE COVEN, MUCH LIKE ANY CITY OR TOWN, HAD A SOCIAL HIERAR-chy. As Vorce had mentioned, spies are on the bottom, then merce-naries with assassins being on top. But even among the assassins, there was a different hierarchy. The assassin hierarchy was not based on wealth or nobility so much as age and the number of con-tracts one had fulfilled. The Master was a man of sixty-one with over five hundred successful contracts in the thirty-five years that he was active. He was third in command only under The Fist, sixty-eight with five hundred-thirty contracts, and The Wind, seventy with almost six hundred; and above two others, The Gallant, fifty-five with a few over five hundred contracts and The Mountain, fifty-six with exactly five hundred contracts.

But that was not all that was required to gain a seat among the five. If one of The Leaders were to pass away, they would be replaced by someone they had previously nominated. If they passed away with-out having a nomination, the remaining four would come together and decide on a replacement.

The five of them do not participate in training or interaction with the trainees at all. They are mostly there for politics, making deci-sions, observations and showing up for events. They are the ones that decide how to title the ones who make it to the end of training. They are also the ones that decide on how to discipline and whether a trainee will become a spy, mercenary, or assassin.

Occasionally, you would see them walking the streets silently surveying the scenes before them, but rarely would they speak to the children. You had to gain a title or gain notice for The Leaders to acknowledge you.

It was true what The Master had said about his bond with The Tigress. Before he was deactivated and became one of The Leaders, he would come back to Dead Man's Rest after missions with stories and little gifts for her. He had given her her first knife, even helping her practice using them. It was this that made her so partial to knives and throwing knives. Though the trainees are trained to use a variety of weapons, after a certain age they tend to favor or develop better skills with one.

It was The Master who helped make knives her weapon of choice.

The Master did help to shape her. He taught her things that she did not learn during her lessons. When he went away on missions for months at a time, a year being the longest, she missed him.

Looking back, she knew that he did not treat any of the other trainees the same as he did her. For some reason she was different, special to him. It never mattered to her why until this moment, until she found out about her past.

She thought about all of the questions she had swimming through her head and how she was going to find the answers to them when a gentle hand was placed on her shoulder. She looked up, awakened from a trance, to see an older woman smiling at her.

"The Tigress, welcome home," she said in a voice as soft as her touch.

The Tigress immediately put her fist over her heart and bowed her head. "The Wind," she said. "I am honored that you remember me."

She gave a chuckle that made her sound younger than she was. "If I remember correctly, you were always getting into trouble during your time here. Not because you were a bad child, no, you just had a difficult time with one of the rules."

The Tigress bowed her head to hide her smile.

"It is difficult to forget you," she replied. "You gave us such trouble when you were a trainee, yet, showed great promise." The Wind held her hand out motioning for The Tigress to continue walking with her.

The Tigress obeyed. "Do not help those that cannot help themselves," she said citing the rule The Wind was pertaining to. "It is a concept I am still not comfortable with, ma'am, even after all of the lashings and years that have passed."

She nodded her head. "And like a tigress you defended the younger trainees as if they were your own cubs."

The Tigress gave The Wind a side glance. "Yes," she replied after a short thought-filled silence. "And it got me in trouble on more than one occasion."

"And yet it never deterred you from doing it," The Wind said picking up an orange from one of the fruit stands.

"I guess I am a slow learner."

The Wind turned and took her by the hand, her wrinkled, dark skin cool in her own. "Perhaps you are the only one to truly understand the lesson we were trying to teach."

The Tigress gave her a strange look. "I am not sure I understand what you mean, ma'am."

The Wind squeezed her hand gently. "Maybe one day you will," she replied turning to walk again. "The Master tells me that you are here only for a visit. I wonder if you might be interested in helping with some of the trainees."

"Forgive me," The Tigress responded. "But like I told The Master, I do not believe I have the patience necessary to deal with large groups of children."

The Wind laughed. "But you seem to be a fair enough teacher," she said.

The Tigress furrowed her brow.

"Tell me, dear," she started, "do you know how one of the young boys obtained dragon bane's poisoning?"

The Tigress shifted her gaze.

"Seems a strange business since the coven only has a small amount of dragon's bane. And it is kept in the forbidden garden on the other side of the village from where the boy was found, and the children know they are not allowed to enter its perimeters," she said. "When asked where he received this cut from which the poison entered his body he would not answer. He just said that he deserved it."

"I will not insult you by lying, ma'am," The Tigress finally said. "It was me who poisoned the boy."

She laughed again. "My loss of youth does not mean loss of intelligence," she replied. "When I figured out that he had been bullying another boy and I heard that you were back in town, I put two and two together."

"Forgive me, I was merely teaching the boy a lesson as he said he was teaching the other boy one. It was only a small cut with a minimal amount of dragon's bane. I would never truly maim a child."

"No, I do not believe you would. Do not trouble yourself," The Wind said after a moment. "Some children can only learn the hard way."

The Tigress did not respond, just merely walked with The Wind to the end of the lane, turning with her toward the piers.

They stopped at the end of the longest pier watching the waves dance in the Dormant Sea.

The Wind smiled. "I do believe you made quite an impression on that boy," she said with a soft smile.

The Tigress nodded. "I hope he learned not to pick on someone just because they are smaller."

Her smile broadened. "I daresay that that boy might actually think before he acts but that was not the boy I was speaking of." She made a small gesture with her head indicating for The Tigress to look behind them.

She turned and saw the small boy with the bruised face slip back behind one of the wooden support beams of the pier and frowned.

"Do me a favor, would you?" The Wind asked.

The Tigress turned back around. "Anything, ma'am."

She smiled and nodded. "Look after him."

The Tigress creased her brows. "I am not sure if I heard you correctly, ma'am," she replied shaking her head.

The Wind laughed. "You have heard me just fine," she said. "The boy has been here since birth, but I do not think he will ever fit in. He is only seven, but I do not think he will improve."

"Seven years ago," The Tigress thought. "I remember him," she said. "He is the son of the Mehtian pirate girl who survived that shipwreck and somehow made it to shore."

The Wind nodded. "She gave birth a week later and then died a few days after that. And he has been lost ever since. Sweet boy and painfully shy, he doesn't seem to have the ability to speak. But he is extremely smart. He at least excels in that aspect."

"If I recall correctly, ma'am, he was under your care until he was of age to train."

The Wind nodded, smiling sadly. "As you must know, I have no children of my own," she replied. "Our vows forbid us from ever doing so, but the longing and the need were always there as I believe it to be there for most people, men and women alike." She paused and looked out toward the sea solemnly. "I had just joined ranks with The Leaders a few years before and the month before that had become third in command. I did not have as much influence as the others, say for two, but with me being the only woman I was tasked with his care. And I am not ashamed to say that I grew very fond of our time together and my heart had never been more broken as it was the day I had to send him away to the trainee houses. Send him into the strict lifestyle of the coven that I believed would shape him into a courageous man." She took in a deep breath from her nose, savoring the sea air. "Naturally, as the years passed, and I saw him less and less, he forgot about me. But I have yet to forget about him and that strange feeling to protect him still haunts me."

She turned to The Tigress her eyes shining with tears that she refused to let fall.

"May I have your confidence?" she asked in a serious manner.

The Tigress nodded. "Of course."

"I named him," she said.

The Tigress blinked at her.

"I did not give him a title, but a real name. Dohrrn."

"Like the spring bird?" The Tigress asked.

The Wind nodded. "There was a dohrrn that used to sit on his windowsill every morning and sing the first few months after he was born. He would laugh at it."

"Dohrrns are not usually found this far east in the realm," The Tigress said.

"Yes," The Wind added. "I found it odd as well. But it seemed fitting that a child out of place visited by a bird out of place should be named after it. He is a very special child and he does not belong here."

"What would you have me do, ma'am?" The Tigress asked.

She smiled at her. "I am sure you can find the answer to that on your own," she replied. She took a deep breath before wincing a bit. "Ah, age does not agree with my knees, I am afraid," she said. "All of those years climbing up walls and falling to the ground has done a number on my bones." She gave another wise smile. "But you cannot just let the pain get in your way. Life moves on and so must we." She gave The Tigress's shoulder a squeeze.

"Ma'am," The Tigress started. "I am only going to be here for a week, two at the most. How am I to look after this boy? Surely, I cannot take him with me on my contracts."

The Wind gave another smile. "My dear, there will be more opportunity to talk of such things," she said. "But right now, I have to take care of my knees."

"Would you like me to walk back with you?" The Tigress asked. "We could walk and talk."

"No, I can manage," she replied smiling as she began to walk back toward the village. "I will leave you to your thoughts."

The Tigress stood by herself staring off into the sea wondering once again what she should do.

After she gave herself enough time to think, she turned and walked back toward the village. When she got to the post where the boy was hiding, she stopped and slowly turned her head to look down at him. He had dark skin like all Mehtians, but his eyes were a golden amber color with an orange tint, almost like fire. She had not really noticed them the day before in the dying sun, but now with the sun shining, his eyes, or eye—for the other one was still slightly swollen—truly seemed to glow.

He smiled up at her and she could feel her lips begin to smile back.

She watched as he reached out and grabbed her hand giving it a light squeeze. She looked down at his hand in hers, surprised by its warmth. After a moment she gently pulled her hand from his and patted him on the head as she moved to make her way back through the free market.

Like the village that Vorce had built, the coven was self-sufficient. They grew their own crops and raised their own livestock. All of the trainees, usually under the guidance of one of The Teachers, would tend to the crops or the food stands in the market. Everything at the coven was based on age, strength and discipline.

The older trainees were the ones that typically worked the fields while the younger trainees ran the fruit stands in the free market. Those that had already earned their titles were allowed to take and eat what fruit they pleased but the trainees had to earn tokens from The Teachers and hand them to the trainee manning the product. Theft was not tolerated and was harshly punished in the coven. The Tigress remembered several occasions where trainees were publicly flogged breaking such a rule. Though they were never deprived of food, certain foods, and for that matter other privileges, had to be earned.

The Tigress held up her wrist to show her tattoo and swiped an apple from the stand. The young boy stood on his tip toes staring at the apples smiling.

"Do you have a token?" the elder trainee asked impatiently.

The young boy, Dohrrn as The Wind had named him, took a step back without responding.

The Tigress looked down at him and grabbed another apple from the stand. "He did some work for me," The Tigress said. "I have no token to give to him, but he deserves an apple."

The trainee mumbled nothing more than a "yes, ma'am."

She handed Dohrrn the apple which he took readily and gratefully, shooting her another joy-filled, one-eyed smile before he took a large bite out of it.

Dohrrn, silent except for the sound of his feet and the crunching sound he made while eating the apple, continued to follow The Tigress. After a few more feet she stopped and turned back around to face the little boy chomping away at his apple looking happier than any child she had ever seen.

The Tigress couldn't help but laugh out loud. After a moment, she looked at the sky for the position of the sun. It was a few hours before noon.

"Shouldn't you be on your way to a lesson or training?" she asked him.

He wiped the apple juice from his face and creased his brows shaking his head. He then clapped his hands as best he could with the apple still in his hand twice and held his hands in a praying position.

The Tigress took a deep breath and nodded. "It's Holy Day," she said.

He nodded, too.

Holy Day was not so much a day for worship as it was just a day of rest for the trainees from training.

She rubbed her temples and looked around the market. "There is no duty or chore that you need to get done?" she asked remembering that there was always something for the trainees to do.

He swallowed the last bit of apple and looked up at her before shaking his head.

She frowned at him. "Can you not talk?" she asked the little boy.

Dohrrn blinked at her before shrugging.

"Right," she said remembering The Wind had informed her about his inability to talk. "Okay." She looked around the street seeing other kids fulfilling their tasks for the day. A few yards away she caught sight of Marten talking to another man. He looked up and for a few seconds made eye contact. She scowled and turned to walk further away.

"Come on, kid," she said to Dohrrn who seemed all too happy to oblige.

The streets had not changed since she left two years before. She sighed as she looked around. She could almost see the past image of herself running around these streets, carrying a basket of fruit to the stands or chasing after a boy who managed to steal one of her tokens for fruit. She could see shadows of herself fighting with the other trainees or even walking next to The Master as he told her of his latest mission.

The two of them came to an open hut that started the row of shops and found the blacksmith hammering away.

The Tigress smiled as she walked up. "The Horn!" she said above the pounding of his hammer.

The Horn was one of the coven's weapon makers and had taught The Tigress as well as other trainees how to enhance weapons in the field. It was he who taught her how to lace her knives with dragon's bane.

He did a double take before he registered that it was her. "Well," he said returning her smile. He put his hammer down and wiped his hands on his apron. "Look what the wranglers brought in," he said walking over to her.

They clasped hands bringing their forearms together. She looked up at the boulder of a man and laughed.

"You are in the same place that I left you, sir," she said.

He nodded. "It will be the only place you will find me. It helps clear the mind." He squeezed her arm and gave her a look up and down. "You are looking a bit," he made a face, "scrawny. Have your adventures not been prosperous?"

"Watch it," she replied, a playful scowl on her face.

He laughed. "What is a halfling doing clinging to your skirts?" he asked looking down at Dohrrn.

"Never mind him," she frowned. "What have you got in the way of knives?" she asked him.

"What size?"

"I need new throwing knives, and a new pair of tactical knives for defending myself from swords." She pulled out the knives she was referring to.

"These are kind of small, aren't they?" he asked taking one from her. "This one almost gets lost in the palm of my hand."

She huffed through her nose taking the knife back and putting them all away. "Says the man with hands the size of two ordinary men's," she said smiling. "The blade is as long as the tip of my finger to my wrist. It is a very sufficient size for throwing and it gets the job done very well, thank you."

He laughed at her. "Let me find you something just a little bit bigger," he said walking back toward his inventory. He pulled out a large curved knife with a dark, polished wooden handle and handed to her.

She weighed it in her hand to check its balance. "It is pretty, but not easily concealed or easy to throw. It is more of a short sword than it is a long knife," she said. "It is not exactly what I am looking for."

"What are you looking for?" he asked her, taking the knife back.

"I want knives like the one I showed you," she replied.

He wagged a finger at her. "How boring," he said. "Don't you want something with a little more flash?" he asked with a smirk.

"No," she replied with a smile. "I am more of a traditionalist."

He sighed and then nodded. "How many do you need?" he asked.

"Four throwing knives and two tactical ones, please," The Tigress answered looking down at the silent boy patiently waiting next to her.

"That is doable," he said nodding. "Should only take me two or three days if I start now, three at the most."

"Many thanks, old friend," she said walking off.

"Old is a little harsh," he called after her.

"But accurate," she replied back.

The Tigress and the silent boy continued to walk through the streets until she came to six small, simple houses arranged in three rows of two and then two larger houses off to each side of the rows. These were the trainee houses.

They were not separated by sex but by experience. The longer house on the left was for the most experienced, or the ones that were closest to receiving their titles, while the one on the other side was for the children and their caregivers that were not quite old enough to train. The houses in the middle were for the trainees that fell in between the two.

They stood in front of the buildings for a bit, watching the children and a couple of The Caregivers talking outside.

The Tigress held her hand out. "Well, kid, this is where we part ways for the day," she said. "I have things to do and they don't quite include you."

Dohrrn was not deterred by her blunt words, he merely smiled. He motioned for her to bend over.

She paused but knelt down in front of him.

He placed a warm hand on her cheek and gave her a sweet, simple smile. He then placed the same hand over his heart and rubbed it.

She blinked back at him. "Are you saying, 'Thank you'?" she asked.

He nodded and reached out to pull on one of her curls gently just so he could watch it bounce back.

The Tigress felt herself smile once again.

Dohrrn then gave a look of surprise at her necklace as it dangled from her neck. He gently reached out and took it in his hand. He gave The Tigress a look between wonder and delight. His grip around the silver wing tightened for a few seconds and he smiled.

"Do you like my necklace?" she asked him.

Dohrrn flashed her a set of brilliant teeth and nodded before letting go. He then waved and took off running toward the houses.

The Tigress watched the boy go, curious but amused by his reaction.

She smiled all the way back to the market where a tall shadow blocked her from the sun. She looked up and saw The Gallant, fourth in line of The Leaders, standing in front of her blinking at her.

The Tigress was taken aback but pressed her fist to her chest and bowed. "The Gallant, sir," she said as he slowly approached her. In all of her time at the coven, The Tigress only saw The Gallant a handful of times. He was tall and lean, but muscular.

"I hope your travels have been prosperous," he said to her, his eyes seeming to size her up.

The Tigress nodded. "Yes, sir," she replied.

"We have heard many stories of your adventures," he told her.

The Tigress bowed and started a moment as The Gallant reached out his hand and touched her hair. She was not sure what to do when he produced a small beetle and flung it on the ground.

He gave a quick smile. "They are everywhere this time of year," he said. "The trainees cannot seem to keep them off the crop this year."

The Tigress blinked and forced a small smile. "Yes."

The Gallant opened his mouth a moment as if to speak, but, thinking better of it, he gave a small nod and quietly moved away leaving a cloud of confusion in his wake.

The Tigress watched him go for a few moments before thinking nothing more of it.

CHAPTER 21

THE TIGRESS WALKED UP THE GRAY STONE STAIRS TO THE COLD-LOOK-
ing library. She pushed her way through the doors as the smell of old
paper and dust rushed over her. She sneezed and shook her head.

She could not remember the last time she walked the boundless
shelves of this building brightly illuminated by several windows and
lamps. She moved through the sections, not knowing where to begin
her search.

She stood for a moment at one end scanning the large open area
with her eyes, watching several trainees dust books, or replace them
in the correct spot. Some of them were even reading, sitting at large
tables, lost among the words.

"Might I help you, miss?" came a small voice almost taking The
Tigress by surprise.

She turned and saw a young girl trainee by her elbow. "Yes, they
call me The Tigress. I was looking for The Book of Seals and The
History of Banners. Do you know where I can find these?"

The girl nodded. "Yes," she replied. "If you take a seat, I can go and
find them for you."

The Tigress nodded and watched as the girl quickly made her way
through the rows of books. In less than five minutes, she returned

with the books that she wanted.

"Here you are, The Tigress," she said handing them to her. "Please let me know if I can find you anything else."

"Do you have any paper and writing utensils?"

The girl bowed. "I shall bring them to you."

The Tigress opened the first book, The Book of Seals, and breathed a sigh of relief when her family seal looked back at her.

"The silver wing of the house of Mahrkai," she read. "This is an ancient house founded by the original prophet Strahm Mahrkai who predicted the coming of the gods and the destruction of the realm. He took his insignia from a dorrhn bird whom he claimed brought him his visions."

The Tigress arched a brow at the passage. She wanted to read more, but the next page had a different seal on it. She closed the book and pushed it away unsatisfied by it. She went to grab the other book and open it when the girl came back with her stationary. She thanked her and told her that she would have a note sent saying she deserved a token.

The girl beamed and bowed, but just as she was going to turn away to go, The Tigress stopped her again.

"Might you be able to find me whatever books we have on Strahm Mahrkai?"

The girl bowed and was off again on her quest.

The Tigress then opened The History of Banners. She thumbed through the pages trying to find the banner she saw in her dreams, the banner that Vorce described seeing. She skimmed through the brilliant blues and greens and reds and mixtures of them, but halfway through the large volume, she had not found the one she wanted.

She sighed and rubbed her eyes slightly annoyed at what she thought would be a simple task when the girl returned empty handed. She looked embarrassed and ashamed. "Forgive me, The Tigress," she explained, "but the books that you have asked for are in the forbidden section."

The Tigress blinked at the girl. "The forbidden section?" she repeated.

The girl nodded. "Yes."

"Why is there a forbidden section?" The Tigress asked rhetorically.

The girl shrugged. "I do not know."

The Tigress sighed. "Well, how do I get books from that section?"

The girl licked her lips and pressed them together. "You have to get permission," she replied.

"Permission from whom?"

"From The Leaders."

"Of course, I do," The Tigress replied blandly. She sighed and shook her head as she tapped her finger on the table. "You wouldn't know what land a banner of yellow and orange with a black bird in the middle comes from would you?" she asked her.

The girl thought for a moment before shaking her head. "No, but you can look banners up by color, or animal," she replied.

The Tigress blinked at the girl. "I can?"

The girl nodded, happy to be of use again. "May I?" she asked motioning to the book.

The Tigress slid it toward the girl who flipped it to the back and skimmed through the index. "There are three with black birds," she said after a moment. She flipped to the first one but shook her head. "Not the right color." She then flipped to the second one and smiled. "Is this it?"

The Tigress's heart dropped. "Yes," she replied breathlessly. "Thank you." She scribbled a quick note and gave it to the girl. "Give this to any elder with tokens so that you can receive what you deserve. If they have any questions, I am staying at The Master's house."

The girl's eyes widened in surprise and bowed. "I thank you humbly for your generosity, The Tigress," she told her before she turned and all but ran off.

The Tigress then turned back to her book and looked down at the banner, the black bird looking as if it were screaming at her.

"The Banner of the Isle of Zeln," she said reading the description below it. "Said to be where the gods were born, Zeln is a sacred place inhabited by the true children of Vron. The great black hawk on the banner is seen bursting through the flames of the god Vremir, representing Vron is his victory over his brother."

The Tigress brushed her knuckles across her lips pensively. She knew the legend of Zeln being the birth place of the gods, but she was not aware that it was a real place. She had never heard of anyone coming from or going to Zeln.

She turned the page, but just like The Book of Seals, the next page was a different banner. She slumped in her chair, disappointed, and tapped her fingers on the table again. Something told her that any book with information about Zeln was to be found right next to the books about Strahm Mahrkai in the forbidden section.

THE TIGRESS DIDN'T RETREAT FROM THE LIBRARY UNTIL JUST BEFORE sundown. She sighed as she left with more questions than answers. And the books she needed to answer her questions were locked away in the forbidden section of the library. She chuckled in disbelief.

Now she must ask permission to gain access to those books. She did not even know that a forbidden section even existed; the thought had never crossed her mind. Why would anyone need a forbidden section in a Library? While she was busy going over these thoughts, she ran into Dohrrn.

She looked down into his sweet little face that always had a smile for her and patted him gently on his head.

She was going to continue down the street when he pulled on her tunic to get her attention.

"Yes?" she said.

He opened his mouth as if he was going to speak but like usual he closed it and instead made gestures with his hands. He put his fist over his chest as if saluting a member and held up three fingers with his other hand.

"The Master?" she said.

He nodded and then held his hands out palms up and opened and brought them toward his chest before pointing to her.

"The Master wants me," she said.

He smiled at her.

She smiled back. "Thank you," she said. "Come." She waved him along with her hand. "I will walk you back to housing before I go see him."

She began to enjoy her time with Dohrrn. He followed her almost everywhere she went around the village, somehow always finding her in the streets. And looking down at him now with his strange child-like demeanor and happiness, she felt like he was truly the only person in the world whom she could trust. The only person who hadn't let her down. Granted, he was a child and, perhaps, she had not known him long enough, but she still felt as if he was the only person whom she truly cared for.

He was a lot easier to deal with than Tristan whose memory made her flush with anger. And Marten, whose conversations always ended with her feeling reprimanded, could not compare to the innocence that the child brought.

He trotted along side of her.

"Anything exciting happen today?" she asked him.

He nodded as he made a circle with his thumb and forefinger and placed it on his other hand before holding up two fingers.

"You earned two tokens today?" she asked lifting an eyebrow.

He nodded again.

"Impressive," she said. "What lessons were those earned in?"

He pressed his palms together and held them in front of him as if he were praying.

"Religion."

He then lifted his hands up making a circle then made a half circle with one hand behind him.

The Tigress pursed her lips slightly creasing her brows as she tried to figure out what he meant.

He moved his mouth to the side thinking of a different way to try and explain. He pointed to the sinking sun and then made continuous circling motions with his finger moving away from it.

"Ah," The Tigress said. "History."

He nodded.

The rest of the way to the housing The Tigress would ask Dohrrn questions and he would answer her with his hands or a nod or shake of his head. Except for a few obscure gestures, The Tigress understood everything that he tried to convey to her.

By the time they made it to the housing area for the trainees, his gestures and hand motions became faster and longer and still she understood them.

Dohrrn looked at his housing and then back at The Tigress with a sad sigh. She softly smiled and knelt down so she could talk to him.

"I know you don't want to go, but you have to. You don't want to miss curfew, do you?"

The boy shook his head.

"Good," she replied, placing a gentle hand on his cheek. "Now, stay out of trouble and I will take you to the gardens soon."

Dohrrn beamed in delight. He then, as he had gotten into the habit of doing, reached out and wrapped his little hands around her necklace before waving good night and returning to the houses.

Walking back to The Master's house, The Tigress realized how much more she was at ease after talking to the young boy. Though there had been a strange moment when he asked her what was on her mind and she thought, or felt, that he somehow knew what she was thinking. But even after that brief alarm, she felt like a weight was lifted off of her shoulders.

She thought about this as she walked, smiling and musing to herself when the sound of footsteps alerted her to someone else's presence. She turned to see The Gallant approaching her. He gave her a fleeting smile.

"It's a beautiful night," he commented.

She gave a nod. "Yes, it is."

"Do you mind if I walk with you?" he asked. "We appear to be going in the same direction."

"I don't mind at all, sir," she replied, though feeling strange by the encounter.

"Have you been far on your travels?" He asked her after a minute's silence.

"I have been as far as Ganavan," she responded. "I think it's one of my favorite places."

"The hot springs and spice-scented streets of Ganavan have always been a favorite of mine as well."

The Tigress smiled and nodded. "You have traveled further, I imagine," she added.

"Past the Dormant Sea to the black sanded beaches of Drenoo."

There was a brief pause.

"The Gallant, sir," The Tigress hesitated.

He turned his head to look at her. " Yes?"

"Perhaps, this might seem strange, but," she hesitated again, looking him in the face so she could gauge his reaction, "does the Isle of Zeln exist?" She didn't know why she asked him. It was odd, but felt she *had* to ask *him* and not The Master.

The Gallant looked a little startled at her question. "What makes you ask?" he replied, clearing his throat.

"I was researching a specific banner and came across one for the Isle of Zeln," she told him not untruthfully. "I tried looking up more information on the Isle of Zeln, but I could only find that of legend."

The Gallant didn't reply, seeming pensive.

"I was just wondering why a banner for a place based on legend would be in a book called History of Banners," she continued.

"I suppose it does seem curious," The Gallant finally remarked. "I have never been to such a place, but that doesn't mean it does not exist."

She nodded.

There was another brief pause.

"This is where I shall leave you," he told her, stopping in front of what she assumed was his house. "Thank you for the company."

She bowed and bid him a good night, turning to leave.

"You should keep looking," The Gallant said, causing her to stop. "The answers you seek are out there." With that, The Gallant turned and vanished inside his dwelling.

The Tigress stood dazed for a minute, taking in what The Gallant had just told her, before she turned and left.

WHEN SHE GOT BACK TO THE MASTER'S HOUSE, SHE FOUND HIM SIT-ting at his desk in the study.

He was leaning over his desk fingering some amulet or medallion that he wore around his neck. Her entrance must have surprised him because he jumped and hurriedly stuffed the rounded, gold object back into his shirt.

"There you are," he said in a slightly heightened voice. "Come in! Come in!"

"I am not interrupting anything, am I?" she asked with a raised brow.

He shook his head. "Gods, no," he replied. "If anything, your entrance has given me a reason to take a break from this atrocious letter of business."

She looked at the untouched piece of paper sitting on the desk in front of him. "Where did you get that medallion?" she asked, curious as to his reaction when she entered the room.

He cleared his throat and forced a smile. "This old thing?" he replied, taking the object back out of his shirt. "It is just something I picked up years ago." He bobbled his head for a moment. "It is a trifling thing of no importance," he continued, turning it over in his hand.

The Tigress caught a small glimpse of the object before The Master hid it away again. It was the size of a coin, gold, and adorned with black stones that were arranged into the shape of, perhaps, a wing.

Was it a wing like the one she wore?

She wanted to press about it further but The Master had already moved on from it.

"So, where have you been all day?" he asked her. "I did not see you this morning. I did not even see you with that strange little boy that seems to follow you around."

She suppressed a smile when she thought of Dohrrn. "I took my horse out for a morning ride, sat in on a few training sessions and then went to the library," she replied.

The Master laughed. "The library," he repeated. "You were never one for that place, were you?"

The Tigress smiled guiltily. "No, you're right," she responded. "The smell of old books made my skin crawl."

He nodded with a smile. "I am the opposite," he told her. "I have always preferred to bury my head in a book."

The Tigress nodded and frowned. "I was not aware there was a forbidden section in the library," she said. "There are a few books I had asked about that are located in there."

The Master lifted his eyebrows curiously. "Oh?" he asked. "And what books are those?"

"Historical books," she told him not sure why she didn't want to tell him more than that. "I was told I need permission from The Leaders to gain access to them."

The Master gave a slow nod. "That is true," he replied. "You have to argue your case as to why you need them as the information hidden inside of them are considered sensitive."

The Tigress blinked at him incredulously. "Do you think you could give me access?"

He shook his head. "I alone could not," he responded pensively. "I do not even have the key. You must argue your case in front of all of us."

The Tigress was taken aback. "I have to request an audience with all five of you?" she asked in surprise.

He nodded. "Yes, and if we agree with your reasoning you will gain access."

The Tigress sighed. "Would you mind getting me an audience with the rest of The Leaders then?" she asked.

The Master held his hands out palms up. "Of course, my child," he told her. "I am going to be meeting with The Wind tomorrow to discuss some things. I shall bring this up."

The Tigress bowed. "Thank you, sir," she replied.

"Yes, yes," he said waving a hand in the air, a distant look on his face.

There was a brief pause between them.

"Oh, you wanted to see me, sir, before I brought up the forbidden section of the library," The Tigress said.

"Ah, thank you for reminding me," he replied. "I know recently you were caught in a Mehtian Pirate raid."

The Tigress nodded.

"I was wondering if you perhaps thought that these raids might be on the rise?" The Master asked. "We have a numerous amount of reports from the past two months alone. I wanted to know your thoughts on them."

The Tigress lifted her brows in surprise. "I do not believe the raids to be any more numerous than the previous year, but I have only been active for three years now. I do not have much in the way of comparison." She gave a soft smile. "Honestly, I believe they are always on the rise."

The Master nodded at her response. "That is true. It seems like every year their numbers grow along with the number of raids." He sighed. "I hope to discuss this with The Leaders as well," he continued. "I want to discuss the possibility of sending some of our mercenaries out to the neighboring kingdoms to see if they will buy their services for protection. Or to perhaps send out our own teams to investigate these raids ourselves. They seem to be hitting a lot closer to home lately. Just this morning The Bull came back with some trainees and told me they ran into a destroyed caravan not twenty miles from here."

The Tigress thought for a moment. "You mean, use our mercenaries as guards for the local villages?" she asked lifting a brow.

The Master smiled. "If it comes to that," he replied. "We certainly cannot have them coming any closer to The Rest, can we? We need to make sure they know we do not tolerate unnecessary murder and theft on our shores."

The Tigress nodded.

"But," The Master continued, "more importantly, we find out if they are trying to ally themselves with Bornnen again. Just a few weeks ago, there was a report of a pirate raid near Grey Town."

The Tigress frowned. "That's over tree hundred miles from the coast," she told him. "The nearest river is almost half a day away. What are they doing so far from their ships?" She shook her head. "That doesn't make sense."

"Unless something is bringing them up there," The Master added. "Like desperation or the promise of riches."

She nodded. "I will be on the lookout for more information on my next contracts," she told him. "What do our spies say?"

"Well, The Monk, by far our best spy, cannot find out anything about it yet," he replied. "He says he has heard rumors that a poor harvest and harsh winter has left the people of Meht desperate, but he does not know for certain if that is the case."

"Have we not sent anyone to Meht to find out?" The Tigress asked. "They do have a port with semi-civilized people. I am told that the pirates only raid because they themselves are so poverty stricken, but the kingdom itself does live lavishly as long as you have the money."

"Yes, that would be something to discuss when I bring it up," he said rubbing his chin. He smiled after a moment. "Enough of that, though. I shall see to dinner. You must be starving."

The Tigress smiled. "Yes, I am, actually," she replied, not realizing how hungry she was until he said something.

"Come, then," he said stretching out his hand. "Let us eat."

CHAPTER 22

THE TIGRESS WATCHED THE SUN SINK FROM THE WINDOW OF HER room in The Master's house. She had already been at Dead Man's Rest for a week and it had been four days since she asked The Master about gaining an audience with The Leaders for access to the forbidden section of the Library.

She still had not received an answer, leaving her discouraged and impatient.

Whenever she asked him, he would say The Wind had not gotten back to him about it yet, or he had been too busy to meet with the others. Though she was confused at his apparent resistance, she did not question him to his face. A few times she thought of going to The Wind or The Gallant to talk about it herself, but she did not want to go behind The Master's back.

So, to pass her time and keep her mind occupied, she roamed the streets of the village, watching the trainees during training sessions, or catching up with some of those she had left behind.

All of this was done under the careful watch of Dohrrn, who followed The Tigress around wherever she went, silent and always smiling at her. A couple of days she took him to the ranges where she taught him how to throw knives or shoot a bow. Another day she took him riding.

There was no shaking the boy. Even when one of The Teachers scolded him for missing his lessons her sympathy kicked in and she vouched for him. She found within the small boy a sense of companionship, though there was something curious about him.

Besides the fact that he never spoke, The Tigress had already thought that there was something different about him, like The Wind had told her. She could not quite figure out what it was, but the more the boy hung around her the less she cared. The boy simply made her feel needed.

But there was something bothering her about her time back at The Rest.

Vorce told her that her father was of the coven. That he had married her mother in secret and hid them away to keep them safe. She wondered if The Master might know who her father was or give her what information she needed to figure it out herself. Part of her even hoped that *he* was her father.

It was the one piece of her past that she had yet to uncover, the piece that continuously ran through her mind keeping her up at night.

"Tonight," she thought to herself as she watched the fishing boats returning, "I will approach The Master once more about my past." He was due to come back from a meeting with The Leaders at any time.

The Tigress watched the sun as it finally sank into the horizon with the same feeling she had for days running through her mind. She was missing something.

The Leaders were meeting right now about the pirate raids and whether or not there was anything to be done about them. The Tigress hoped The Master would mention her plea about the forbidden section, so she might find out who killed her mother and how to track them down. She reminded him about her plea as he walked out the door before he left.

Mirabelle Mahrkai, her mother. AnnJella Mahrkai, herself.

She thought over and over what she would say to The Leaders if they were to give her an audience. Would revealing her lineage help her or hurt her?

Finally, after the moon had completely taken over the sky, she heard the front door open and someone enter. She quickly exited her room and turned down the hall. She followed the sound of footsteps to The Master's study and entered.

She bowed and pressed her fist over her chest. "Forgive my intrusion," she began, "but I believe we must speak and speak now before I lose my nerve to talk."

"The Tigress," a familiar voice that did not belong to The Master said.

She looked up in surprise to see the prince of Skahrr smiling back at her. "Prince Mohrr," she said in an astonished voice. "What are you doing here?" she asked, her cheeks flushed in confusion. "How did you get past the watcher at the gate?"

He walked toward her, the smile still glued to his face as he took her hand and gave it a gentle, lingering kiss. "You look well, if not but a bit surprised," was all he said in response.

She felt her blush deepen. "I- I," she shook her head. "Yes, your highness, I am very surprised to see you here in Dead Man's Rest," she finally replied. "And I will not say that I am unhappy to see you, but I just wonder as to how you came to be here. You should not have been able to come into the village," she said.

He nodded and gave her hand a squeeze before letting go and walking back toward the fireplace. "Yes, I am not of the coven and, yet, I am somehow still here," he said. "It seems a curious business, does it not?" he asked in his charmingly vague way of answering questions.

She looked at him hoping that he would answer her, but he only continued to smile at her.

"I heard your travels to Bornnen were not so prosperous," he said changing the subject after a moment or two.

"Yes, your highness, you heard correctly," she responded. "I ran into some trouble. The information that was fed to us was false."

He nodded. "Yes, that would hinder any mission," he added. "And where is Tristan?" he asked turning to look at some of the books that The Master had on his shelves. "He is not here, is he?"

She shook her head. "No, your highness, he is not," she replied blandly.

He looked over at her from the books. "Please, no more formalities," he said. "They are boring and you are way too interesting for them. Call me Mohrr," he gently insisted, softly smiling at her.

The Tigress felt herself blush again. "Mohrr," she said nodding. "May I ask why you are here, Mohrr?"

He nodded and looked back at the books. "I am here on business, believe it or not," he replied. "I am meeting with The Master about a possible," his eyes darted to the floor, "transaction."

She gave him a confused look. "Transaction."

He shook his head. "That is not quite the word I am looking for," he replied rubbing his mouth and turning back to the fireplace. "Proposition, perhaps, is a better way of putting it."

She saw him give her a side glance.

"The other reason was to see you again."

She felt her blush deepen. "I am honored that you would want to see me, but I am just confused at to why—"

He put a hand up to stop her from talking, turning to her once again. "Because you are by far the most interesting woman I have ever met, and daresay, shall ever meet again."

The Tigress could feel her heartbeat quicken.

"I thought of you often while we were parted," he told her. "It's strange to me."

She blinked at him.

He gave a small laugh. "I sound like a fool for sure."

Before she could respond, Marten and The Master walked in through the door.

"Ah," The Master said looking at the prince. "You are here a day earlier than I had expected you. Forgive me for making you wait." He walked up to the prince and shook his hand while Marten made his way silently across the room to the fireplace.

The prince bowed. "There is nothing to forgive," Mohrr replied. "As you said, I am here earlier than expected."

The Master walked up to The Tigress and placed a soft hand on her back. "I assume you know The Tigress here?" he asked the prince.

The prince nodded. "Yes, I have had the extreme pleasure of meeting her before, sir," he replied, shooting The Tigress a smile making her avert her eyes.

The Tigress's stomach was in knots, her expression riddle with confusion.

The Master nodded and then turned his attention to her. "Your request has been granted, my dear," he said to her. "The Leaders will hear your proposal on why you should gain access to the forbidden section of the library."

Marten shot her a surprised look.

The Tigress let out a sigh of relief. "I thank you, sir, for taking the time to ask of my request," she replied.

"Yes, of course, my child," he said. "I can deny you almost nothing."

She looked over at Marten who was looking at her pensively. "The Master," she began. "I really must speak with you," she said turning her attention away from Marten.

"Speak! Speak!" he said going to pour the four of them drinks.

"I would much prefer if this conversation was done in your confidence and in your confidence alone," she said.

Everyone in the room stopped and turned to her.

The prince nodded. "Our discussion can surely wait until the morning," he said. "It has been a long journey and I am in need of a much-deserved rest."

The Master nodded. "Yes, perhaps you are right," he said. "The Monk, would you be so kind as to find the prince a room?"

Marten shot The Tigress a worried look, but nodded at The Master's command. "Yes, sir," he replied. "Prince Mohrr, if you would follow me out into the hall?" Marten walked toward the door only to stop and whisper in The Tigress's ear. "The Master will not have for you the answers you wish to know," he said. "I can tell you more about Mahrkai if you just wait for me."

The Tigress gave him a surprised look. "How?" she whispered back breathlessly.

He gave her arm a squeeze. "Later," he mouthed to her and walked out the door to show the prince to his room.

The Tigress stood half confused at the exchange between her and Marten while The Master was busy stoking the fire.

Questions swam through her head. How did Marten know about Mahrkai? Has he known the whole time who she was? She felt a surge of anger rise within her at the thought.

"Are you going to speak, child?" The Master finally said poking away at the fire. "Or are you expecting me to guess what is on your mind?"

The Tigress took a deep breath, surprised at the interruption of her thoughts. "Yes," she said finally, trying to think quickly as to what to tell him. "I just wanted to know the details of what was said tonight. About my audience with The Leaders."

He laughed and looked up at her from the fire. "I wonder why you had to speak with me alone for this."

She gave a weak smile and bowed her head slightly. "I did not want Marten to laugh at me."

The Master raised a brow at her. "Marten?" he repeated scornfully.

"The Monk," she replied quickly. "Forgive me. I have forgotten that his name should have been lost the day he was given his title."

The Master gave a nod. "And so, you fear The Monk's remarks, do you?" he asked her jestingly.

The Tigress shifted her gaze. "His jokes can grow rather tiresome," she replied.

The Master chuckled. "Understood." He finally stopped playing with the fire and moved to pour himself a drink. "Now," he started, "about this evening, there is nothing much to tell. I merely brought up your desire to speak to them and they acquiesced." He took a sip. "They shall hear you out in the next couple of days."

"It is as simple as that?" she asked him.

He nodded taking another sip. "Getting the audience might have been simple but getting permission to take books from the vault might not be so."

"Of course," she replied. She ran things through her mind to break the silence that had fallen, watching The Master drink and move about the room inspecting his books. "I did have a thought the other day," she started.

"Oh?"

"We were talking about the raid that I was in not too long ago and it slipped my mind to mention how unprepared I felt. I was thinking how we needed to train more for battles and not just assassinations."

He looked at her pensively.

"Most of us who are training to become assassins train for stealth, a quick in-and-out job, but battles are not in-and-out," she continued. "They are long and drawn out, and weapons built to preserve our speed and agility, are not always suitable for fighting in those circumstances."

He smiled at her, a proud smile. "I agree with you," he told her. "And I will push for this. You make a valid point. Everyone, not just the mercenaries, should be prepared for a battle if a battle shows itself." He shook his head still smiling. "I like the way you think. You would make a fine leader one day." He looked down at his glass for a moment as if to avoid her gaze, letting silence fall between them.

"What business do you have with the prince of Skahrr?" she finally asked giving time for the air to clear out.

The Master cleared his throat. "I am not sure," he replied. "I have yet had time to sit down with him."

The Tigress thought he was lying. "Why was he allowed through the gate? If he was to have business with you, why would you not have met with him outside of The Rest's boundaries?"

"The Monk vouched for him," The Master replied. "And one does not refuse a prince."

The Tigress regarded him skeptically. "What aren't you telling me?"

Before The Master could answer Marten walked back into the room clearing his throat. "Excuse my intrusion," he said.

The Tigress did not really register Marten's entrance. She just continued to size up The Master from where she stood.

"Your intrusion is not unwelcome, The Monk," he said staring back at The Tigress. "I am done talking for the night anyways. It has been a day of many talks." He gave himself a small nod and then walked toward the door.

The Tigress stood there knowing, had they not been interrupted, she was not going to like whatever The Master was going to tell her.

"T," Marten said after The Master's footsteps disappeared. "Shall we take a walk?"

She sighed as she turned to him. "I am not in the mood, Marten," she said.

"Mood or not," Marten replied, "we need to talk and I do not think we should do it in here."

She took a deep breath and nodded walking out with Marten into the cool summer night air.

A few steps out of the door, Marten took hold of her hand much to her surprise but she did not pull it away. His hand was warm and comforting, and, after a moment, she allowed her hand to relax in his.

"I am sorry for what you might believe about me, T," he said. "But I would never in my life betray you."

She nodded.

"You must know that," he continued, "above anything else. Everything, outside of my private assignments, I have done for you. Everything I have or have not told you has been for you."

She looked over at him. "Marten," she started, "what are you talking about?"

He gave her hand a squeeze. "There are things that I was never before able to tell you and even now I know that I should not, but sometimes you have to break a few rules to make something right."

She continued to stare at him. "I still don't understand."

Marten held up his other hand. "Just allow me a moment to gather what I am trying to say."

The Tigress didn't reply as they continued down the street, hand-in-hand.

He took a deep breath, keeping his gaze in front of him. "I have never openly lied to you. I may not have always been forthcoming with information or have been as vague as possible with what I have given you, but I have never lied," he said clearing his throat.

"Marten," The Tigress said a little more sternly when he didn't continue, "are you going to get to the point soon?" she asked. "You are never one to beat around the bush either."

He gave what could have been a smile. "No, I am not." He gave himself another moment to catch up with his thoughts. "I have a gift," he said nodding. "It is not a physical gift but more like a spiritual one."

"A spiritual gift?" she said almost laughing. "As in from the gods? Please tell me you are joking! You aren't going to tell me that you're the next prophet, are you?"

He finally looked over at her, a hurt look on his face. "I know you never believed in the gods or goddesses," he said. "You listened to and learned the stories, but they have been nothing more than that to you. But I believe they are real. And I believe that they, more specifically, Vremir has presented me with a gift."

"You're serious?" she said incredulously. "You really do think you are a prophet?"

He shook his head. "Prophet, no," he replied. "I am a soothsayer."

The Tigress stopped walking letting her hand fall from Marten's. "You have visions?" she asked him, her face just visible in the glow of the street lanterns.

He nodded. "And I saw you," he started, his voice dropping to a whisper, "dead on the side of the road, a banner of yellow and orange with a black bird on it flapping in the wind."

The Tigress gawked at him, unable to understand what he was telling her. "What are you talking about?"

"It is difficult to explain," Marten said trying to think of another example. "A few days ago, I saw you talking to a man, Vorce, and I heard him telling you about your mother Mirabelle. How he loved her. How your father is of the coven. I heard him tell you that you are a direct descendant of Strahm Mahrkai. I now know you know who you are"

The Tigress felt sick all of a sudden. "How can you know all of this?" she asked him, shaking her head. "I have told no one."

"I saw it," he replied tapping the side of his head. "I have been trying to talk to you about it for days, but you have been heartily avoiding me. I know why you want to get into the forbidden section of the library. I know that the Order of Zeln killed your mother."

"I don't believe you." She shook her. "I can't believe you."

Marten took a deep breath and nodded understanding that there might be some hesitation. "A month or so ago, while on the road to Thren, I warned you about that man you were traveling with, Tristan," he told her.

The Tigress thought back to that night sitting by the fire with him, the look on his face when he touched her shoulder.

"I saw him betraying you to the Bornnenians," he told her.

"Wait. What?" She frowned at him. "You mean to tell me, you saw him—and you didn't—you just let me—," she took a deep breath trying to regain her composure. "Why didn't you say something then?" she asked, trying to keep her anger at bay. "Why would you have just let me go with him?"

He shook his head. "It is not that simple," he replied.

The Tigress groaned. "Yes, Marten," she replied furiously. "It is that simple. Sometimes it is just as simple as saying the whole truth to someone." She wiped her mouth angrily, trying to take in calming breaths through her nose. "Have you known this whole time who I was? Who I *am*?" she asked, looking him dead in the face.

Marten looked down at the ground.

"You son of a bitch," she said coldly. "All of these years I have asked you, begging you to tell me, and time and time again you lied!"

"No!" Marten started, defending himself. "I have not lied. I merely told you that sometimes it is best not to know."

"You told me that I could be the daughter of a whore and that was not worth knowing!" she retorted heatedly. "You never told me that I was the great-great-great-great-great granddaughter of a prophet!"

"The seven-times great granddaughter of a prophet whose family was ordered eradicated," he corrected her. "I didn't tell you because I wanted to protect you, T," he told her, his eyes glimmering with emotion.

The Tigress ran her fingers through her hair and shook her head. "I," she paused taking another deep breath, "I am not saying that you are lying but I just don't know how to believe you," she said.

"You have always wondered how I seem to know everything," he told her. "Would me being able to see visions, or moments in time that are happening apart from where I am, make sense?"

The Tigress thought for a moment and considered what he said. After a moment she seemed to relax a little. "I am always asking you how you know everything, aren't I?" she replied. She nodded after a moment. "Alright," she started. "If you are truly a soothsayer, then tell me something that you shouldn't know. Something that you should only know if I tell you." She looked at him with a subtle challenging intensity.

"It does not really work like that, T," he said. "I see visions. Past, present, future. I cannot read minds."

She frowned, disappointed more than angry. "There is nothing you can tell me to prove to me that you are truly a soothsayer?"

"Has nothing else I said proven it?"

She lifted a brow. "Hardly."

He licked his lips and thought for a moment before nodding and clearing his throat. "All right," he started, "give me your hand."

She looked at him skeptically.

He lifted a brow at her. "It helps the process," he explained. "Please just trust me."

The Tigress pressed her lips together for a moment before complying.

Marten took her hand in his and closed his eyes. "Before you came to The Rest, you were in a hidden village deep in Vron Wood." He frowned for a second. "While there, you spent your time in a garden sitting next to a statue of a woman holding a small child."

The Tigress started and pulled her hand back. Her breath caught in her chest and her heart skipped a beat. She stared back at Marten, her eyes wide.

"I see Tristan rolling around crying in the grass from a wound that you inflicted on him. Something about dragon's bane."

She gave a small, uncomfortable chuckle.

"Your mother named you AnnJella after her grandmother on her mother's side."

"Marten," she said, shaking her head, "you are amazing. How come you have never told me this before?"

"I was forbidden not to," he answered.

She shook her head again. "Knowing this about you would have made things a lot easier."

They had finally made it to the pier where they looked silently out into the water, the moon's reflection stretching out into the distance.

"You mentioned earlier you saw me," she said hesitantly. "Do you really believe that will come true? Am I going to die soon?"

He shook his head. "Sometimes the visions change," he explained. "If I warn or somehow divert a person's course or even thoughts it changes the course of events."

The Tigress nodded, trying to hold back a shiver.

"When the coven saved me from that man," he said pausing as he always did when he talked about the man his father sold him to, "they first decided that I was too old to take back and train. But on the way back I had a vision. I saw the coven members getting caught in a battle with a group of bandits as they made their way down the Mahk River. I was able to prepare those brothers for a fight that they did not know was coming, saving their lives. And instead of dropping me off at the Behr temple to live amongst the monks, they brought me to the coven."

"This is why you are the most trusted and successful spy," she said with a smile. "You're a spy who can see the future."

He nodded. "It certainly doesn't hurt," he answered. "So, knowing the future sometimes helps prevent it. But there is more."

She looked over at him. "Yes?"

He took a deep breath before letting it out slowly. "I was the one that led the coven to your family," he said, still looking off into the distance. "I was the one that found you. At least I found you here." He pointed to his head.

She gaped at him. "Tell me you don't mean it," she finally replied breathlessly.

He nodded. "I do," he replied. "I saw your mother running with you in her arms, trying to save you. It was strange, but even at that young age, I knew that you were important, that you needed to be saved. So, I told The Master and The Gallant, who were among the ones that saved me, and they rushed to the village where the carnage took place, but it was too late. Luckily, you mother had hidden you and I was able to direct The Master to you."

The Tigress closed her eyes to force back her tears.

Marten took a deep breath and turned to look out into the Dormant Sea. "I am sorry that I have never told you any of this before, T," he told her softly. "But you must understand that I was unable to."

The Tigress nodded.

He shook his head. "You are the most important person in my life, T," he told her taking her hand again. "I did not want to put you at risk. If it was understood who you were, the Order might come after you as they did your mother." He shook his head. "I couldn't let that happen."

She tried to smile at him. "I know, Marten," she replied. "But that does not make what you did right. I had a right to know about who I was."

He gave another nod. "I wanted to be the one to tell you," he said. "I just wanted to make sure you were ready before you knew."

The Tigress squeezed his hand. "I forgive you," she told him.

He gave her a weak smile as they fell into a brief silence.

"Do you know who my father is?" The Tigress then asked.

Marten looked her in the eyes. "I do not," he told her with sincerity.

She sighed. "I know he is of the coven. Vorce told me so, but he would not tell me who he is."

Marten nodded.

"Do you think The Master could be my father?"

Marten shrugged. "I cannot read The Master," he told her.

She frowned at him. "What do you mean?" she asked.

"On most people, I can touch them and see a vision of their past, or future, but with The Master, I cannot even discern what he is to eat for dinner the next day." He shook his head. "It's strange. When I first came to The Rest, I was able to read him, or, I at least read him once. Then, he went away on a mission or on some business and I wasn't able to read him again. It's as if something is keeping me from reading him. It's strange. I have shaken his hand on several occasions and have gotten nothing."

The Tigress nodded. "Earlier you said that you believe your gift to be given to you specifically by Vremir," she said. "Why do you think that? Why would Vremir give you or anyone a gift? Is he not the undesirable god? The god of rage and jealousy?"

Marten shook his head. "No," he told her simply. "The temple has it all wrong. Vremir is the god of truth and rebirth. It is Vron who is the jealous god."

The Tigress shook her head. "Why would the temple lie? What is there to gain?"

"Mahrkai knew," he replied. "He saw Vremir's first coming, to free the people from the of tyranny of Vron. He gave us the knowledge, the will to rebel against Vron, ultimately giving his life for our freedom."

"But, again, why is this not more widely known?"

"Because the victor writes history, T," Marten replied simply. "Vron, though he could not take back what Vremir had given, our free will, he was able to write the story the way he wanted it to go, making him seem the hero."

"So, the other prophet, my grandfather, I guess, or whoever set out to try and correct this wrong causing the church to fear him so much that they wanted to eradicate his entire family?"

Marten blinked at her. "You know about that?"

"Vorce told me."

He gave a weak smile. "Your descendant, the second prophet, not only wanted to correct this wrong, but foresaw the second coming of Vremir. The Temple wanted to stop this from spreading, so they saw to it that your family name was ripped from the history books. But the coven knew that your bloodline was important. They knew that in order to better prepare for Vremir's second coming your family needed to live."

"And the Order of Zeln?" The Tigress asked. "Did the temple hire them after the coven refused to take the contract?"

Marten shook his head. "They must have."

"I read they are the true descendants of Vron," she continued. "But there was not much else about them. Do you know anything else? I have never heard of them before. Honestly, I thought the Isle of Zeln to be nothing but a legend."

Marten shook his head. "There is still much I don't know yet," he told her. "But I am glad you have an audience with The Leaders and I hope you gain access to the books you seek."

"Perhaps, I should make a proposal for the both of us to look at them," she said with a smile. "They will certainly prove more useful to you than they would me."

He gave a small smile himself. "It would certainly be helpful to have a second pair of eyes looking over the documents." He shifted his gaze for a moment. "There is something else I need to discuss with you," he told her. "I wanted to be the one to discuss it with you."

The Tigress looked at him skeptically. "Why do I feel as if I am not going to like what you have to say?" she asked.

"This second coming," he started, "you play a big part in it."

The Tigress didn't reply.

Marten rubbed his lips together. "The reason the prince of Skahrr is here is because he is here to buy your release from the coven."

The Tigress made a face between anger and confusion. "What are you talking about?" she asked in a venomous whisper.

He held his hands up in a calming motion. "Now, hear me out," he said. "You cannot freely do what needs to be done for the greater good of the realm if you are still working within the limits of the coven."

She blinked at him and shook his head. "I am as much of a free woman as anyone else I know," she retorted.

Marten sighed. "You are not free to love," he told her softly.

The Tigress frowned. "I don't understand what that has to do with me being sold to the highest bidder."

He shook his head. "You are not expected to marry the prince—"

"No, but I am to be a different kind of slave to him?"

"No!" Marten told her. "You will truly be free from everyone."

The Tigress opened her mouth, perturbed, but closed it again, unsure of what to say.

"I know it seems strange," Marten told her. "But you must trust me."

The Tigress regarded him for a moment, seeing the sincerity in his eyes. "And what does he get out of it?" she asked him a little more calmly. "He is paying for my freedom and just expects nothing else in return?"

"Yes, but not from you," he replied.

"From the coven then?"

He nodded. "I know you have heard the rumors about a war starting between Bornnen and the rest of the realm."

She nodded. "The Master said that they held no weight."

He shook his head. "He is wrong," he replied. "A war is coming, T. Not only can I see it, I can feel it."

The Tigress didn't reply.

"The prince is giving the coven fifty cows and four bulls, twenty oxen, a hundred chickens, a hundred and fifty pomegranate trees, twenty sheep, building materials and the promise of cheaper trade of Bornnenian steel after the war. And in exchange, he is asking that you be released from your vows and that the coven side with him when the war finally hits."

The Tigress rubbed her mouth with her hand. "I don't understand what part I am to play in all of this," she finally said. "How does me being bought by some prince have anything to do with my role in the second coming?"

He blinked at her. "Though I thought your part would be some-what obvious, I don't fully understand, yet, either. Not all has been revealed to me," he told her.

"Well, that's convenient," she muttered.

He gave her a stern look.

She took a deep breath. "Do you at least know when Vremir is going to come?" she asked.

He looked at her, a sincere look on his face. "Vremir is not just coming, T," he said in a serious tone. "He is already here."

She furrowed her brows at him. "I was at the Oasis not too long ago and the grass where he is buried still grows."

Marten shook his head. "No, it is growing again," he replied. "His will and spirit have been released over seven years ago. He is already among us." He took her hand and she watched as his face changed, his eyes glazed over as he looked beyond her. It was the same look he had on his face that night on their way to Harpren. "You must accept this deal with the prince of Skahrr," he said coming out of his trance.

She gently took her hand back. "Why?" she asked. "I need to know why. I cannot live on faith as you do, Marten. What did you just see?"

He shook his head. "I can give you no other explanation than to trust me," he replied fervently. "I know in the past I have told you to trust no one, but I hoped beyond reason that you would not see me the way you see everyone else."

The Tigress was at a loss. Accepting this bargain to release her filled her with a strange dread. The coven, the place that took her in and raised her, that made her self-sufficient and strong, was all she knew.

"You must be relieved of your vows. If I did not see it leading to a fortuitous outcome, I would not have suggested it to the prince in the first place."

She narrowed her eyes at him. "Selling me was your idea?" she asked.

He shook his head, slightly defeated. "I wish you would not see it that way. It's not as bad as it sounds."

"Am I expected to marry the prince?" she asked. "To stop my life and breed just so my bloodline continues?"

"No, there was no talk of marrying the prince. Having children, however, would be recommended at some point in time. The bloodline of the first prophet must continue."

The Tigress leaned against one of the wooden posts on the pier. "I am so lost," she said. "More than I feel I have ever been." She looked at him, his features just visible in the moonlight. "It's strange, funny almost, how I have looked for a life outside of the coven for so long and now that it's here, I am almost scared to take it." She gave a small chuckle.

"There is no shame in what you are feeling," he told her. "We all fear the unknown."

"I have finally found out where I came from, who I am, and I feel no less lost than I was before," she said shaking her head. "The whole thing seems almost pointless to me now."

Marten shook his head. "Everything happens for a reason, T," he said. "You will see that this journey was not in vain. Everywhere you have been has led you to where you are now and where you are going."

"Tell me, Marten," she said taking a step closer to him. "Where am I going?"

Unexpectedly, Marten pulled The Tigress into him, wrapping his arms around her. He held her to him firmly, but gently. "Only the gods know, T, but only you can decide." He then let her go leaving a kiss on her cheek before he walked back through the dimly lit streets.

CHAPTER 23

THE TIGRESS HARDLY SLEPT AS THE CONVERSATION WITH MARTEN played through her mind again and again. She thought about what he had said about taking the opportunity to be relieved of her vows, to gain her absolute freedom. She rubbed the 'X' tattoo on her wrist, the symbol of her brotherhood, absentmindedly.

Her thoughts then drifted to the prince somewhere in the same house. Her cheeks burned when she thought of leaving here with him. Her heart thumped in her chest and her head spun, but in the pit of her stomach she felt that something was off that she should not trust these feelings to guide her decision.

Next, her thoughts fell on Dohrrn. She thought of his sweet little smile and strange sunset eyes always following her closely. The Wind had asked her to look after him and though she hated the idea at first, she hated the thought of leaving him even more. He was in need of someone more than The Teachers to look after him and, if she left, he would have no one.

By the time The Tigress was able to drift off to sleep she had already made up her mind.

"I hope you slept well," The Master said not looking up from his breakfast table as The Tigress entered.

"I did not," she replied. "I stayed up half the night thinking."

"Of what?"

The Tigress told him about her conversation with Marten, pertaining only to the part about the prince and her freedom. She did not mention the part about her past.

The Master looked slightly disappointed. "Ah," he said. "I am sorry he told you. I wanted to be the one to do so."

The Tigress regarded him for a moment.

The Master looked up at her. "And what conclusion have you come to?"

She took a deep breath. "I will go with the prince willingly if I can take the boy born of the Mehtian pirate woman with me," she replied.

The Master lifted a brow at her. "That is a strange request," he responded. "Why is it you want to take him? What interest do you have in him?"

The Tigress licked her lips and then rubbed them together gathering her thoughts. "He is not flourishing here, and I think that he would do better outside of this environment."

He blinked at her. "You have grown rather attached to him, I know, but is this wise?" he asked her. "Is this really what you want, my child?"

She thought for a moment. "Yes, I must do this."

A flash of what could have been disappointment passed over The Master's face.

"Could you at least bring it up with The Leaders?" she finally asked after he didn't respond.

He nodded silently.

She thanked him and turned as she made her way out to the courtyard in the back of the house. She took a seat in the sun soaking up the morning warmth. She had made the right decision, she knew it, felt it, but still her stomach churned and her heart raced with anticipation.

What was she doing, she thought?

Patience, you must have patience.

The Tigress started at the sound of a voice. She stood from her seat and looked around her, but she was alone.

Had she imagined it?

She shook her head. No, she thought. She has heard that voice before. But where?

She sat back down on the bench unsure about what just happened when The Master sat down next to her.

"There is a lot that I need to say to you," he started. "More than I can perhaps ever explain. But I want you to know that everything I have done since I have known you has been in your best interest."

She looked at the earnestness of his eyes and nodded, her heart pounding. Was he going to tell her he was her father like she believed he was?

"And for reasons I cannot explain to you or to myself, I have only ever wanted for you health and happiness. It is all I can hope for you."

"It is all I can ask for myself," she replied slowly, half disappointed when he didn't continue.

He reached out and patted her hand before getting up. "There is more breakfast in the dining room. I am going to show the prince around while we talk. The meeting with The Leaders will be later tomorrow. I shall see you between now and then."

He did not give her time to respond before he walked back the way he came.

She gave a sideways glance in that direction. She had no doubt that at least one of The Leaders would approve of her choice. The Wind did not seem to think that Dohrrn belonged any more than The Tigress did.

Soon after The Master left, The Tigress made her way out to the free market. She grabbed a few of the fruits from the stand and then made her way to the housing units. It was there that she found Dohrrn hovering over the ground looking intently at something.

She called to him and watched as he slowly turned to smile at her and wave his greeting. She walked over to him curious as to what he was looking at but before she got to him he stood and ran to her. He rubbed his stomach and grimaced. She smiled and handed him the plantain that she had grabbed for him.

"Come," she said. "Today we are going to the forbidden gardens."

Dohrrn wriggled his nose in pleasure as he turned with her.

The Tigress, before they walked around the corner, looked over her shoulder to catch a glimpse of smoke dissipating above the ground where Dohrrn had been hovering. She creased her brows in confusion but continued to walk away.

Dohrrn slipped his hand through hers and she was surprised at the immensity of heat that came off of it. She took his hand and examined it making sure that there was no injury, but there wasn't a mark on him.

She looked down into his amber-orange eyes. They always seemed to be changing in color. "How is it your hand is so warm?" she asked him.

He shook his head and made a twisting motion over his lips with his fingers.

"Your lips are locked?" she replied with a smile.

He nodded.

"Are you hurt?"

He shook his head.

"Alright," she said as they walked the path that led to the forbidden gardens.

The day was warm, but the shade provided by the trees was pleasant. To get to the forbidden gardens you had to walk through the free garden where herbs, vegetables and fruits grew. Dohrrn watched as the older trainees tended to the plants, picking what was ripe or removing weeds.

After the free garden was the flower garden which gave life to a variety of flowers in all different colors. As they passed a rosebush,

Dohrrn plucked an orange rose from it and handed it to The Tigress. She smiled and thanked him for the sweet gesture.

As they left the fountains of the flower garden, they came to a gated area and stopped. The Tigress scanned beyond the gate seeing a woman just beyond tending the large tree in the middle.

"Might you allow me access, please?" she said getting the woman's attention.

When the woman approached The Tigress smiled.

"I thought you looked familiar," she said.

The woman smiled back. "The Tigress," she replied opening the gate. "It has been a long time. Have your travels been prosperous?"

The Tigress nodded. "The Rose, are you the caretaker now?"

She nodded and a strand of red hair fell loose from her head. "The Crow passed to the gods a few months ago and I was asked to take over."

"He was a good brother," The Tigress said as she ushered Dohrrn in.

"What can I help you with?" The Rose asked as she led them further into the forbidden gardens.

"I was hoping to see if you had some dried dragon's bane and some bitter-herb."

The Rose turned and lifted a brow. "It wasn't you, by chance, that poisoned that boy with dragon's bane, was it?" she asked. "I had to make a salve for him, but he cried for hours."

"Children need to learn not to bully those they believe to be helpless," she replied.

She led them into a little hut lined with shelves and drawers. "Agreed," she replied as she searched the shelves for what The Tigress asked for.

Dohrrn looked around in amazement looking at all of the jars and fingering the names.

"No touching please," The Rose said without looking his way.

The Tigress lifted an eyebrow at him and smiled.

"Did you come back to teach then?" The Rose asked as she pulled a jar from the shelf.

"I did not," The Tigress replied. "I am just passing through, taking breaks between contracts."

The Rose nodded as she poured a few of the dragon's bane berries into a small bag and pulled it closed. "I had a good two years on the road and I fulfilled a good amount of contracts, but I am happy here taking care of the plants. It is more fulfilling doing what you love."

The Tigress nodded though she did not understand. She did not know what she loved, yet.

"Now, bitter-herb," The Rose said turning back to her jars and drawers. "I have been here a few months, but I still have not figured out where The Crow stored everything. His system for organization is confusing, but soon I will have everything set up to my preference." She opened the fifth drawer and pulled out what she was looking for. "Ah-ha! I found it." She put the bitter-herb in another bag and handed it to The Tigress.

"Thank you," she replied taking it.

"Anything else I can help you with?"

The Tigress looked around at all of the jars until a name caught her eye. "Is that hallows breath?" she asked pointing a little excitedly.

The Rose turned and nodded. "Yes, The Crow finally got some to grow before he passed away."

"Might I take some of that as well?"

The Rose raised an eyebrow. "Do you know how it is used?" she asked.

"You might have been the best grower in the class, but I did just fine memorizing the poisons," The Tigress replied with a smirk.

The Rose nodded. "All right. I will give you a few doses. You only need a seed or two per person. Boiling it in tea is the most effective way to use it."

"Thank you," The Tigress said taking the bag from her. "I will keep that in mind."

"Oh, here is some sweet-herb and yellow grass," The Rose said turning and taking a few more things down. "They are great for healing."

The Tigress thanked her again as The Rose gave her a few more instructions on how to use everything she gave her.

"I know that you say you know how to use them, but it is part of my duty to explain use."

"Understood. I thank you again," The Tigress said. "May your travels be prosperous."

"As may yours."

The Tigress ushered Dohrrn out of the little hut and back through the forbidden gardens.

"Be careful not to touch anything," she told him. "Sometimes just touching the plants can cause irritation to your skin."

Dohrrn nodded staying close to her. He then pointed to her bags and shrugged.

"Why did I get poisons?" she asked looking down at him.

He nodded.

"Because you never know when you might need them," she replied.

CHAPTER 24

THE NEXT DAY THE TIGRESS WAS CALLED IN FRONT OF THE LEADERS. They first heard Prince Mohrr talk about an alliance with him when the war broke out. He spoke of the inevitability of the Bornnenians invading anywhere they could along with the help of the pirates.

"I have also heard some disturbing rumors about a possible alliance with other realms," the prince said as he stood before The Leaders.

"The other realms?" The Gallant repeated. "Do you mean the Lost Tribes? What would any of them gain from helping Bornnen?"

"Not the tribes," the prince said. "The godless."

There was a murmur among The Leaders.

"I heard the godless were afraid of the sea," The Fist said straightening his robes. "They would never journey on a boat anywhere."

"The godless come from a barren land not too different from our Desert of Vremir," he replied. "It is difficult to grow food and they are more often than not going through a famine. It is why so many of them have resorted to the unspeakable."

"Cannibalism," whispered The Mountain.

"I would bet for a chance for good farming land and hunting territory they would do just about anything," Mohrr said.

The Tigress looked about the room at The Leaders to gauge their views of what the prince was saying.

"Still," The Fist said, "I do not see them being much of a threat. They are undernourished and feeble."

"Yes," The Wind said cutting in, "but they also have nothing to lose. Men who have nothing to lose are often the most fearsome in battle."

The Tigress looked to see how The Master felt but he seemed to be deep in thought.

The Gallant nodded. "The Wind is right. The godless are also lawless and will fight back without reserve. I have no doubt of that."

"That might be true, but how long will the fires inside them last if they have not the nourishment to fuel it?" The Fist asked. "They will not last long in battle."

"This goes to say if the rumors about the godless joining Bornnen are even true," The Mountain added. "They could just be words in the wind for all we know."

"The Master," The Wind said turning to him, "What say you?"

The Master turned and looked at them all before shooting a glance at The Tigress. "I think that we have a lot more to gain from this than to lose," he replied, his tone bland, almost vacant. "War with Bornnen has been brewing for a few years now. Though we make it a rule not to choose sides, we have never been on friendly terms with Bornnen. It will only be a matter of time before they make their way down the Mahk River and knock on our door. We should be ready for them." He nodded. "With the prince's proposition we will be able to better fortify ourselves and stock up on reserves."

"And what of The Tigress?" The Wind asked. "She is part of the prince's deal."

All of them looked up at her.

The Master nodded.

"The Tigress," The Mountain said motioning for her, "come forward so that you may speak."

She did as she was told and stood in front of them next to Mohrr.

"Do you understand what the prince's proposition entails?" The Fist asked her.

She looked from one to the other. "I believe I do, sir," she replied. "The prince asks that I may be relieved of the vows I took to the coven, the vows I took when I received my title and accepted my role in The Brotherhood of The Nameless."

"What are your feelings on this issue?" The Gallant asked her softly.

"At first I was angry," she replied. "I felt as if I was being sold like cattle and then I was confused. I did not know how I would ever be able to leave the only thing that I ever knew. How would I be able to drop my old life for a new one so completely different?" She paused and caught The Master's eye. "But after some consideration I realize that this is not about me and what I want. It is about the greater good of the coven and those that we serve; it is about the children that we take in and train; it is about the greater good of the realm." She gave a side glance to the prince who nodded.

"Then you have agreed to be released?" The Mountain asked.

The Gallant shifted in his seat and shot The Master a look.

"If The Leaders accept Prince Mohrr's proposition, yes, on a special condition that I might be able to take a young trainee with me," she replied.

A few of The Leaders lifted brows at her.

"There is a young boy who was given birth to by a Mehtian pirate, I have grown fond of him and see that he does not fit in or I have noticed that this is not the place for him," The Tigress continued. "I feel he would benefit more if he were to come with me." She looked at The Wind who smiled at her.

"I don't like this," The Fist said after a moment. "We cannot just release anyone of their vows. Vows are taken for a reason."

"There have been special occasions where vows were allowed to be broken," The Wind said. "Historically, when the realm was in need, we have been known to sacrifice."

The Gallant nodded. "It is true," he replied softly, vacantly.

The Mountain shook his head. "But to be released of all of your vows?" he said. "What is the point of ever having made them?"

"Desperate times, my friends," The Master said. "Desperate times."

The Wind stood. "Shall we vote then?"

"Wait," The Tigress said interrupting them. "Am I still to be heard on the issue of the forbidden section of the library?"

The Leaders exchanged glances with one another.

"You ask to be released of your vows, but still wish to gain access to books that are only accessible to those of the coven?" The Fist asked.

"I originally asked for an audience with The Leaders for that specific purpose," The Tigress replied. "The prince's request was not made until after mine. I believe that should be taken into consideration."

The Wind looked from one leader to the other. "I see no reason why we cannot hear her reasons for wanting access to the vault," she replied.

"I second that," The Gallant said.

The Mountain and The Fist nodded.

"Prince Mohrr, please excuse us, will you?" The Wind asked with a nod.

"Most certainly," he replied bowing deeply. "I thank you for the honor of hearing me out." He then turned and briskly walked out.

"What are your reasons then?" The Fist asked a little impatiently after the prince was gone.

The Tigress took a deep breath and let it out slowly. "In that vault are books with information on a secret society, perhaps not unlike our own, that have committed several heinous crimes. I was commissioned by someone to find out this secret society, so they can be punished for their crimes."

The Gallant leaned forward in his seat as if to try and hear her better.

No one spoke for a few minutes.

"Sounds like a rather vague explanation," The Mountain replied finally.

"Commissions or contracts are confidential as you know," The Tigress replied. "Therefore, I cannot give further information about it."

"You are currently under a contract while asking for a release from your vows?" The Wind asked skeptically. "You cannot legally fulfill a contract without the protection of your vows. It would be murder, otherwise."

The Tigress pressed her lips together. "It is not a contract for an assassination," she explained, "but for information."

"Then why would the person not hire a spy?" The Fist asked.

"He does not trust anyone to get the correct information but myself," The Tigress replied.

"What books specifically are you looking for?" The Master asked, finally saying something.

The Tigress hesitated. "I-I am not sure I can tell you without compromising my client."

"Then we cannot give you access to the vault," The Fist said. "It is as clear as that."

"Agreed," The Mountain said nodding his enormous head. "Those are barely reasons at all. Find out information so what? So someone else can take their revenge?"

"It is understandable she would not want to give up information on her client," The Gallant added. "They are not unjust reasons."

The Wind nodded but said nothing.

The Master looked at her pensively.

"My vote is 'no,'" The Fist said after a small disagreement among them.

"Mine as well," said The Mountain.

"I see no reason why she couldn't take a look," The Gallant replied. "Perhaps for just a day."

The Wind took a deep breath. "I am inclined to agree with The Fist and The Mountain," she said. "Especially if we agree to release you from your vows. You will be forced to break any contract you have formed."

The Tigress looked at The Master who looked disappointed.

"This meeting is adjourned," The Wind said. "We will begin discussing your release after you leave."

The Tigress did not move, unshaken by what had just transpired. "Recently, I have met with a man from my past," she started getting the attention of everyone in the room again. "He told me who my mother was and where I came from." She lifted her necklace from her neck.

The Master's eyes grew wide while The Gallant and The Wind exchanged glances. The Fist and The Mountain remained motionless.

"My name is AnnJella Mahrkai," she continued. "And I am the seven times great-granddaughter of Strahm Mahrkai, the original prophet."

The Master stood from his seat and walked to a window, his back to everyone.

The Gallant seemed frozen where he was while The Wind became pale. The Fist and The Mountain sat further back in their chairs.

"Over twenty years ago, my mother was murdered by the Order of Zeln," The Tigress said. "They were sent by the temple to stop my bloodline. A contract they took after it was refused by the coven."

The Gallant closed his eyes.

"How do you know this?" The Wind asked sternly, looking from The Master and The Gallant.

The Tigress shook her head shooting her own glance at The Master who had not moved from the window. "My client told me," she replied.

"Can you not give us his name?" The Fist asked.

"I cannot."

"Then how can we verify this as being true?" The Mountain asked.

The Tigress shook her necklace. "This was my mother's necklace, Mirabelle Mahrkai," she explained. "This is the seal, the house crest, of Mahrkai."

The Fist, The Mountain and The Wind whispered amongst themselves while The Master shifted uncomfortably by the window. The Gallant stared distantly at her.

"I know the coven saved my mother years before her murder when they turned down a contract from the temple," The Tigress continued, "and I know the temple sent the Order of Zeln in your place. I also know that they succeeded in killing my mother years later. But what I don't know is what the Order of Zeln is, where they come from or how to find them."

"Perhaps, you already know too much," The Master said softly still looking out the window.

The Gallant shot him an indiscernible look. "I believe we must adjourn this meeting and discuss what all this means amongst ourselves," he said returning his eyes to The Tigress. "This is a sensitive topic. If The Tigress is who she believes to be, there is potential for her life to be at risk. Especially if this information were to fall into the wrong hands."

The Wind nodded. "Agreed."

"This will, of course, affect our decision to release you from your vows," The Fist said.

"We would not be able to offer you the same protection if you are released," The Mountain added.

The Tigress looked from one leader to the other. "I am not asking for protection," she replied. "I am asking for knowledge. To know my enemy."

"The Order of Zeln is a legend, nothing more," The Master replied finally turning about, fire in his eyes. "There is nothing to know."

The Tigress shook her head. "Their banners were seen the night my mother was rescued by the coven and then again when she was murdered a few years later," she retorted. "There is nothing legend about that."

"Enough," The Gallant said gently but forcefully. "The Tigress, please leave, so we can discuss this meeting amongst ourselves."

The Tigress stood for a moment with her mouth slightly open, an angry, hurt look on her face as she stared at The Master. After a moment she turned and left.

CHAPTER 25

THE TIGRESS WALKED QUICKLY THROUGH THE STREETS BACK TO THE village. She had not gotten far before Marten met up with her.

"You told them who you are?" he asked her a little incredulously. "What made you do that?"

She gave him a strange look, forgetting for a moment his ability to 'see' things. "I need access to those books, Marten," she blurted out. "They weren't going to give me a chance if I was released from my vows." She took a deep breath and let it out, exasperated. "I didn't know what else to do."

Marten nodded. "How did they take it?"

She shook her head. "Mixed feelings," she replied walking quicker. "Some were silent, others were shocked. I was so taken up by the heat of the moment that I hardly know what happened or what I said."

"T, where are you going?" Marten asked when she passed the turn to go to The Master's house.

"To the library."

"Why?" he asked alarmed.

"I need access to those books," she said matter-of-factly.

"So, you think you're just going to go in and take them?" Marten asked sardonically.

She finally stopped and faced him. "I don't know, Marten," she said. "What would you suggest?"

"Literally, anything except for what you are about to do," he told her. "It will not end well."

"You see what would happen then?" she asked.

"You don't need to see the future to know that," Marten told her blandly.

She cursed and tried to take a calming breath. "Can you see what they are going to do?" she asked after a moment holding out her hand for him to take. "Can you tell what they are going to decide?"

"T," he said softly, looking her in the eyes, "come back to the house. There has to be another way to gain access to that information."

"I am so close to unravelling this mystery, Marten," she told him. "The information I need to find out about the people who killed my mother is in there," she pointed in the direction of the library, "and I can't get my hands on it."

He nodded. "I know," he replied. "But that is not the end." He gave her a soft smile. "If this is just another obstacle for us to climb over, then we will, together."

She regarded him for a moment. "No more half-truths or omitted information?" she asked.

He shook his head. "I will reveal to you everything." He held out his arm for her to take.

She took a deep breath and let it out slowly before she wrapped her arm around his and allowed him to walk her back to The Master's house.

THE TIGRESS FINGERED THE SPINE OF A BOOK IN THE MASTER'S STUDY.

"I guess, this is farewell," The Master said watching her. "Though I am sorry you were unable to gain access to the forbidden section."

"You did your best to stop me," she replied.

The Master pressed his lips together. "For reasons you will

probably never understand," he replied trying to keep his emotions in check. "You at least gained your freedom from the coven."

The Tigress nodded.

The Leaders voted three to two on the condition that The Tigress never returned to Dead Man's Rest.

The Master cleared his throat. "I am happy for you," he said, a little strained. "You can now live your life the way that you want."

She turned to him. "What I want," she started, "is to find who killed my mother and perhaps find out who my father is."

He rolled his shoulders, seeming uncomfortable, and nodded turning from her. "Why wouldn't you?"

There was a heavy silence as she waited for The Master to speak.

"Who was he?" he said after a moment.

"Who was who?" she asked, confused.

"Your client," The Master continued a little strained. "Who was your client who told you what your name was before the coven?"

She gave a small laugh. "Why?" she retorted bitterly. "Do you think you might know him?"

He rubbed his beard at a loss of what to do or say. "I do not want you to leave on such terms," he told her. "I wish you would trust me."

She nodded and walked over to him stopping a few feet away. "I want to thank you for always being kind to me and for your never-ending guidance. I am not sure I ever would have made it far if it had not been for you."

The Master forced a smile knowing she was not going to tell him what he wanted to know. "Your success was and always will be important to me," he said. He slowly and almost cautiously, as if he were afraid to touch her, placed his hands on the sides of her arms giving them a light squeeze. "May your travels be prosperous," he all but whispered.

The Tigress nodded as she turned to walk out of the house where her traveling partners were waiting for her. She mounted her horse and gave one last look at The Master, who watched her go through a window in his study, as she rode toward the border of Dead Man's Rest.

The four of them, Marten, the Prince, The Tigress and Dohrrn, were all silent as the village slowly disappeared behind them. It was not until they reached the bridge to cross the Mahk river did they begin to relax, but before they made it over, Dohrrn brought The Tigress's attention to a horse quickly approaching.

"That is The Gallant," Marten said squinting in the sun.

"The Gallant?" The Tigress repeated. "What could he want?"

After a minute, The Gallant caught up to them looking uncertain. He nodded to them all, finally resting his eyes on The Tigress.

"Forgive me for delaying your travels," he said.

"There is nothing to forgive, sir," The Tigress replied.

The four remained silent, waiting for him to speak but he looked flustered.

"Mohrr, let us continue," Marten said after a moment. "T can catch up."

The prince nodded and the two of them turned leaving The Tigress, except for Dohrrn who shared a horse with her, alone with The Gallant.

"I fought for you," he told her after a minute. "I wanted you to be able to gain access to what you should already know."

The Tigress blinked back at him not sure what to say to him in response.

He nodded and pulled from his saddle bag a bundle wrapped in cloth. "These will not be missed," he told her handing the bundle over. "There is not a decent record of what books are in the vault, so their absence should go unnoticed for some time."

The Tigress looked at the bundle in astonishment. "Are these—?" She looked up at him.

He gave her a smile and a nod.

She shook her head in disbelief. "Why?" she asked. "Why would you take such a risk for me?"

He averted his eyes for a moment. "Perhaps, I am making up for past grievances," he replied.

"Thank you," she finally managed to get out. "I do not know what I have done to deserve such recognition from you, but thank you."

His eyes seemed sad, but his smile deepened. After a moment he placed his fist over his hand and bowed. "We shall meet again, but until then, may your travels be prosperous." The Gallant lingered only for a moment before he turned his horse and rode back to the village.

CHAPTER 26

DOHRRN NESTLED AGAINST THE TIGRESS AS THEY RODE ALONG WITH
Marten and the rest of the prince's entourage. He was excited to
be leaving Dead Man's Rest, taking no convincing or encouragement
to join the travel party. She looked down at him as he ruffled the
horse's mane.

Though the prince was not against Dohrrn joining them, he did
not altogether seem pleased at first.

"What is your attachment to this boy?" he asked cautiously when
they first left The Rest.

"I made a promise to look after him," she replied.

Mohrr only nodded in response. "Well, T, if that is what you would
still like me to call you, he will, of course, be welcome."

"Thank you," she said with a nod, then after a moment, "my real
name is AnnJella."

He raised his brows.

"But it sounds foreign to me."

He laughed through his nose. "To be truly honest," he started, "I
very much liked Tristen's name for you. I would hate to agree with
him on anything, but it suits you much better."

She looked at him rather surprised.

245

"At any rate, I am glad that you decided to come. I have not been able to think of anything else since you left me at Harpren over two months ago."

She gave a small laugh. "How long ago that feels," she replied. "How was your sister's wedding?"

"Wonderful ceremony," he said. "King Caston spared no expense for his son. And my sister made a very beautiful bride."

"I hope that they will be happy," she said shifting a little on her saddle. Dohrrn was as hot as the sun against her.

"I believe that they will be," he replied. "It would be lucky for her. Not many arranged marriages are happy."

They drifted into silence for a few minutes.

"What is it you want with me?" she asked suddenly. "Why did I have to be part of your deal?"

He gave a small laugh. "There are many questions to answer on our long journey back to Skahrr. But some will have to wait. Some I cannot explain on my own."

"How do you know Marten?"

"The Monk and I met a few years back and I have frequently hired him to spy for me or to trade information," he replied. "He has quite a gift."

The Tigress shot him a look wondering if he knew about Marten's ability.

"He can find out or figure out anything."

She nodded. "Yes, he has always had a knack for it," she said. "Perhaps he might be able to figure out who tried to have your father killed."

The prince straightened his back and shifted his shoulders. "The Bornnenians sent your fellow assassin, I thought. We found the Bornnenian coin on him."

"I still am not sure about that," she replied. "Anyone could have planted the coin on him."

"Of course," Mohrr said. "Maybe we should ask him later."

The prince looked tense, so she decided not to press the issue.

Dohrrn turned and took The Tigress's necklace in his hand for a few moments before motioning to her that he was hungry.

She looked down at the boy. "I have some jerky and cheese in my saddle bag," she said to him.

He wrinkled his nose in displeasure.

"How about an apple?"

Dohrrn nodded, his eyes lit up with joy.

She handed him the apple and smiled as he ate, gently petting the horse they both rode on. He was as content as she ever saw him. She realized that she had yet to tell him his name, the one that The Wind had given him. She patted his back to get his attention. He smiled back at her.

"Do you remember The Leader titled The Wind?" she asked him. "She is an older woman, darker skinned, with long gray hair that she wraps in a bun on her head."

He nodded. He made a cradle out of his arms and rocked them back and forth as if he were holding a baby before pointing to himself.

She nodded back confused. "Yes, she took care of you when you were a baby," she replied not sure how he remembered. "Well, she gave you a name while she looked after you. She told me about a rare spring bird that would sit on your windowsill by your crib and sing to you. And, so, she named you after that bird. Dohrrn." She gently pulled on his ear causing him to smile. "So that is your name. That is what I will call you by."

He made a few more motions with his hands and, at first, she didn't understand what he was trying to tell her until the words themselves formed in her mind.

I like it, but I already have a name.

The Tigress started. It was the same voice she heard in The Master's garden.

Dohrrn turned his attention back to the road ahead pointing out things for The Tigress to look at.

She followed his finger wherever he pointed in a daze. "Where had that thought come from?" she asked herself. "It was as if it was placed there in my mind."

THE FIRST NIGHT THEY MADE CAMP WAS COLD. THERE WAS A CON-stant breeze coming from the Dormant Sea sending chills down The Tigress's back that even the fire she had built could not prevent. She sat perched up on a rock staring into it and rubbing her arms trying to keep the cold at bay. She looked over at Dohrrn to see how he was faring, but he was fast asleep.

She looked down at one of the books The Gallant had given her earlier that morning. It was a book authored by her ancestor himself.

In it, Mahrkai describes what it was like to speak to the gods. He says at first they come as signs, signs that one might not notice or take for granted and ignore, and then they start out as thoughts in your head.

He described talking to Behr and Gehr as poetic, their voices as soft and warm as a lover's. They often spoke through memories and dreams.

Mahk liked to play harmless pranks and spoke through the wind and nature.

Talking to Vremir was like talking to a friend, appearing as a small bird or dog.

Vron never spoke, but often appeared to him as a black hawk clutching a small animal in its talons.

Mahrkai then went on to explain the things that Vremir would tell him. He would tell him how Vron controls the people of the realm, blinding them to his abuse of them, making them mine all hours of the night for beraxium, a mineral that gave the gods strength. But instead of sharing the mineral with his brothers and sisters, he took it all for himself.

This mineral can be found off the coast of Skahrr and deep into the jungles of Meht.

She took a deep breath and rubbed her eyes. The book was old and not in the best condition. The pages and ink were worn making reading slow and tiresome in the dying light of the sun. She yawned after a moment and stared back into the fire focusing on the sound of the wood crackling. In the distance, she could just hear some of the Skahrrian guards laughing. For some reason her mind kept focusing on Tristan. She wondered where he was and what he was doing. She wondered if he had kept true to his final words to her that he was a changed man. She chuckled to herself at the thought.

"What is so funny?" Mohrr asked approaching her camp.

She removed her hand from her knife. "You startled me," she said. "You move very quietly. I did not hear you approaching at all."

"Losing your touch already?" Marten asked as he came up behind Mohrr.

"No, just relaxed for once, I guess," she replied pensively her brows slightly creased.

"You and the boy are more than welcome to join me at my campsite," the prince said. "I have a tent and there is plenty of room. And it is a lot warmer."

"Sharing a room with a man is no longer forbidden, T," Marten said in a hushed voice.

"Old habits die hard," she replied slightly annoyed by his remark.

"I can vacate my tent for you," Mohrr suggested. "I can share a tent with one of my captains or sleep out under the stars for a change. I only want to make you comfortable."

She gave a small smile. "Thank you," she replied. "But, honestly, I am fine." She looked over at Dohrrn. "And it doesn't appear he is complaining either."

The prince bowed. "As you wish."

"What is that?" Marten asked motioning with his head to the book.

"Oh," she said almost breathlessly. "I forgot to tell you the reason The Gallant rode after me. He brought me three books from the forbidden section."

Marten looked at her in surprise. "Might I see one?" he asked eagerly.

She nodded and handed him the one she had been reading. "I have not found anything useful, yet, and they are not in the greatest condition being as old as they are."

Marten ran his hands over the cover. "This was written by Strahm Mahrkai himself," he said in an excited voice.

The Tigress smiled at his enthusiasm.

"The Gallant has done you a great honor," Marten told her handing the book back gently.

"Yes, he has."

"Are they the books you asked to see?" Mohrr asked.

She nodded. "They certainly would have been ones I would have looked at," she replied.

"They might tell us things we need to know," Marten added.

She pulled another book from the small stack and gave one to him. "I will certainly need help deciphering everything," she told him.

Marten's eyes grew wide as he took the book proffered him. He nodded. "Yes, certainly." He gently ran his hand over the cover.

"So, what brings the both of you to my humble camp site?" she asked after a moment.

"We have come to talk," Mohrr said. "There are things that you need to consider on your way to Skahrr. There are some," he paused trying to find the right word, "truths that we need to make known."

She looked from Mohrr and then make to Marten. "Bornnen was not the country who hired The Shadow, was it?" she asked.

Marten, finally looking up from the book, exchanged glances with Mohrr.

"No," Mohrr said shaking his head. "It was me."

The Tigress shook her head. "You tried to have your own father killed?" she asked him incredulously.

He nodded. "For good reasons," he said holding his hands up in defense. "Not just for the crown or for the crown at all, but for the greater good of the realm."

She shot a glance at Marten who nodded. "'For the greater good of the realm,'" she repeated. "I seem to be hearing that phrase a lot lately, but I don't understand. How would killing your father be for the greater good of the realm?"

"The death of my father was essential to stopping this war," Mohrr said.

The Tigress creased her brows. "I thought you wanted to start a war?" she said. "Is that not why you gave all that money, cattle and fruit trees to the coven? So they would stand by you when the war breaks out?"

The two of them shook their heads.

"That trade was for you," Marten said. "The talk about war was only a ruse."

She shook her head. "If you are trying to confuse me, it's working," she replied. "What is so important about me that you needed to make up a lie about an impending war? And why leave a Bornnenian coin on The Shadow if you did not want to frame that country and lead everyone to war?"

"It is not a lie," Marten said. "The war is impending. And we could not pay The Shadow with Skahrrian money. That would lead to unwanted attention."

"The death of King Ahlenwei was a blessing to the people of Bornnen," Mohrr said. "I have made several trips to those lands and saw in disgust the waste that most of his people live. He was a greedy and selfish king."

"Is there any other kind?" The Tigress asked with a raised brow.

"If you were not released from your vows, there was a good chance that you would have been killed," Marten asked forgetting her question. "If that were to happen, your mother's bloodline would have stopped and so would the magic inside of you."

The Tigress laughed. "What magic could you possibly be referring to?" she asked shaking her head.

"Your ability to talk to the gods," Marten replied.

"Without your ability we would be lost when Vremir gains his full power," Mohrr added.

She shook her head again. "I have no such ability," she replied. "I barely believe in the gods much less talk to or with them."

Marten smiled, his features dancing in the glow of the fire. "The gods speak to you every day," he responded. "Have you ever felt something, a nudge or a whisper, telling you or warning you of impending danger guiding you to safety or putting you on alert?"

The Tigress averted her eyes for a moment before giving a small shrug.

"Those are the gods, T, warning you, guiding you to the right path," he said.

She shook her head. "Or that was my training," she said. "Instinct even."

"I understand your doubt," the prince said looking into the flames. "But I have faith in Marten and his abilities. If he tells me that you are the chosen prophet of this realm, then I believe him."

She gave another nervous laugh. "What has he told you that made you believe anything that he said?" she asked.

Mohrr smiled, a deep smile that struck to the core of The Tigress. "He told me that I would fall in love with a woman as beautiful as the sunset but as dangerous as a tiger."

The Tigress blushed, her cheeks and face warmer than they had been all day as she averted her eyes to the ground. "Dangerous sunset," she thought to herself. "Dahlen."

"And he was right. It is why I needed no convincing to buy your freedom from the coven," he replied.

The Tigress could still not look up from the ground.

"I expect nothing in return but your kindness," Mohrr continued. "I want nothing to be forced upon you."

"What is to be done now then?" she asked trying to change the subject. "If your father is the reason this war breaks out are we going to try and kill him again?" she asked.

Mohrr shook his head. "We have missed our chances with that plan," he replied. "Since that night, he has tripled his guards everywhere."

"Yes," Marten replied. "It was foiled by yourself."

The Tigress made a face. "Yes, I suppose I hindered your plans a bit," she said. "But how would the outcome not be the same if he were killed tomorrow or three weeks from now?"

"The tension between the countries has already escalated," Marten replied. "King Breht's death would have decreased it substantially."

She frowned. "Decreased it, but not got rid of it all together?"

"It would have given us at least a couple more years," Marten told her.

She sighed and rubbed her forehead. "You said it would have stopped the war," she responded. "You didn't say it would have delayed the war." She looked from one man to the other. "Why do you really want your father dead?" she asked the prince. "What is the full story?" She looked at Marten. "You promised no more half-truths."

The two men exchanged glances.

"Well?"

"My father is looking for beraxium," Mohrr replied finally.

The Tigress blinked in surprise having just read about it. "The mineral?"

They both nodded.

"He wants to mine it and use it as a bargaining tool," Marten replied.

She stared from one to the other. "For what?"

Mohrr cleared his throat. "He wants to offer it to Vron in return for his help in conquering not just this realm, but the western tribes, Ganavan and beyond."

She gave an exasperated sigh. "Vron?" she repeated. "The god Vron?"

They nodded.

"Where the hell does he come in?" she asked getting heated. "Is he 'coming again' too?"

"No, T," Marten told her softly. "Vron never left."

A strange chill ran down her spine.

"We need my father dead because he plans on conquering the world," Mohrr told her. "But he has not even considered how helping Vron could mean bringing about the collapse of life as we know it."

"This is the real reason King Breht hired you to kill King Ahlenwei," Marten added.

"Because of Vron?" she asked hesitantly.

Mohrr nodded. "It was not to save my sister's virtue or a treaty with Thren," he continued. "It was because Ahlenwei was looking for beraxium too."

"So, he was cutting down the competition," she said shaking her head.

Mohrr and Marten nodded in response.

"And with the competition out of the way, there is no one to stop Breht from giving Vron exactly what he wants," Marten told her. "Vron is a destructive force unlike any other, and, without Vremir being ready to oppose him, there will be no stopping him."

"And then Vron will enslave us all again," Mohrr added.

She shook her head. "I still think we can move to have Breht killed. I have faced greater odds and have come through." She thought for a moment. "Do you know if your father," she paused for a moment, "hires women of the night?" she asked Mohrr.

Mohrr looked uncomfortable for a moment. "I can't say that is a conversation that has come up between us," he replied.

"Well, there has to be a way," she told him. "I will figure out a way to get to him and then kill him."

"T, you can't just kill people anymore," Marten told her. "You are no longer protected by the coven. Killing anyone, other than in self-defense, would be murder. And to kill a king even, you can't."

"That's right," she replied softly. "I forgot." She took a deep breath and let it out. "Why not just hire another assassin from the coven?"

"We cannot take the chance this information might get out," Mohrr replied. "Bringing in another party increases that risk."

"Then you do it, Marten," she replied. "You are still protected by the coven."

He shook his head. "It is not my thing," he replied. "I am a spy, not an assassin. I was never trained to be."

She gave him a serious look. "So you are not going to assassinate someone just because you do not bare the title of assassin?"

"I am not going to kill someone because I have never had the stomach for it and never will."

She gaped at him. "Have you never killed anyone before?" she asked, astonished.

He shook his head. "I have never killed anyone," he replied. "Is that so difficult to believe?"

She looked away and blinked into the darkness. "Would it be sad of me to say that it was?" she asked.

"One day the world will no longer need the coven, T," Marten said. "There will be a world where assassins, mercenaries and spies are unneeded. There will be a time where all the lands are joined together and peace will rule."

She gave a hearty laugh. "What dreams you have, Marten," she replied. "As long as men exist in this realm and the next, greed, selfishness, pride and hate will rule. Peace is just a myth we tell our children to help them sleep at night. But it is nothing more than that."

Marten looked discouraged. "I am sorry the realm and everyone in it has treated you thus so that faith no longer lives in you."

She shook her head. "Says the man who wants to kill a king for his own designs," she replied.

"To save the realm," Mohrr interjected. "My father, as much as I respect him for being so, is just as you say, greedy, selfish, proud and hateful. We cannot expect great things to happen under such a man's rule."

"So we kill him and you are to be king because you are none of those things?" she asked sardonically.

He gave a weak smile. "Perhaps I am all of those things as well," he replied. "That is why I do not wish to become king or stay king."

"You want to gain the throne just to abdicate it?" she asked shaking her head in disbelief. "To whom do you expect to give it to?"

"We wish to make one country out of this realm under the rule of King Castuhl and his wife Queen Rain," Marten replied.

"With their forgiving, fair and understanding tempers we could all live in that peaceful realm together," Mohrr said.

She stared into the fire for a few moments. "Is that what you see, Marten?" she asked looking at him. "Do you see this peaceful realm if every country were to be placed under King Castuhl's rule?"

"I see a chance for it, yes," he replied focusing his eyes on the sleeping child.

"A chance?" she repeated her voice heightened. "You want to bet all of this on a chance?"

"People have betted on more with less," Mohrr said.

There was a short silence between all of them, the sound of the fire the only noise.

"And what of Vremir?" she asked. "You say he's already here. How will we find him?"

Dohrrn gave a soft whimper in his sleep causing them all to look over at him.

"When he is ready, he will reveal himself to us," Marten said, his eyes still on the child.

CHAPTER 27

MARTEN SHOOK THE TIGRESS AWAKE A FEW MORNINGS LATER IN A panic. "Wake up, T," he told her anxiously. "We need to keep moving."

She sat up, seeing that almost everyone else was awake, readying themselves for the day's journey. "What's amiss, Marten?" she asked as she rubbed her face, noticing his strange demeanor.

"They have found us," he told her.

"What?" she said still blinking in the early light of the sun.

"They have been tracking us," Marten continued. "Have been almost since we left Dead Man's Rest. I don't know how they found out, but they must know you're among us."

Dohrrn, who had been awake for some time, began helping The Tigress pack their things.

"What are you talking about?" she asked in a low voice so as not to alarm Dohrrn.

Marten nodded. "They will try and take you."

"Who?"

"The Order of Zeln," he said. "They have found you."

The Tigress looked at him for a moment, her mouth slightly gaped. "But how?" she asked almost breathlessly.

Marten shook his head. "I don't know," he told her. "But we have to get out of here."

"Does Mohrr know?" she asked him.

Marten nodded. "Yes, there is no time to talk," he told her with urgency. "We have to leave now!"

We should avoid the coastal road, came a thought to The Tigress. She looked around confused. *We can better lose them if we head north through the woods.*

She looked at Marten. "We should take the road through that small wood," she said nodding with her head.

Marten looked where she indicated and frowned. "That trail leads north and will add days to our journey," he replied.

She shook her head. "I know," she told him, "but something tells me that is where we want to go."

Marten and The Tigress both turned toward the far end of the camp where shouting could be heard.

"They're here," Marten said looking worried.

"There is no time to argue," The Tigress told him, boosting Dohrrn onto the horse before jumping on herself. She steered her horse toward the woods. "Hang on, Dohrrn," she said as she dug her heels in and let out a yell. Her horse gave a small whinny as it lunged forward kicking up sand as it went. She traversed through the men who were running about trying to pack their things, shouting. She made her way up a steep hill pushing her horse to climb. Once they reached the top she stopped for a moment to look behind her.

She could just make out Marten and Mohrr on their horses following her and, in the distance, gaining ground was a horde of horsemen, their banners flapping in the wind. From where she stood, she could not discern what was on the banners, but she knew they were the yellow and orange banners of the Order of Zeln.

"Go!" she could just hear Marten yell. "Go!" his arm motioning for her to continue.

She watched as Mohrr's men were taken down by the invaders, their glistening armor useless against their opponents' weapons.

"Go, dammit!" Marten yelled breaking her thoughts away from the carnage below.

Just then, an arrow landed a few feet from her, letting out a soft 'fthm' as it hit the ground.

"Yah!" she shouted as she turned her horse again and ran along the path into the woods. "Keep your head down, Dohrrn!"

They raced through the trees, jumping over fallen branches, scattering the wild life in a fury of speed. After what seemed like miles at a gallop, she could see a split in the road forming ahead.

Turn left, came the voice from before.

She turned left and continued to gallop at full speed. Seeing a stream just off the path she steered the horse toward it, hoping to hide her tracks. She could feel the sweat pouring off of her horse, but still she pressed it forward. After a bend in the stream, she slowed the horse down to a trot letting herself and the horse catch their breath.

"Are you all right, Dohrrn?" she asked looking down.

The boy nodded but turned and reached for her necklace as if to comfort himself by holding it.

The Tigress removed it from her neck and placed it around his.

"I need you to hold onto this, okay?" she told him. "It's very important to me, so I need you to keep it safe."

He nodded and hid the necklace in his shirt, holding his hand over it.

After a short distance she could hear the sounds of a horse coming up the path by the stream. She cursed and steered the horse to the opposite bank where she hid behind a bush. She jumped down from the horse motioning for Dohrrn to stay and keep quiet.

She then crept closer to the stream, staying close to the trees. She slowly took out her bow and aimed it at the bend in the path, waiting. She sighed a breath of relief when she saw Mohrr coming up the road.

He looked around confused when she whistled. He looked up relieved.

The Tigress and Dohrrn remounted her horse and met him in the middle of the stream. She searched the path confused that it was just him.

"Where is Marten?" she asked.

"He went right at the fork to throw them off your trail and split their forces," he told her.

"What?" she asked in angry surprise. "He went down that path alone?"

"He did not give me time to argue," the prince replied.

The Tigress turned her horse around.

"Where are you going?" Mohrr asked, his voice heightened.

"Marten is not a fighter," she told him. "I'm going back for him."

Mohrr reached out and grabbed her saddle bag. "Don't be foolish," he told her. "He knew what he was doing. He did what he did to save you, not so you could risk your life even more by trying to save him."

The Tigress hesitated when the sound of multiple horses was heard running their way.

"We must go!" Mohrr said kicking his horse into another gallop.

The Tigress followed him as yells were heard behind them. Mohrr slowed a moment to allow her to pass him.

"Keep going!" he shouted.

The Tigress leaned forward on her horse and dug in with everything she had. Arrows whizzed by her, Mohrr continued to scream for her to continue, Dohrrn grew warmer by the second.

A large tree blocked their path and as she jumped it, an arrow sunk its way into her horse's hindquarters causing it to collapse as it landed.

The Tigress and Dohrrn fell from the horse and tumbled into the water. The Tigress quickly jumped up and grabbed the boy's hand pulling him through the water into the trees. She pulled them to a thicker part of the woods where horses would not be able to ride, all the time her heart racing, her face hot with anger.

"Keep going, Dohrrn," she said to him. "Everything is going to be all right."

She could hear running behind them and took a moment to pause and shoot an arrow, hitting their pursuer in the neck.

"Keep going up!" she yelled to Dohrrn who had not stopped running. She turned to run with him when a man charged at her, sword raised. She parried and struck him with her bow, giving her enough time to pull out her long knives and block his next attack.

The man pushed down on his sword, but she kicked him in the stomach causing him to stumble backwards down the hill. She then quickly pulled her bow back out and put an arrow in his chest.

Another man came out of nowhere lunging at her when Mohrr tackled him to the ground and stabbed in the throat. He stood from the man and the both of them continued running up the hill. He picked up Dohrrn once they caught up to him and ran with him under his arm.

After they crested the hill they came to a large clearing pausing a moment to figure out where to go when a booming voice called for them to stop and a spear landed next to them. The prince gently put Dohrrn back on his feet and drew his sword as he turned around. The Tigress had her bow ready, keeping the boy behind her.

"It would be foolish to resist us," said a man motioning to the other men to form a circle around them.

The Tigress counted twenty of them. She turned, her back to the prince's, Dohrrn between them.

"What do you want?" she asked.

The man laughed. "Is it not obvious?" he asked. "We want you. Give yourself up and we might let the other two live."

"You will not take her while I am alive," replied Mohrr readying himself.

"That can be arranged." The man raised an arm signaling for the other men to raise their bows.

"No!" The Tigress yelled.

The men pulled back on the strings, but before they could release, the ground began to quake. It was a slight tremor at first, but soon grew. All of them looked down at the ground in surprise, watching as stones danced across the grass on their own.

Then the archers let out a cry as their bows burst into flames, the strings snapping in the heat. The men dropped them to the ground and watched as they turned to ash where they fell.

No one moved or said anything for a few moments until the leader of the men stepped forward and drew his sword. "Then we will just have to chop you down," he said.

Just then, The Tigress noticed movement in the trees around them. Large shapes moving in the shadows.

Hope.

"Bring me the woman!" their leader shouted causing the men to rush at them.

She shot two of the men before they reached where they stood in the center on the circle. She then pulled out her long knives, a present from The Horn, and slashed at the man who drew near her, blocking his sword with one hand and cutting with the other.

Mohrr fared just as well, bringing down men of his own.

In the heat of the battle, however, they lost sight of Dohrrn who moved from in between them. He watched silently as the two of them killed man after man sustaining only minor injuries when he was picked up by the waist.

He let out a strange squeal of surprise causing The Tigress to turn and giving her opponent the opportunity to cut her leg. She dropped to one knee for a moment before rolling out of the way and thrusting a knife into the man's side. She then turned toward Dohrrn.

"Stop," cried the man holding Dohrrn, "or I will slit the boy's throat."

The Tigress held out her hands to stop him. "There is no need to hurt him," she replied. "He is just a child."

Just then a rain of arrows came from the forest followed by the sounds of hooting. Large fur-covered creatures ran from the woods yielding swords.

The field rang out with the sound of clashing steel as the creatures cut down the men. Grunting and screaming rant out in a macabre symphony of death.

The largest of the men came and stood by The Tigress, pushing back his masked hood. It was Vorce.

"You will not leave these woods in one piece if you harm that child," Vorce said in a growl.

"I will not leave these woods alive either way," the man said pressing a knife to Dohrrn's throat.

"No!" The Tigress yelled taking a step forward.

But she had not moved any closer when the ground shook with a greater force than it did before.

Everyone stood still, their eyes and mouths wide as Dohrrn's eyes glowed and in an instant, the man's yellow robes caught on fire and set him ablaze. The man screamed and dropped the child who did not move as the man fell to his knees and perished in a smoldering pile of embers.

The Tigress, whose leg pulsed with pain, fell to her knees, staring slack-jawed at the child before her.

"He has come," Vorce finally said after a moment. He took a step toward the boy and knelt.

The Tigress watched as the rest of his tribe followed suit and bowed before Dorrhn while she continued to stare in astonishment. Even Mohrr knelt before him.

Dohrrn stood there with a close-lipped smile at everyone before walking up to the Tigress and placing his hand on her cheek.

The Tigress almost flinched at the intensity of heat from his tiny hand.

"It is he," Vorce said approaching her. "The prophecy has come true. This child is Vremir."

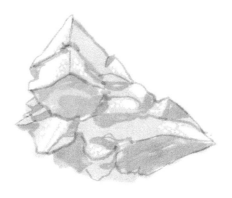

CHAPTER 28

AFTER THE SHOCK OF WHAT HAD HAPPENED WORE OFF, THE TIGRESS remembered Marten. Panic stricken, she looked at Vorce and asked him for his help.

"He took a different path from me to split their forces and now he is out there alone with them," she told him. "We have to go find him and help him."

Vorce nodded. "I will send my men out to find him, but you will not go," he told her.

She frowned. "I cannot leave him out there."

"The cut on your leg is rather deep," Vorce replied. "You will accompany me and two of my men back to our camp and get your wounds cleaned."

The Tigress opened her mouth to protest when Mohrr cut in.

"He is right, T," he told her. "Go and take," he hesitated looking down at the small boy beside her, "Dohrrn with you. I will go with these men for The Monk."

Again, she hesitated, but after a small tug of her hand from Dohrrn, she relented. "I have some yellow grass in my saddle bag where my horse fell," she told Vorce. "It should help with healing."

He nodded. "We shall get it," he told her.

The Tigress turned to make her descent back down the hill when her leg gave out, the effects of adrenaline having worn off.

"You need to tie off your leg," Mohrr said, quickly ripping fabric from his sleeve. "You're losing too much blood." He quickly secured a tourniquet around her leg.

She gritted her teeth through the pain as he helped her up. "There will be time for this later," she told him, "but right now we *must* find Marten."

"You will take my horse," Vorce said whistling for the animal.

She mounted the horse with his help and led them to the area to collect her things. Her horse, only wounded, was lying in a patch of grass eating. She smiled, relieved to see her alive.

"Which way is this friend of yours?" Vorce asked.

"I can show them," Mohrr said approaching Vorce. "Just get her and," he paused still unsure of what to call the child, "the boy to safety." He looked at The Tigress and smiled. "I will be back."

He then mounted his horse and charged down the path, Vorce's men following behind him.

She watched him go with a wrenching feeling in her stomach, scared as to what might happen. With regret, she turned down the path Vorce led her to and followed him.

They rode in silence for a while. All of them, she was sure, thinking the same thing. Who was this child riding with her?

Part of her still couldn't believe what she had seen in that clearing. Dohrrn had set a man on fire using... what? Magic? And those bows, did he do that as well? Is everything that Marten had been telling her true? Is this child Vremir, god of fire, truth and knowledge?

She glanced down at Dohrrn who had fallen asleep against her. He looked so innocent, it was hard to believe he burned a man alive not an hour ago.

"The Monk is an assassin as well?" Vorce asked breaking her from her thoughts.

"He is a spy," she replied.

Vorce nodded. "I did not expect to see you coming so soon from Dead Man's Rest," he told her. "Did you find the information that you needed so quickly?"

"Not quite," she replied.

She then relayed the whole of what happened since she left Vorce.

He looked at her, astonished. "You have been released?" he asked her. "Just like that?"

She nodded. "Yes," she replied. "But they would not allow me access to those books and be released at the same time. But one of The Leaders took books from the vault himself and gave them to me. He heard my plight and took pity on me, I guess."

"Who was this leader?"

"The Gallant."

Vorce shot a glance out of the corner of his eye. "The Gallant is one of The Leaders now?" he asked.

She nodded. "He was nominated by The Ghost maybe a year before I received my title."

Vorce nodded. "He will do well as a leader," he replied. "He was always thoughtful of others."

"He had always been rather quiet. He would often watch us train, but would not approach."

Vorce cleared his throat. "And what books did he give you?" he asked bringing the subject back on track.

"A book written by Strahm Mahrkai himself, one of the legend of Zeln, and another about beraxium."

"Beraxium?" Vorce repeated, startled.

The Tigress nodded. "According to Strahm, beraxium is some sort of mineral that is an energy source for the gods."

He nodded pensively. "Yes, I know," he replied. "Have these books been helpful?"

"I have only been able to read a few chapters of Strahm Mahrkai's," she replied. "It's difficult to read while riding a horse and when we stop to camp I only have so long until the sun sets. I gave one of the books to Marten in the hope we will discover something sooner. He has a," she hesitated, "gift for figuring out things."

Vorce gave another nod. "While you were gone, we were busy too. We intercepted a few letters coming from Bornnen," he said.

"Anything interesting?"

"We now know why they wanted you," he replied.

The Tigress flinched as Dohrrn readjusted in the saddle, knocking into her hurt leg. "And?"

"It was not to put you on trial for the King's death, but because they know who you are too."

The Tigress looked confused. "How is that possible when I didn't even know who I was until just a few weeks ago?"

"They have a soothsayer," he replied.

"What?" she asked in surprise.

Vorce nodded. "She has been tracking you."

"Another soothsayer," she whispered to herself.

"Another?"

She nodded. "Marten is one as well."

"Good," Vorce replied. "We will have one on our side then."

"Is that all you found out?" The Tigress asked pressing for more information.

He shook his head. "We found a letter without an address, but it was obvious who it was for." He looked at her. "Bornnen is seeking an alliance with the Order of Zeln."

The Tigress stared off into the path in front of her, her lips slightly parted, a sinking feeling in the pit of her stomach.

"They were trying to offer you to them in return for an alliance."

The Tigress thought for a moment. "How big can the order be?" she asked. "The Isle of Zeln, according to the legend, is not even that big. Their forces cannot be great."

Vorce nodded. "Unless they do not reside on the island and only take their name from it."

The Tigress let out a sigh. "All I know is that we are lucky you found us when you did."

Vorce bowed. "I told you I would protect you."

"How did you find me, by the way?" she asked, trying to move the tourniquet that was tied too tightly around her leg.

Vorce squared his shoulders. "I had received word that you were leaving Dead Man's Rest and that you might be in need of assistance."

The Tigress sized him up for a moment. "It was my father, wasn't it?" she asked him. "He saw me while I was at The Rest, didn't he?"

"Our camp is just ahead," Vorce told her ignoring her question.

The Tigress sighed, disappointed, knowing that Vorce was not going to tell her anymore than what he already had. "You know, for once, I wish someone would just give me a straight answer instead of dancing around the truth!" she sternly stated.

"Come," he said, unfazed, directing her off of the path. "We must see that your leg is tended to."

CHAPTER 29

AFTER THE TIGRESS'S LEG WAS PROPERLY CLEANED AND BANDAGED, she was allowed to walk, or limp, around the camp, which was all she could do anyways, as she waited for the return of Marten and Mohrr. Fifty men made up the camp, Vorce had told her. Fifty of his best men came to hers and her friends' aid.

She thanked him heartily.

He smiled at her with glistening eyes. "I told you, I will not lose you again."

The Tigress paced up and down the tents, her head swimming with the worst images imaginable. She wished, for a moment, that she had Marten's gift of vision, just so she could see whether or not they had made it out of harm's way.

"They should have been back hours ago," she said restlessly.

"AnnJella," Vorce said calmly, "you are making me nervous with this pacing. Please take a moment to sit and rest. You must take care or you will cause your wound to bleed again."

The Tigress sighed but she did as he asked and sat, but no sooner had she touched the ground was she up again.

"I cannot sit and wait anymore," she told him. "I am going looking for them."

Vorce reached out and took her by the wrist. "You will do no such thing," he said raising a brow.

The Tigress looked at him in surprise.

"I have confidence that my men will bring back the prince and your friend alive," he told her. "You running off will only cause more confusion. And if I have to tell you one more time to sit and rest your leg, I will tie you to a tree."

The Tigress bit her lips to suppress a reply and sat down again, nervously tapping at her leg.

"Did I tell you before how I taught you to swim?" Vorce asked pulling an apple from the bag next to him and cutting it with a knife.

The Tigress gave him an incredulous look. "No," she replied a little dryly.

Vorce gave a laugh. "I threw you into the lake near our home in Alavan. Your mother was so angry with me," he said laughing again. "You were too scared to venture in on your own, so I just picked you up and tossed you about five yards away." He laughed again. "You cried the whole time, but you swam without help to where you could stand."

She blinked at him, her eyes slightly narrowed. "Wonderful parenting skills. It is a wonder I didn't drown."

"Oh, there was no chance of that," Vorce replied tossing an apple slice in his mouth. "I would have pulled you out if you needed me to, but you didn't."

"Luckily."

Vorce shook his head. "No, you were always very self-aware, and you learned very quickly." He smirked. "There was nothing I couldn't teach you."

The Tigress didn't reply.

"That child you have brought with you is very special," he said after a moment. "It seems as if your family's bloodline lives through you, for he is certainly Vremir."

She looked over at the tent Dohrrn was still sleeping in, tired, no doubt, from his earlier exertion.

"And it looks as if you two have a bond of some sort."

She looked back at Vorce who fed the core of his apple to his horse. She couldn't deny that she felt more at ease around him and that she always seemed to understand what he was trying to say without him actually speaking.

She opened her mouth to comment on this when the sound of hooves reached them. They both stood and walked to the path, ready for a fight or ready to greet whoever came around the bend.

To her relief, it was Mohrr and the others with Marten. She rushed over to meet them, forgetting for a moment about her leg.

"You made it," she said choking back her tears.

Mohrr jumped off his horse and helped Marten down, who was badly bruised, his face swollen and caked with dry blood. The Tigress embraced her old friend who closed his eyes and let himself relax in her arms.

"I cannot believe you would have been so stupid as to go off by yourself," she said angrily, blinking back tears. She pulled away so she could see his face.

He gave her a weak smile through the blood and smeared dirt. "It's all right," he told her. "I feel worse than I look."

The Tigress gave a small laugh. "Then you are certainly in a lot of pain."

He reached out and cupped her face in one of his hands. "It was worth it." He knees buckled and the prince caught him.

"Come," Mohrr said, "we must get you cleaned up."

"Yes," Marten agreed. "A nice ale and a soft bed would be nice."

"He is going to be all right," Mohrr told The Tigress after walking out of the healer's tent ten minutes later.

"What happened?" she asked him.

Mohrr took a deep breath and sighed. "The Order caught up with him and it seems they knew he is a soothsayer." He rubbed his lips together. "They had him strung from a tree, the rope long enough so his feet could just touch the ground. They then took turns hitting him and asking him to reveal what he saw in their future. They were laughing while they did it."

The Tigress's breathing quickened in anger as he told her.

"We finally killed all of the men and cut him down, but we did not want to put him on a horse until he was able to stand on his own," he said. "It's what took us so long."

The Tigress's lips quivered in anger as she balled her fists. "I should have come with you," she said through clenched teeth.

Mohrr took one of her hands in his. "No, you should not have," he told her. "You were where you needed to be."

She softened for a moment. "I thought none of you were going to make it back," she told him. "I would never have forgiven myself if something had happened and I had not been there to help."

"It doesn't matter now," he told her. "We're all safe."

The Tigress squeezed his hand. "Thank you for saving him," she said.

He smiled at her. "I was not lying that first night at camp," he told her quietly brushing back a lock of her hair. "I would do anything for you." He leaned in and pressed his lips gently on her forehead.

THAT NIGHT, THE TIGRESS, T, DAHLEN, ANNJELLA, FOUND IT DIFFI-cult to sleep. She tossed and turned wishing sleep would take her, but after what felt like hours, she got out of bed and crept past a sleeping Dohrrn into the night air.

She took a deep breath in and let it out slowly as she looked around the silent camp. The only movement was the changing of the guards, but their furs were so dark against the forest, the movement was unnoticeable.

She rubbed her lips together as the she stood there deciding what she wanted to do when she remembered Marten's words from the other day.

"Sharing a room with a man is no longer forbidden, T."

She shivered as she let out a ragged breath. She had never felt this urge, this ache before and it almost scared her, but at the same time it filled her with a desire and excitement she had to fulfill. She lingered for a moment in front of her tent, wondering what she should do.

Finally, she gave herself a nod of encouragement as she made her way a few tents down. The soft glow from a candle told her the occupant was awake. She took another deep breath as she pushed aside the cloth opening and let herself in.

Mohrr sat up in surprise. "T, what are you doing here?" he asked her.

The Tigress fell to her knees by his side. "Call me 'Dahlen,'" she told him before planting her lips on his.

DAHLEN EMERGED FROM THE PRINCE'S TENT THE NEXT MORNING TO see Marten staring in her direction, a sad smile on his face.

Dohrrn then skipped over to her happily, taking her hand and placing it on her belly.

It will be a girl, said the voice.